Dear Reader,

Having recently moved to Savannah, Georgia, a much warmer climate than I have ever lived in before, I find it ironic that the first book I am writing for the Tearoom Mysteries is set smack in the middle of a Maine winter. My family has vacationed in Maine, in a cottage on Swan Lake, a real lake not far from where our fictional Chickadee Lake is located. There, we spent peaceful hours swimming and canoeing, futilely chasing the loons that pop up in one location, only to dive and surface an amazing distance away. However, while I have never wintered in Maine, I have shoveled quite a bit of snow in the mountains of central Pennsylvania before migrating south.

Here in Savannah, tucked away in the air-conditioning while outside it was 110 degrees, I enjoyed celebrating Elaine and Jan's first Valentine's Day as the owners of Tea for Two. The cousins serve special Valentine-themed tea blends and display a charming poster of some of their customers' favorite photos, while bundling up to investigate the disappearance of a young local man who, they believe, was kidnapped. And of course, we can't forget that sapphire ring they found... Are the cousins' sleuthing skills up to the task of solving such a long-ago mystery?

Anne Marie Rodgers

# *Tearoom Mysteries*

TEAROOM
mysteries

# On Thin Ice

## ANNE MARIE RODGERS

**Guideposts**

New York

## Acknowledgments

Every attempt has been made to credit the sources of copyrighted material used
in this book. If any such acknowledgment has been inadvertently omitted or
miscredited, receipt of such information would be appreciated.

Scripture quotations are taken from *The Holy Bible, New International Version*.
Copyright © 1973, 1978, 1984, 2011 by Biblica, Inc. Used by permission of
Zondervan. All rights reserved worldwide. www.zondervan.com

Cover and interior design by Müllerhaus
Cover illustration by Ross Jones, represented by Deborah Wolfe, Ltd.
Typeset by Aptara, Inc.

Printed and bound in the United States of America
10 9 8 7 6 5 4 3 2 1

# CHAPTER ONE

Elaine Cook, co-owner of Tea for Two—the Victorian mansion in Lancaster, Maine, that she and her cousin Jan Blake had converted into a tearoom and their residence nine months before—was in the dining room of the tearoom late on a February Sunday afternoon dusting a display of Nanking teapots their grandmother had left them. Outside the house, the Maine winter had a deep, inexorable grip on the landscape and the lake behind them, although for once there was no snow forecast for a day or two.

Elaine smiled as she worked, moving on to another antique. She loved the teapot she was cleaning now. Although it was blue and white like many of the others, this one had what was known as a strap handle. Additionally, portions of it, including the spout, the handle, and the rim, were heavily covered in handsome gilt. It must not have been often used on a daily basis, because the gilt was still in excellent shape and hadn't worn away even in the areas where it would have been most commonly touched.

A distant shout from outside startled her, and she lifted her head, feather duster suspended in midair.

What was that? It had sounded like a man who was annoyed or startled. Angry, even. Cleaning equipment still in hand, Elaine went to one of the west windows. She looked out at the back of the bookstore that was their nearest neighbor on that side and then past it to the Pine Tree Grill. Nothing seemed out of place, and no one was moving around outside. Not unusual, given that it was a typical winter Sunday nearing suppertime. The sun was fast sliding toward the horizon; all too soon it would be dark. It was bitterly cold out there with below-freezing temperatures, although inside their home/business, Elaine and her cousin Jan were toasty and warm, particularly in the kitchen, where the oven often was on, baking goodies for the patrons of the tearoom.

Frowning, she walked to the front windows and peered out. Again, nothing seemed out of the ordinary along Main Street. An SUV moved sluggishly past the library and on down the street, and she could see lights still on inside Gift Me, a Maine-items-exclusive gift shop beside the library. Even as she glanced, the lights went out, signaling that it must be five o'clock, when the shop closed. The owner insisted on staying open from noon to five on Sundays even in the depths of winter when there was next to no tourist traffic.

She moved on into the east parlor, and as she did, she thought she heard another muffled shout. Quickly, she peered out the window. Frost crept around the edges, narrowing her view to an oval in the center of the pane, but she still could see in the other direction along Main Street, and her nearest neighbor, Sylvia's Closet, a vintage clothing shop which, like Tea for Two, was usually closed on Sundays.

Concern deepened. Was someone out there hurt? She hurried into the commercial-grade kitchen, where Jan, wearing an apron over her corduroy slacks and a white shirt with the sleeves rolled up, as well as a hairnet over her short dark hair, turned from the large granite-topped work island, where she was busy using a large stand mixer. Jan glanced up and saw her, indicated that she should wait, and after about ten more seconds, turned off the mixer.

Silence fell. "What's up?" Jan asked. "I'm making raisin bread. It's so much easier to knead it in the mixer when I'm in a rush."

"I heard a sound," Elaine said. "A shout or something. And then I thought I heard it again. Did you?"

Jan shook her head. "I've had this mixer on several times. This last time, it's been kneading for nine minutes."

Elaine walked past her and peered through the kitchen door's half-pane of glass out the screened porch windows beyond. "Maybe it came from the lake."

"I doubt it," Jan said. "It's getting dark, and you know people don't go out on the ice when it's..."

"Hey, come look," Elaine interrupted.

Jan came to the door, narrowing her eyes. "There are a couple of people still out there, aren't there?"

"Yes. One, two men, right? Coming off the lake."

"The one on the right is pretty big," Jan said, "so probably men, but look. Did he just stagger? Is he hurt?"

"Oh, I hope no one was injured." Elaine was concerned. "He does look like maybe he's hurt, doesn't he? Or maybe he just had too much to drink. A lot of the fishermen seem to think alcohol is part of the experience."

"They do," Jan agreed. They continued to watch. The person helping the big guy along was not nearly as large, making his assistance unwieldy.

The two walkers had reached a public parking lot over by Green Glade Cottages by now. It was easier to see them beneath the overhead lights that brightened the lot, and it seemed to take no time at all for the men to climb into a vehicle and head out on to the street.

"If he was hurt," Elaine reasoned, "they're probably heading for the hospital now."

"And if he just had a little too much to drink, it's a good thing he's not driving. He'll sleep it off overnight."

"I imagine we'll hear about it tomorrow if it was anything unusual," Jan said. News traveled fast in the tiny Maine town of Lancaster.

"What smells good in here?" Elaine sniffed the air, distracted by the scent now that she knew she couldn't be of immediate service to anyone.

Jan grinned. "Pizza. I made whole-wheat dough in the stand mixer before I started the raisin bread. It'll be ready in about ten more minutes."

The pizza, which Jan had topped with spinach, banana peppers, and mushrooms, was delicious. As they ate, the cousins firmed up their plans for Valentine's Day at the tearoom. The special event was coming up on Saturday, and they had planned several ways to promote the tearoom with a Valentine theme.

The discussion continued after they had cleaned up the remains of their meal and settled themselves in the sitting room upstairs.

Jan picked up a cross-stitch pattern she was working on; it was a lovely picture of a small round wicker table covered with a lacy cloth set for two with a charming rose-patterned tea set. Wicker chairs were visible, and a large Boston fern stood on a tall stand off to one side behind the table.

Elaine stopped to study it for a moment. "That's really coming along. You're going to be done in no time."

"Not really," Jan said. "This week I need to concentrate on getting our Valentine décor and costumes finished, and I need to finish Tara's birthday sweater. I was just excited about doing a little more of this."

"Wednesday is the cut-off date for photograph submissions," Elaine said. "So we can work on that display Wednesday night." They had decided to ask patrons to share Valentine photos they would place in a poster in the entryway.

"Yes, and..." Suddenly Jan stopped. "What is that noise?"

Both women fell silent. From above their heads, they could hear something moving around in the attic. Goosebumps rose along Elaine's arms. "That's no mouse," she said in a low tone.

Jan nodded. "That's something bigger. Not human," she said hastily. "At least, I don't think so."

The sound came again, as if something was thumping across the floor. Then a skittering noise followed.

"A cat chasing a mouse? Maybe we'd better go look." Elaine rose. "I'll get a flashlight. Back in a minute."

When she returned from the kitchen with two large flashlights, the cousins quietly went to the attic door. Jan turned the knob and the hinges of the old door squealed as she pulled it open. "Well, that should scare anything up there into hiding," she whispered over her shoulder as she began to ascend.

Elaine had to agree. "Between that and these creaky steps, we're not exactly going to be sneaking up on anything." She snapped on the light that illuminated the attic.

At the top of the steps, they paused and looked around. There were no further noises. The bare lightbulb cast a pool of light around the center of the space, but there were deep shadows beneath all the eaves and behind assorted pieces of furniture that had been left up there over the years. Behind them, the brick column of the old fireplace chimney rose, casting a deeper shadow behind it.

Jan took the right side and Elaine the left. They trained their flashlights into the shadows as much as possible, but Elaine was quite aware that there were many hiding places up there for creatures of all sizes. Even a person could probably hide successfully up here short-term. Although, she assured herself, that sound definitely hadn't been human.

"Nothing over here that I can find," Jan commented.

"Not on this side either," Elaine said. "Daylight would help, but we may need to get a handyman or someone up here to try to figure out what that was."

"The go-to guy for wildlife is Jack Weston, the game warden. He's a Jack-of-all-trades, so to speak." Jan smiled. "I'm sure he'll be able to relocate whatever it is if it's bigger than a field mouse."

"Whatever we heard was definitely bigger than a field mouse," Elaine said. "It sounded like a baby elephant rummaging around."

"I'll call Jack first thing in the morning," Jan promised. "After we get back from checking out the ice where that man was hurt."

"What? Why?" Elaine raised her eyebrows.

Jan shook her head. "I don't know. I just have a funny feeling about it. That tall fellow looked barely conscious. You said so yourself."

"He did." Elaine couldn't disagree. "Maybe there was some sort of accident. He could have slipped and fallen on the ice."

"Unlikely," Jan said, "and you know it. It's not smooth and polished like an ice rink, and nearly everyone wears ice cleats. But it's possible that he had an accident. I would just feel better if we walked down there tomorrow."

"It's going to be frigid first thing in the morning," Elaine said. "Sunrise isn't until nearly seven, so I guess we'll go then."

As the cousins resumed their seats in the sitting room, Elaine said, "Have you thought any more about what we learned about the Wood family?" She was referring to the cousins' ongoing interest in figuring out why a sapphire ring had been secreted in the wall of their home. They'd discovered it when they first began renovating, and they were determined to solve the mystery of how it had gotten there.

Jan pursed her lips. "The only thing," she said at last, "that I can think to do is to try to find out more about who lived in the house through the years."

"That's as good a direction to check out as any," Elaine agreed. "Let's try to find a time this week to go…where? Probably not the library."

"The courthouse," Jan said. "I think the courthouse would be the place for property records. That way, we can make sure that we know who all the previous owners were."

PROMPTLY AT SEVEN on Monday morning, the cousins met at the foot of the stairs. Both already had eaten. They were warmly dressed in turtleneck sweaters even before they donned long down parkas with hoods that would come up around their faces and high boots with clip-on ice cleats on the bottoms. Waterproof mittens and thick scarves Jan had knitted herself completed their outdoor gear, and a minute later, they stepped out the front door of Tea for Two.

In better weather, it would be an easy walk down the back steps of their house to Lake Chickadee. But in the winter, there was no need to constantly shovel off those steps and the dock, so there was no way to get to the lake by the stairs. Today, they walked along Main Street until they reached the parking lot where the two trucks had been parked the evening before and then moved on to the edge of the lake.

Anyone born and raised around Maine lakes knew how vital it was to exercise caution and common sense when stepping out on to a frozen lake. Warm spells could weaken even the thickest ice and make it unsafe. Fortunately, it had been well below freezing since the first day of the new year, so it was unlikely that there would be flaws or weak spots in the lake today.

Added to that, Bud Wattings, the owner of a fishing rental business in town, had several ice shanties placed at intervals in the area toward which they were headed. They knew Bud to be sensible and careful with his equipment; if his ice huts were out there, it should be safe.

Stepping on to the ice, Jan and Elaine carefully headed directly for the hut farthest to their right. That one, closest to the tearoom as the crow flies, was the hut where they had seen the two men last night.

"You freezing yet?" Jan asked her cousin as they walked.

Elaine laughed. "Actually, since we've been walking steadily, I'm almost too warm. But better too warm than chilled. Did you notice the temperature before we left?"

Jan grinned. "A balmy ten degrees. As long as it doesn't get windy, that's not too bad."

As they drew close to the ice hut, Jan pointed. "No lock on the door, so it must not be rented out right now." If someone was fishing for a period of several days, Bud would rent locks so fishermen could leave their gear in the shanty overnight instead of dragging everything back and forth.

The ice shanties Bud had out on the lake ranged in size from small ones, maybe six feet by five feet, designed for one or two people, to larger eight-by-ten ones that would accommodate three people and a small wood stove. Although they could be made of many materials, Bud had chosen to make his shanties of wood, which he then covered with vinyl siding. Each shanty had a single door and one or two Plexiglas windows. They stood on runners that would allow them to slide across the ice behind a snowmobile or an SUV. Elaine hadn't been in one for years, but she knew the ice shacks usually had a bench seat across one side.

There was no visible evidence of the men's presence at the narrow front door of the hut. Jan started around the side. Following her, Elaine nearly walked right into her cousin when Jan stopped suddenly.

"Oh no," Jan said.

"What?" Elaine stepped to the side. At the back of the hut was a dark, brown-red frozen splotch the size of a grapefruit on the surface of the ice. "Is that blood?"

# CHAPTER TWO

J an cautiously surveyed the dark, reddish blotch on the ice near Elaine's foot. "It sure looks like blood to me," she said. "I can't imagine what else it would be."

Both women started forward. At almost the same moment, they became aware that something was crunching under their feet.

Looking down, Elaine saw odd little pockmarked patterns in the ice. "Is this ice melt?"

Jan froze. "Some form of it. It's hard to tell since it's already melted down into the ice. Stop. Don't go any further. We should get away from it, just in case it has weakened the ice."

"Is that possible?" Elaine asked. It was hard to envision tiny pieces of ice melt doing significant damage to many inches of thick ice. She didn't know as much as Jan did about the subject, not having lived in Maine her entire adult life, but she did know that Bud Wattings didn't set out his ice shacks until the ice was at least eight inches thick for several yards around the perimeter and could support the weight of a snowmobile with ease.

"I don't know," Jan said. "But I don't want to risk it. Let's beat feet."

Following Jan's lead, Elaine backed away from the ice-melting substance. Once the cousins were back around the side of the ice shanty, they "beat feet," as Jan had said, back to shore and then toward their large Victorian home.

Jan sighed. "I was going to call Jack anyway this morning about our visiting critter, but I guess I'll ask him who we should call about the blood and the salt on the ice."

"We need to tell Bud too," Elaine said. "He's going to want to move that shanty, I imagine. Even if it doesn't weaken the ice, that stuff's a pollutant."

"But I think we should talk to Jack before we call Bud. If he thinks we should call the police, they'd probably prefer the scene be undisturbed, right?"

"Probably," Elaine said.

They walked on silently, thinking of what they'd found. Just before they stepped inside the house, Jan blurted, "Who would want to melt the ice around a fishing shack? Maybe it was an accident? Someone spilled the ice melt?"

But Elaine was consumed by a far more pressing question. "And whose blood is that on the ice?"

Jan placed a call to Jack Weston as soon as she and Elaine had divested themselves of their outdoor gear. She got his voice mail, so she left a message saying that she and Elaine had a couple of concerns to share with them.

Aware that such a message could get low priority, Elaine muttered, "Tell him it's urgent."

Nodding her agreement, Jan spoke into the phone again. "One of them is urgent, so if you can call or stop by this morning, we'd appreciate it."

Afterward, Jan headed for the kitchen and wrapped herself in a large apron to work on a new recipe and get a few tried-and-true ones ready for the day's clientele, while Elaine went to the office to look over some orders they had decided to place.

When she looked up, an hour had passed, and it was close to opening time. After shutting down the computer, Elaine went to the kitchen.

"No Jack yet?" she asked, seeing Jan brushing maple syrup on a plaited maple pecan danish.

"He just called." Jan reported. "He's ten minutes away. I told him what we found, and he's going to check it out."

"I can't stop thinking about that mess on the ice," Elaine said. "I really hope no one was hurt."

"Jack will know what to do," Jan assured her. "I suspect he's going to notify Trooper Benson, but I'm glad he's going to see it first."

"I agree." Elaine stopped in her tracks, diverted by the sight before her. "Oh my. That looks heavenly." She mimed wiping drool from her chin. Jan had created a braided handmade puff pastry filled with a blend of toasted pecans, maple sugar, white sugar, and cream cheese down the center. Now that it had baked, she was brushing the top with maple syrup for a lovely shiny glaze.

"It needs to cool and then you can be my taste-tester. I wanted to try a different maple recipe, and Rose suggested this. It looked interesting, so I gave it a shot," Jan said, smiling.

The back door opened before Elaine could reply, and Rose Young, one of their two employees, entered. She unwrapped the scarf that muffled half her face, her blue eyes crinkling in a smile. "Good morning. It smells great in here."

"It's your braided danish idea," Jan told her.

Their young employee paused as she shucked outer layers and tucked her multicolored woolen earflap hat and mittens into one sleeve of her coat before hanging it up. "Oh, did you try it? I hope it'll be as good as it smells."

"I can't imagine it won't be," Elaine said.

"I think it's going to be well received," Jan told Rose. "Next time, though, we'll have to triple or quadruple the recipe, especially if we make it in the summer, because this isn't going to last long once people hear about it."

Rose took an apron from a hook on the wall and slipped the loop over her head and tied it snugly around her waist. "I'll get started on those baked apples I talked about yesterday. I think they'll be a great winter recipe."

"I like baked apples," Elaine said.

"These aren't just any old baked apples though," Jan said. "You're really going to love these."

"It's a German recipe," Rose said. "You know how much I love specialties that reflect my German background. This baked apple recipe has rum raisins, peppered honey, and a walnut-and-blue-cheese stuffing. I tried a small batch of them at home, and they were fantastic."

Elaine's mouth was watering. "I wonder if that would be an acceptable lunch. Lots of fruit, and the blue cheese and walnuts have protein in them."

Jan laughed. "You go right ahead and call it whatever you like," she said as she picked up a stack of folded napkins and walked into the front hallway.

"You're going to be a natural when you start culinary school," Elaine remarked as she watched Rose begin to assemble the baking dishes and utensils she would need.

"I hope so," Rose said, crossing to the industrial refrigerator and pulling out several packages of cream cheese to soften. "I sent in my application at the beginning of January and I hope to hear soon. They said they try to process applications within thirty business days."

"Where is this place?" Elaine asked. "I hope you're not planning to leave us."

Rose flashed her a smile. "Not a chance. It took some doing, but I found a school that offers night classes. It's called the Maine Institute for Culinary Excellence, and it's located in Augusta." She leveled a spoon at Elaine. "The acronym is MICE, but you're only allowed to laugh once."

Startled, Elaine let out a yip of laughter. "This is my 'once.' I just hope there are no rodent dishes on the menu."

"There aren't. I may have asked." Rose grinned. "They have a pastry chef teaching there who is supposed to be one of the best. He taught at one of the top-ranked culinary schools in the country. When he semiretired and moved to Maine, he began teaching one course each semester at MICE. I am so excited to meet him I can hardly stand it." Her voice rose with anticipation.

"Meet who?" Jan came back into the kitchen, having placed the extra napkins on a sideboard they used for clean place settings when they turned over tables.

"A highly esteemed professor at her culinary school," Elaine said.

"It's not my school yet," Rose said modestly. "I can't wait to hear about my application. I did receive an e-mail saying they'd started processing it. I'm really hoping to know something within a week."

"They'd be crazy not to take someone with your drive and skills," Jan said. "It's a done deal."

Elaine nodded. "I agree."

Heavy footfalls on the back porch signaled Jack Weston's arrival. He gave them a brief wave through the back door window before he stepped into the kitchen.

"Ah, smells great in here. And it's warm," he said, removing his fleece-lined aviator cap with its snap-up brim and long ear flaps. He tugged down the half-face ski mask that covered his nose, mouth, and chin, and dropped heavy fur-lined mittens atop his hat on the table.

"How about some tea and a muffin?" Jan asked. "Have you been down on the lake?"

Jack nodded his thanks for the mug and plate she extended to him. "I have, and I'm sorry to report that I think you're right. That's definitely blood on the ice."

"Did you see the ice melt?" Elaine asked.

"Sure did. But it's rock salt, not ice melt."

"Rock salt?" Jan sounded shocked. "Hardly anyone uses that anymore."

"I sure don't recommend it," Jack said. "It wreaks havoc on asphalt and macadam, and it's hard on dogs' paws for those who walk them on sidewalks. But it will melt ice."

"Enough to weaken the lake ice?" Jan frowned.

"I doubt it," Jack said. "In large quantities, yes. But what was scattered around out there wasn't enough to do any damage. Anyway, I called Trooper Benson, and he's on his way here to take a look."

"I'll feel better once he's seen it." Glancing at the clock, Elaine saw it was barely a minute before ten. "I need to go unlock the door."

"I'll catch Jack up on the noise in the attic," Jan volunteered.

Elaine nodded, heading for the foyer.

This was their first winter as proprietors of Tea for Two. Summer and fall had been gratifyingly busy, but they had braced themselves for a significant downturn in business during the winter months when there were fewer tourists to swell the population. To their pleasant surprise, many of the Lancaster and surrounding area residents had embraced tea and pastries. Elaine suspected their little tearoom was becoming known for being a nice, cozy place to gab as much as for a spot to drink good-quality tea.

Business had been steady, and different from their summer experience. It was nice to have folks coming by on a regular basis and to have a chance to chat with them. In the summer, they'd had a larger proportion of tourist business. Tourists were interesting, to be sure, but just as one got to know them, their vacations were over and they left again.

Elaine went through the large foyer to the front door, checking to be sure Jan had written the daily "special-teas" on the chalkboard in her pretty calligraphy script. Through the sidelights to each side of the heavy front door, she could see fresh snow had fallen, even though there had been none forecast. She unlocked the deadbolt, turned over the Open sign, stepped out on to the porch, and picked up the broom they kept off to one side of the door. It was in the low twenties now, and the blue fleece North Face zip she wore over her turtleneck was warm enough for a few minutes outside, since the wind wasn't blowing and it wasn't snowing.

Earl Grey, the cat who had adopted them when they moved into the house, came padding around the corner from the back of the house, where they had set up a shelter for him on the screened porch behind the kitchen. Unless the weather was really bad, they left the door to the porch slightly ajar so he could come and go as he liked. The big cat chirped and meowed affectionately, and Elaine scooped him up for a quick cuddle.

"How are you this morning, buddy?" she asked him, stroking his lavish gray fur and the tufts at his ears. "Are you warm enough at night?" She wasn't really worried, because she'd made him a warm little home using recommendations from the feral cat research she'd done. He seemed perfectly comfortable in his weatherproofed home even when the worst of storms blew.

The big cat leaped from her arms and trotted across the porch. Quickly and efficiently, Elaine swept the edges of the porch clean of the dusting of fresh snow that had fallen overnight. Several times she had to shoo Earl Grey gently out of the way when he chased the broom, apparently convinced she was sweeping just for his enjoyment.

Then she switched her broom for the shovel and removed the snow from the front walk and sidewalk. She barely had finished shoveling when she saw Macy Atherton and Rue Maxwell approaching.

"Good morning, ladies," she said. "Just wait until you see Rose and Jan's new recipe for a braided maple danish. Jan hasn't let me taste it yet, but the smell is beyond wonderful."

Macy groaned. "I don't need more of Jan's pastries. I think I've gained five pounds since you two opened this place."

Rue chuckled, elbowing her friend. "But that hasn't stopped you from coming back again and again and ordering them, now has it?"

Macy narrowed her eyes at her friend, but as Rue had observed, she marched right on up the steps and into the tea-room after stopping to stroke Earl Grey. Behind her back, Rue shot Elaine a big grin and a thumbs-up gesture.

Elaine bit her lip. It wouldn't do to laugh at one of her best customers, particularly when that customer frequently threw business their way by encouraging summer guests staying in Green Glade Cottages to check out Tea for Two.

"Where's Zale?" Elaine asked as she followed the pair inside. Macy's daughter-in-law Azalea frequented the tearoom nearly as much as Macy and Rue did, and she often came along with Macy.

"She's coming over soon. We have a new renter, and Zale offered to walk with her. I think she knows her from her college days. She was waiting for her in the office."

"A new boarder? What's she going to do in town this time of year?" Lancaster had little in the way of tourism for vacationers in the dead of winter. The question was reasonable; most of the visitors at this time of year were ice fishermen who had rented some time in one of the huts on the lake.

"She's some college teacher who says she's here for the peace and quiet so she can do some writing and maybe a little ice fishing," Macy said.

"True," Elaine grinned. "Unless you ski or snowboard, we're not exactly a hotbed of winter fun."

The women hung up their down jackets, scarves, and caps. As they were about to head into the east parlor, the larger of the two tearooms where Jan had built up the fire again for the day in the large fieldstone fireplace, Macy stopped dead. "What's this?"

# CHAPTER THREE

Macy stood in front of a poster Jan had made and set on an easel.

"It's an invitation," Elaine said, although anyone reading it could see that for themselves. Her heart sank as she realized that for divorced Macy, this wasn't the most welcome idea. She thought quickly, realizing the photos could include more than just romantic love. "For Valentine's Day, we thought it would be fun to display some of our local friends' photos that celebrate love. We'd love to have lots of submissions. I think it could be a photo of their parents' fiftieth anniversary a photo of their children or grandchildren, maybe sisters or brothers, or a favorite cousin. It could even be a picture of you and your pet, if it's the love of your life."

"*Hunh.*" Macy grunted and walked on past. "How about a picture of my divorce decree from that miserable good-for-nothin' I married?"

"Macy." Rue hissed the name as she hurried after her friend. "Don't talk like that. You know Zale's coming along in a few minutes, and you don't want her to hear that. The man is her father-in-law, regardless of what you think of him." Over her shoulder, she said to Elaine, "I think it's a lovely idea. I'll look through our pictures and find a good one of Ned and me for you."

"Thanks." Moving back toward the door, Elaine welcomed a few more early-bird customers and directed them to choose any table they liked. A few more folks settled in the east parlor while one couple found the far corner of the west parlor and held hands across the table, making Elaine smile.

"Good morning," Elaine heard Jan say. "Our 'special-tea' of the day is Drum Mountain White Cloud. It's still grown on the same mountains where monks from the Buddhist Drum Mountain monastery grew it for centuries. Let me bring you a pot and you can smell the wonderful aroma—sweet, nutty, and even a little fruity all at once."

"Might as well bring us some, and we'll try that braided maple danish thingy too." That was Macy, making Elaine smile again to herself as she recalled the conversation outside a few minutes ago.

The door in the foyer opened and closed again, and Elaine retraced her steps. Zale, Macy's daughter-in-law, had entered with another woman. Both of them were removing down parkas and caps. The newcomer was about Elaine's height with a mass of dark curls caught back in a clip, emphasizing her large, dark eyes.

"Hi, Elaine," Zale said, finger-combing the long brown hair she'd had bundled beneath her knit hat. "I'd like to introduce you to Dr. Fredericka Donnett, who has decided to vacation in the cottages with us."

Elaine held out a hand. "You're a brave woman to choose central Maine at this time of year, Dr. Donnett."

Dr. Donnett smiled, stuffing her mittens into her pockets before shaking Elaine's hand. "Please, call me Freddie. I'm taking a sabbatical from the University of Rhode Island and currently teaching a night class at Colby College, so I'm used to the cold, harsh weather. But Maine cold is noteworthy, even for me."

Elaine laughed. "I imagine so. That answers part of my next question. I was about to ask what sort of doctor, but you're a professor, right?"

Freddie nodded. "My specialty is nautical archeology. My dissertation was in the field of shipwreck locations off the Maine coast."

"That's unusual," Elaine said. "I don't think I've ever met anyone who studied nautical archeology before, although I do know some people who are fascinated by shipwrecks."

The woman smiled. "I've been interested in them since I was a very little girl. I grew up on Lake Michigan, and of course I heard a lot of shipwreck tales there. I guess that's what caught my interest."

Elaine was delighted. This was exactly why she had been excited about the idea of opening a tearoom. What interesting people they met!

"I'm also planning to do a little ice fishing while I'm here," Freddie said. "I don't often get much time to relax in mid-February, so I intend to take advantage of it."

Elaine smiled. "To each her own. Sitting in a tiny hut on a freezing lake isn't my preferred method of relaxation, but I wish you luck."

As Zale and Freddie Donnett went to join Macy and Rue at their table near the fire, the front door opened again. To Elaine's surprise, it abruptly banged back against the wall.

A small, dark-haired woman entered, clearly distraught. Elaine recognized her as Shelba Wattings, the wife of the fishing gear rental shop owner and a casual customer who had begun coming into the tearoom almost every week since the beginning of the new year. "Is Macy here?" she asked.

"I'm in here." Macy had seen the newcomer and immediately recognized her distress. "Why, what's the matter, Shelba?"

"My son's missing." And the woman burst into tears.

"What?" Macy demanded. "What do you mean, 'missing'?"

"Come in," Elaine said. The poor woman looked as if she might faint. "Let me get you some tea."

The woman's lips trembled. "Thank you." She clutched at the hand Elaine extended. "Gleason didn't come home last night."

Macy glanced at Elaine. "Gleason is her son."

Elaine's eyes widened. "Have you called the police?"

"Not yet." Shelba shook her head. "Bud's been calling his friends. I've been stopping anywhere I know there will be local folks and asking them to keep an eye out for him."

"Gleason's an adult," Macy said. "You know, hon, there comes a time in a young man's life when he may choose not to come home at night. It's the natural order of things."

Shelba jerked away from Macy, looking shocked. "It most certainly is not. Gleason was brought up better than that. Besides, he doesn't even have a steady girl *and* he always calls if he's going to be late or staying with a friend. Always."

Macy looked a bit skeptical at the pronouncement, but she didn't assay another opinion. "Come sit down," she said. "Let Elaine bring you some tea."

Elaine hurried to the kitchen and filled a teapot, adding a high-quality kava blend to help decrease anxiety, and carried it back into the east parlor.

Shelba Wattings had removed her coat, and Macy had pulled up another chair and placed it at her table.

"I'm sure he'll be in touch any time," Rue said in a soothing tone.

"Bud tried his cell but it just went to voice mail," Shelba said in a quavering tone.

"When was the last time you saw him?" Elaine asked.

"I saw him at dinner two nights ago," Shelba said. "But Bud saw him yesterday afternoon. Gleason works afternoons in the rental shop. He was going out on the lake before dark to check the ice around all the rental shanties."

A cold chill ran up Elaine's spine. She couldn't help thinking of the two men she'd seen coming off the ice at dusk yesterday. "What does Gleason look like?" she asked. "I don't believe I've ever met him."

"He's tall with dark hair and a close beard," Macy told her.

"And blue eyes," Shelba said. "He has beautiful blue eyes."

Jan had come to the door of the east parlor in time to hear Shelba's words, and Elaine's gaze met hers. In Jan's eyes Elaine saw the same apprehension she herself was feeling.

"Bud came home after that, and Gleason was supposed to lock up. But when Bud went down to the shop a bit ago, it was still unlocked. So Gleason never locked up last night.

Bud's madder'n fire. He's calling Gleason's friends, but so far, no one's seen him. I'm sure something terrible has happened to him."

Over Shelba's head, Jan made a tiny come-here gesture and disappeared into the hallway. Excusing herself, Elaine hurried after her cousin.

"We need to tell Trooper Benson that Gleason Wattings may be missing," Jan whispered to Elaine. "Daniel's standing in the kitchen. He came in the back way."

"What did he say about the blood?"

"He took a sample and had someone take it to the lab. But after hearing Shelba Wattings's story, I'm afraid we may know whose blood it is."

"You could be right, but let's not leap to conclusions," Elaine said. "Do you know Gleason Wattings?"

Jan nodded. "Mostly just from seeing him around town with his folks when he was growing up. But as Shelba said, he still helps out at the rental shop. He's as big as his dad. They look a lot alike, except Bud's hair is getting gray at the temples now."

Elaine had met Bud Wattings once last summer and had seen him down on the docks. He was a tall, broad fellow. "The two men we saw," she said, keeping her voice low. "One was a big man, much larger than the other. He could have been Gleason."

Jan nodded. "Most definitely."

Elaine sucked in a breath of concern. "You're right. We have to tell the police what we saw. It sounds like he could be in serious danger."

When the cousins pushed through the door into the kitchen at the back of the house, Trooper Daniel Benson already had removed his hat and coat and was jotting notes as Jack Weston spoke.

He turned to look at the two cousins. "So you two discovered the blood on the ice?"

At their nods, his brow creased. "Why were you out on the ice just after dawn? Seems like a walk around town would be an easier trek."

Elaine and Jan glanced at each other.

Elaine took a deep breath, seeing that Jan had elected her spokesman. "We saw someone being helped off the ice at dusk last evening, at about five o'clock."

Daniel's eyebrows had climbed halfway to his hairline at the revelation. "Helped how?"

"Half-carried, I suppose," she said after a moment's thought. "As if he was injured or drunk."

The words appeared to electrify Daniel and Jack.

"What?" Jack looked stunned. "Why didn't you tell me that?"

Jan put out her hands in a dampening gesture before Jack could get too fired up. "We haven't really had a chance. And I suppose we didn't want to assume the worst."

Elaine took the floor again. Starting from the shout she had heard last evening while dusting, she led them through the cousins' sighting of the two men and their assumption that he might have hit his head or—more likely—was tipsy. She explained that they'd felt uneasy enough to decide to take a walk on to the lake at first light to see if there was anything, any reason to believe there was something amiss.

"And when we found that spot of blood," she concluded, "we knew we needed to report it."

Jack cleared his throat. "If it makes you feel any better, the amount of blood spilled doesn't indicate a significant trauma."

"There's not enough blood," Daniel clarified, "for us to be concerned about a fatal injury."

"Whew," Jan said. "That's a relief."

"There's something else," Elaine said, clearing her throat.

Daniel's gaze sharpened. "What is it?"

"One of our customers came in today and said her son is missing."

"And you think the person you saw on the ice might be her son?"

"The missing man is Gleason Wattings," Jan said quietly. "You know him," she said, turning to Jack. "Gleason helps his father, Bud, with his fishing gear rental business, and apparently Bud left Gleason to close up late yesterday."

"Gleason's a college student," Elaine added, "and wasn't expected home for dinner, but apparently he never came home at all last night, and his mother insisted that he would never stay out all night without letting them know."

Jack frowned. "Gleason Wattings is a pretty big guy. It's hard to imagine someone doing serious damage to him without a weapon. You didn't hear any shots or anything, right?"

"No." Elaine shook her head. "But when we saw the two men coming off the ice, the one was much larger than the other, and he's the one who was staggering. The smaller man was supporting him."

The trooper was busy taking notes. "And you said they got into a vehicle and left."

"Yes," Jan said, "but just one vehicle. What does Gleason drive?" she asked Jack.

"A Jeep," he said immediately.

"It wasn't a Jeep. It was a car," Jan said definitely.

Elaine nodded. "That night, we assumed that either the one was taking the other home to sleep it off, or that possibly he intended to seek medical help for his friend."

"And that still could be the case," Trooper Benson said. "Sometimes things add up, and sometimes they really are just coincidences."

He consulted his notes. "Tell me more about the car."

Elaine hesitated, turning to her cousin. "It was just a small car. I have no idea of the make or model. And the sun had just set, so I can't even guess at the color, except that it was sort of dark."

Jan nodded. "It was some kind of little-ish car. Not an SUV."

Jack rolled his eyes. "Any other details that might help us?"

*"Hmm,"* Jan said. "The big guy sat in the front passenger seat and the little guy drove, if that helps at all."

"The smaller man helped the bigger fellow into the car," Elaine added.

Daniel nodded. "Okay."

But Elaine could see that his expression was troubled. "Are you going to talk to Bud and Shelba?" she asked. "Shelba said they were contacting his friends and alerting people around town but they hadn't made a report yet."

Daniel hesitated. "Yes. I think it might be a good idea for me to stop by there before I head back to Augusta." The state trooper was headquartered in the larger town. "Maybe he's gotten in touch by now."

"Shelba's having tea in the east parlor right now," Jan said. "If you like, we could let you talk with her in the office."

# CHAPTER FOUR

After Daniel Benson left, Elaine returned to the east parlor to check on the tables she had served. Shelba had hurried out after speaking with the state trooper.

Macy beckoned Elaine over the moment she entered. "Freddie has a question for you," she told Elaine.

"I hate to be a bother," Freddie said, "but would it be all right if I sat in the other room with my computer?"

Elaine smiled. "Sure. Valentine's Day, on Saturday, will be crowded, I suspect, but other than that, it should be more than fine to sit in the west parlor."

"Thanks." Freddie nodded. "This place has a pleasant atmosphere. I think it will be a good place to work."

"Feel free to set up over there whenever you're ready," Elaine said. Before she could ask what Freddie intended to work on, the opening of the front door forestalled further conversation. Returning to the foyer, she smiled as she recognized Pearl Trexler, another friendly face who had become a regular customer.

Pearl entered with her hand under the elbow of a very petite woman. The tiny woman had magnificent silver hair. She looked significantly older than Pearl, who, Elaine knew, was somewhere in her early seventies.

"Good morning, Elaine," Pearl said. She was as tall as Elaine, and every inch radiated enthusiasm and vitality. "I'd like you to meet Nan Colchester. Nan was my mother's best friend and she's practically my second mother."

Elaine extended a hand and carefully shook the fragile, blue-veined hand, while its owner beamed at her as cheerfully as Pearl. "It's nice to meet you, Nan. I think I've heard of Colchesters in the area. Have you lived in the area all your life?"

"Every day of it," Nan confirmed, "and I'll let you guess how close to a century that is." She laughed heartily, and Pearl and Elaine chuckled.

"Please come have a seat near the fire," Elaine said, "and we'll warm you up with one of our teas and a sweet pastry. My cousin Jan made a braided maple pastry I am dying to try this morning."

"That's why we're here," Pearl said. "We go out together once a month, and this is Nan's month to choose. She heard Tea for Two was a terrific place. Since I can't stay away, I could vouch for that, and here we are."

"How nice." Elaine was warmed by the words. They depended on local recommendations from other merchants to bring tourists through the doors, and it appeared that they were benefitting from that with the townspeople as well.

She followed the older women into the tearoom and showed them to a table next to the one at which Macy, Rue, Zale, and their guest, Freddie Donnett, sat. Jan and Elaine both worked the room as more folks entered and found seats. Practically everyone chose to sit near the fireplace or at least in the east parlor where the fire was warming the room. Many people decided to try the Drum Mountain tea, and Jan's braided danishes were a huge hit. Elaine finally had a chance to sneak away to the kitchen and steal a little piece for herself.

Jan came in as she took the first bite.

"Oh," Elaine moaned. "This is fabulous. No wonder the customers are going nuts."

Jan laughed. "Yes, I suspect I am going to be forced to add this to our regular pastry schedule."

"Is it time-intensive?" Elaine regarded the beautiful pastry. "It certainly looks it. I have no idea how you did that braiding."

"It's not nearly as difficult as it looks," Jan said.

Elaine hastily swiped a napkin over her mouth and washed her hands. "All right. Ready to leap back into the fray. Have you met Macy and Zale's guest, Dr. Freddie Donnett?"

Jan nodded. "What a fascinating career. She was telling me about a shipwreck she helped locate in Lake Ontario last year. And have you spoken with Pearl's friend Nan? I bet she's ninety if she's a day, but she's sharp as a tack."

"I hope someone says that about me someday," Elaine said with a laugh.

An hour later, Elaine was preparing tea for another table of newcomers. As she refilled the teapot on the stove, her mind reviewed the morning's shocking discovery of the blood on the ice and the even more concerning news that Gleason Wattings appeared to be missing. She felt a bone-deep certainty that Gleason was the man they had seen being "helped" off the ice yesterday. *Dear Lord,* she prayed as her fingers deftly assembled the tea tray, *please restore that young man to his family unharmed.*

Just then, there was a cry from the front of the house and the chatter of excited voices.

"Uh-oh," Jan said. "Want to check that out or shall I?"

"I'll do it." Elaine stopped what she was doing and rushed into the foyer.

A gaggle of women was standing at the front window in the east parlor, the window that overlooked Main Street.

"What's going on?" she asked.

Macy was struggling into her coat. "Joe Vennard just backed right into Shelba's car and didn't even stop to see if he damaged it. His mother would be so mortified if she knew the kinds of tricks that boy gets up to."

Mrs. Vennard had been the cousins' fourth-grade teacher. She was long since retired, and they rarely saw her around town. But Elaine rather agreed with Macy. Mrs. Vennard had been a strict but pleasant teacher who made her students want to work hard. How she'd raised a son like Joe was difficult to imagine, but Jan recalled talk about mean old Mr. Vennard, who'd died years ago. Maybe it wasn't so difficult to imagine after all.

Shelba had left the tearoom after talking with Daniel Benson, but her intention, Elaine knew, was to walk to the rest of the businesses along Main Street and ask if anyone had seen Gleason or, alternately, if they would keep an eye out for him.

"I'm going to check out that car and then find Shelba. That Joe's a mean-spirited rat," Macy said, stomping out the door.

Elaine's eyebrows rose. Rue, standing in the doorway to the parlor, watched her leave and then shrugged when her eyes met Elaine's.

Rue sighed. "Joe was near my niece in school," she said. "He was a terrible bully, picked on other kids for no good reason, beat up one boy who refused to help him cheat on a test, that kind of thing. He used to own Bud's business, but nobody local would support him because he was always trying to cheat people. Prices were too high; he refused to give refunds when equipment malfunctioned, that kind of thing. He scraped along with first-time tourists, but those that returned year after year didn't like him much either." She shook her head. "You can't run a successful business if you're a miserable human being, you know?"

"I can see how that would put folks off," Elaine agreed. "Poor man. He must be terribly unhappy."

Rue stared at her a minute and then grinned. "You might be the first person I've ever known to have sympathy for Joe Vennard. He married young for love, but his wife ran off with some tourist after about a year. Of course, Joe blamed her, but everybody else in town figured living with Joe for a year was enough to make anybody run away. He's a lot like his daddy was."

Elaine glanced out the window, where she could see Macy examining the bumper of a car she assumed was Shelba's. A moment later, Macy started back up the front sidewalk toward them.

"No damage?" Rue asked as Macy came through the door.

Macy raised a gloved hand palm down and waggled the edges up and down slightly. "There's a scratch," she said, "but

I doubt Shelba and Bud will report it. They've got enough on their plate right now without Joe getting in their faces again, and you know he'd just love a chance to get them worked up."

As Macy took off her coat, Elaine made a beeline for the kitchen. She was dying of curiosity, but she hated to appear too gossipy to their patrons. Asking her cousin questions was another story.

Jan was dumping ingredients into the stand mixer again as Elaine entered the room. "What's the story on Joe Vennard and Bud Wattings?" Elaine asked. She took a minute to recount the scene she'd just witnessed.

"Oh, that Joe," Jan said dismissively. Although she had lived in nearby Augusta until recently, she was far more in touch with their hometown doings than Elaine, who had been far away most of her adult life. "I heard he ran his business into the ground, and Bud bought him out. But Joe can't stand it now that Bud's making something of it and doing well, and he bad-mouths Bud every chance he gets. He's even told people Bud cheated him out of a fair price, but everybody knows it wasn't worth much more than the inventory and the cost of the building because Joe didn't have any clientele to speak of."

Something occurred to Elaine. "Do you think he dislikes Bud enough to have kidnapped his son?"

Jan's mouth fell open. She frowned, closed her mouth and took a deep breath. "Wow. I suppose I hadn't let myself go there. Did we really witness a kidnapping yesterday?"

"I think it's possible," Elaine said. "Maybe not, but we should at least entertain the notion that Gleason was taken away by force."

"I can't imagine Joe would have done that. How would kidnapping Gleason benefit Joe?"

It was Elaine's turn to frown. "There's no plausible reason. If he wants to get the business back, threatening Bud's son seems like an awfully extreme way to go about it."

"Payback?" Jan looked thoughtful. "Would he go to that length to get revenge?"

"Revenge for what, exactly? It's not like Bud did anything terrible to him. Despite what Joe says about being cheated out of his business, Rue says it was failing anyway."

"Revenge for Bud buying it and turning it around?" Jan shrugged. "That's weak. No sane person would consider kidnapping someone's son for something that petty. Maybe he's thinking of getting back some of what he considers his money by asking a ransom."

"That would be pretty hard to pull off without getting caught," Elaine pointed out. "Unless you're a total idiot."

Jan shook her head. "Joe's not an idiot. He's just thoroughly unpleasant."

Elaine returned to the east parlor and took another order, still thinking about what might motivate someone to kidnap a person. It seemed to her that there would have to be a pretty spectacular payoff at the conclusion for anyone to take such a risk.

The group of women around the fire were still talking about Joe Vennard, Shelba, and Gleason when Elaine turned to ask them if they'd like another pot of tea. Everyone declined, and Elaine brought them all their checks before clearing as much as she could and carrying it back to the kitchen.

Rose was preparing an order for a couple from Augusta who had just come in. She looked up inquiringly as Elaine entered. "Any more news about Gleason Wattings?"

Elaine shook her head. "Nothing so far."

Rose hesitated. "I heard his mother was saying he doesn't have a steady girl, but I think she might be wrong."

"Oh? Why?" Elaine recalled Shelba's certainty.

"Gleason works in the kitchen at a little grill in Waterville. When I was taking classes at Colby College, I'd go in there regularly for lunch, and I often saw him getting off the early shift. There was a waitress who got off at the same time. He held her coat and then they'd hold hands walking down the street. Once or twice, I saw them get in a car together. I assumed she was his girlfriend."

"How long ago was this, Rose?" Jan asked, taking a brief break from kneading some dough.

"Pretty recently," Rose said. "I know I was in there right before Christmas, because all the waitresses were wearing big bows on their heads. It was just a silly touch, you know, to make people laugh during exam week. And I remember when she and Gleason left that day, she forgot to take off her bow, and he stopped her in the street and took it off and kissed her." Rose sighed. "It was very sweet."

"So it's likely they're still dating," Jan said thoughtfully. "Maybe we should run over there tomorrow or Wednesday. If we see Gleason, it sure would set my mind at ease."

"If you do, go around one, right after lunch," Rose advised. "That's when I've seen them."

Business slowed down quite a bit as the lunch hour at Tea for Two neared. That was a usual pattern, even in the summer.

Freddie Donnett, the professor from Rhode Island, had stayed after Macy, Zale, and Rue left. She had appropriated a table in the west parlor and was busily tapping at a small laptop computer, a notebook and other items spread out around her, but by one thirty in the afternoon, there was not another customer in the place.

When the front door opened, Elaine hurried toward it with a smile. The smile froze as she noted the disreputable appearance of the man who stepped inside.

# CHAPTER FIVE

The man's clothing, while warm, looked extremely well-worn and none too clean. Ragged dark hair hung lankly from beneath a blue watch cap.

Instinctively, she glanced at Jan and Archie Bentham, their dapper and charming British employee, who were clearing tables in the dining room. Jan had lived in the area all her life and knew many more people than Elaine, who had missed getting to know at least one generation during her years traveling the world as a military wife.

"Hello, Marvin," Jan said, crossing the room to greet him. "Have you met my cousin Elaine Cook?"

"'Lo." The man raised one mittened hand rather than offering a handshake.

"Elaine, this is Marvin Bellamy. You might remember his grandfather, Harve Bellamy, who owned the garage on the corner near my house when we were kids."

"Oh, I do." It was nice to be able to connect this young man—for Elaine could see that he was probably no more than midtwenties—with memories of her childhood. "How is your grandfather?"

Marvin's eyes had followed the conversation from Jan to Elaine with an eager expression that reminded Elaine of a puppy, but now his face fell. He removed his watch cap and ducked his head. "M'granddaddy passed away a couple years back."

"I'm sorry for your loss," Elaine told him.

"It's okay," he said, his voice deep and slow. "When it's yer time, it's yer time. That's what m'grandaddy always said, and I guess he was right."

Elaine wasn't sure how to answer that, but Marvin didn't look as if an answer was expected.

Jan smiled at him encouragingly. "How can we help you, Marvin?"

"I'm, uh, looking for work," he said. "Thought maybe you ladies would need someone to shovel your sidewalks."

Elaine blinked. Surely the shoveled sidewalks spoke for themselves. She usually did it before opening each morning, although when a lot of snow fell, both she and Jan got out there and dealt with it together, and Archie did the driveway with a snowplow on the front of the truck he drove in bad weather.

"I'm sorry," Jan said gently to Marvin. "We take care of that ourselves, and there's nothing else we need help with, is there, Elaine?"

Elaine shook her head. "Not that I can think of. But thank you for checking."

"You're welcome." Marvin turned toward the door with no further ado.

"Where's your brother?" Jan asked him. "Don't tell me Mickey's waiting in a warm car for you." She was teasing, but Marvin did not appear to register the joking tone.

The tips of his ears turned red. "No, ma'am. I'm on my own today. Thank you for your time." And he turned and slipped out the door, cramming the watch cap back on his head.

Jan sighed as the door closed. "I wish we had work to offer him. I feel sorry for those two."

Archie, who had stepped away from the tables and stood in the wide double entry to the east parlor said, "Yes, but you know what would happen. Those two would botch it up entirely, and you'd wind up paying someone else to repair it. I hate to say it, but..."

"...it's true." Jan finished his sentence.

"He did seem a little clueless," Elaine said tactfully. "Although he wasn't here long enough for me to get a clear picture of his personality or his intellect." She tried for objectivity. "Whatever he is or isn't, someone taught that young man good manners."

Archie smiled. "Yes, he does have good manners, even if his mental gears work rather slowly. What you saw was Marvin at his everyday best."

"Sweet, both of the brothers," Jan said, "but frankly, not real bright."

"They tried to open a bowling alley a couple years ago." Rose had come to lean against the kitchen door facing into the hall. "I have no idea how they got the money for that, but I'm sorry to say they clearly had no idea how to run a business and they couldn't even fix the machines when they broke, so they were trying to set the pins by hand, like they did years ago."

Elaine grinned. "Really?"

"I believe it," Archie said.

"They opened an auto body shop," Rose added, "but nobody would go because they knew nothing about fixing cars. Then they tried to be furniture movers, but the company they worked for fired them after they dropped Mrs. Haven's piano into a snowbank."

"Oh my," Jan said.

"They tried to start their own ice shanty rental business last month," Rose added, "but they left a truck on the lake too long and it sank partway. Needed a tow truck to get it out."

"Oh, I heard about that!" Elaine said. "I don't think I realized it was them though."

"Between Bud Wattings and the guy down in Penzance," Jan said, "there's not enough business for another shanty rental anyway. Why would they even try that?"

Rose shrugged. "Their dad was a pretty good carpenter, but ever since he died, those two have been failing at one thing after another. I'm not sure what skills they might have, but I do feel bad for them."

Elaine felt a pang of pity. "Maybe we should try to help them find something realistic."

"Mickey, the older one, seems more capable than Marvin." Rose shrugged. "I don't think I've ever seen him around town without Mickey before."

"Custodial work?" Elaine offered. "Dishwasher?"

"You're right," Jan said to Elaine. "We should try to help them. We'll have to give that more thought."

The door opened again, admitting Daniel Benson. "Hey there," he said. "I'm back again." He offered Elaine a sheet of paper from a stack he held. "Do you have any prominent place you could put this up?"

Elaine took the sheet of paper from the state police trooper. A shock ran through her as she saw the photo of a dark-haired young man reproduced with the caption: MISSING—REWARD FOR INFORMATION. Below the photo was Gleason Wattings's description and the police contact information.

"So you really think it was Gleason we saw last night?" She raised her gaze from the paper.

Daniel shrugged. "We don't know. But I spoke to his folks and he definitely doesn't sound like the kind of person to just take off without letting them know where he is. They asked if they thought they should post these around town, and frankly, at this point, I don't think it's a bad idea. So I told them I'd take some."

The phone on the little table in the foyer rang as if on cue, and everyone stopped and looked at it.

"Excuse me," Jan murmured. She reached out and lifted the receiver to her ear. "Hello?"

Elaine saw amazement streak across her cousin's face.

"Gleason?" Jan asked. "Gleason Wattings? Is that you?" Her voice rose in excitement, and Daniel rushed to her side. But even as he did, Jan was saying, "Gleason? Gleason? Are you there? Gleason?"

Daniel Benson took the receiver from her hand, holding it to his ear. After a moment, he shook his head. "The connection's been broken. What did you hear?

Jan looked stunned. She pressed a hand to the base of her throat. "I heard a male voice say, 'Mom, it's Gleason. I need...' But then someone shouted something, there was a scuffling sound, and the connection died. I think someone took the phone from him and hung it up."

The trooper and Elaine both stared at her.

"Are you sure it was Gleason Wattings?" Benson asked.

"He identified himself as Gleason," Jan said. "But I don't know him well enough to be sure it was his voice."

"Could you trace the call?" Elaine asked Daniel.

The trooper sighed. "We can try. But without getting the FBI involved, we're limited in how much information we have access to." He made a notation in a small notebook he carried. "I think we have to assume that it was a genuine call."

"So that means...," Elaine trailed off.

Slowly, Daniel said, "That means that from this point forward, I'm officially considering that Gleason Wattings may not have gone off on his own." He handed Elaine the stack of fliers. Pulling a notebook from a pocket, he began to jot down notes. "Would you be able to pass out more of those? I need to file a report on this and talk to my captain about how to proceed before I talk to the Wattings family."

Elaine took the fliers Daniel held out. "But why did he call here?" she asked. "Why wouldn't he have called his own family?"

"I think he thought he did," Jan said. "He distinctly said 'Mom.'"

"What's Wattings's phone number?" Elaine asked Daniel.

The trooper flipped through his notebook and almost immediately rattled off a number.

"That's it," Elaine said. "Our numbers are the same except for the last digit. On a keypad, four is directly above seven. Ours ends in four, theirs ends in seven. He misdialed."

Daniel's eyes flicked to hers and then back to the notebook in his hand. "That's it," he said. "Good catch. He thought he had called home."

Jan exhaled a deep breath that sounded relieved. "So he's alive," she said. "Not that I thought otherwise, but I have to confess I was beginning to entertain the notion that he might be in serious trouble."

"He still could be," Daniel said, unsmiling. "If someone took him off the lake and is preventing him from calling home, I'd have to assume that he's being held against his will. The big question is why?"

# CHAPTER SIX

At two o'clock that afternoon, Jan and Elaine had a meeting with a local sugar maker who was hoping to sell them some of his jars of maple syrup.

After the vendor left, Jan and Elaine talked for a few minutes longer about a schedule for adding some things to their inventory before breaking up their meeting. Jan immediately headed for the kitchen to see how Rose was doing, while Elaine closed the laptop and tucked it beneath one arm. As she rose from her seat, she checked to be sure that the table still was pristine for guests.

Entering the foyer, she could see Freddie Donnett was still seated in the west parlor. The woman looked up from her absorption in whatever was on her monitor and waved.

Elaine smiled and altered her intended course from the office toward the woman in the west parlor. "Is there something else I can get you, Freddie?"

"I'm researching an old coin I found," the woman said. "Would you like to see it?"

"Absolutely I would." Elaine leaned closer as Freddie Donnett pulled up an image on her laptop monitor.

The image that Elaine viewed a moment later was stunning. It was a golden coin with what looked like an American eagle on one side, and a sun rising over the peak of a mountain on the other. There was a small nick near one wing of the eagle, and the coin looked to be worn in several places.

"You found this?" Elaine's eyebrows rose. "My goodness, that must have been thrilling. What is it?"

"It's called a Brasher doubloon, and yes, it was beyond thrilling," the woman said. "The only thing that could have been better is if I had found it while diving."

"Oh, I assumed you had." Elaine grinned. "Since you're a shipwreck expert and all that."

"No." The professor shook her head. "I bought a box lot from an antique dealer a while back that had this ratty little wooden box in it. I asked what it was, and the dealer said he had no idea. He'd gotten it from someone cleaning out their attic. I couldn't believe he didn't want to know what was in it, but he was happy to make me a deal. It felt heavier than it should if it was empty, although it didn't rattle, and of course I was curious, but the lock was rusted shut. Eventually I had to break it open, and when I did, this coin was inside, wrapped in an old rag, along with an old journal. Have you ever seen anything like it?"

Elaine shook her head. "It's gold. I'd remember that." She chuckled. "Gold coins aren't exactly something found in the average change purse."

Freddie laughed too. "I guess not."

"It must be valuable. Hard to believe you found it in a box lot."

"I guess that depends on your definition of 'valuable,'" Freddie said. "Actually, this one is an electrotype copy. It's made of brass over a lead base."

"Really?" Elaine peered at the image on the screen. "Oh, I can't imagine how disappointing that must have been," she said with a horrified laugh. "Did you think you had found gold?"

"It occurred to me," Freddie said dryly. "But as I researched it, I learned there are only about half a dozen known 'real' ones, so I suspected this one wasn't real, partly because of this little nick." She pointed to the tiny cut along one edge. "Prior to the 1960s, dealers often cut these to determine if they were pure gold. This one was tested."

"Did the journal you found mention anything about the others?"

Freddie's gaze slid away from Elaine's, focusing on the handsome coin on the screen. "Nothing definitive," she said dismissively.

Elaine heard the front door open. "I'd love to hear more, but duty calls," she said, excusing herself to put away the laptop and greet the newcomers. "Let me know if you'd like more tea or a something else to eat."

"Will do. Thank you." Freddie turned back to the image of the gorgeous gold coin on the screen.

PROMPTLY AT THREE o'clock, Hetta Fishburn and her fiancé, J.C. Grimm, arrived for their appointment to finalize all the arrangements for their wedding reception to be held on the afternoon of Valentine's Day. Elaine welcomed them and showed them into the dining room, where she had set the table for four. A small surge of customers had changed Elaine's mind about meeting in the parlors. She was afraid someone would want to stop and chat with her in the middle of the meeting.

"Hello, hello again," Hetta caroled as Jan entered from the kitchen, bearing a tea tray. The bride-to-be had met with Jan once to discuss the possibilities for food and drink before she made the decision to hold the reception at Tea for Two.

Hetta was a tiny grandmotherly woman with warm brown eyes that always seemed to be smiling, while J.C. was tall and lanky and seemed content to let his intended do most of the talking.

Jan set the tea on a side table for Elaine to distribute while she returned to the kitchen for a second tray with five different types of mini cakes she had made for the couple to taste.

Elaine poured, making small talk until Jan returned.

"Oh, those are gorgeous," Hetta cooed, seeing the simply but beautifully decorated samples. The woman was pink and glowing, and her fiancé held her hand as if she were precious porcelain. "We're just so delighted that we can have the reception here," Hetta told Jan and Elaine. "We're getting married in Waterville at one o'clock, and since it's a small wedding with just our immediate families attending, we anticipate that we should be able to arrive here by two on Saturday."

Elaine made a note on the form she had on a clipboard. "Even with photos?"

"Oh yes." Hetta nodded. "We're going to do a few of just us and then a few family photos. It won't take hours like some of the young people do today." She glanced up at J.C. "He says he only has ten smiles in him before he eats."

Everyone laughed, including J.C., who looked adorably embarrassed. "I just want to marry her and spend the rest of my life with her," he said. "I'm not so keen on all the wedding hoopla."

"How did you meet?" Elaine asked, charmed by the obvious adoration between the pair.

"We were friends in high school," Hetta said. "But we never dated."

"I was too shy to ask her," J.C. said. "I only dated girls who asked me out first."

Hetta waved a hand. "Isn't that the silliest thing you ever heard? Anyway, we both married other people who have since passed away, and when he saw me at our class reunion, he finally got up the nerve to ask me out."

J.C. beamed. "Then two months later I got up the nerve to ask the big question—and she said yes two months later."

Jan gasped. "Really? That was quick."

Hetta shrugged and smiled. "Sometimes you just know."

Elaine smiled, and started down the list of questions she had for the couple. What beverages did they want served? (Hot tea, hot chocolate, and some type of pink punch.) Would there be a garter and/or a bouquet toss? ("No, not at our age. Wouldn't that be silly?") Gift table, sweethearts' table, seating arrangements. Flowers and decorations. Hetta, thankfully, knew her mind and it wasn't a long or tedious conversation.

Jan brought over the tray of cakes and introduced each one. The couple tasted all five. Hetta loved the red velvet with cream cheese icing, while J.C. favored the vanilla with raspberry icing.

"Why don't we do both?" Jan suggested. "We could do the red velvet as a small layer cake and the other as cupcakes. Cupcakes are all the rage for weddings today, and the colors will complement your flowers and your dress." Hetta planned to wear pale pink and decorate with pink, white, and red rosebuds.

"I love that idea," Hetta said, "but it sounds like an awful lot of cake for thirty-some people."

"Three dozen cupcakes, in case there are a few children or folks with big appetites." Jan said. "And we'll save the top layer of the cake for you to freeze and eat next year on your anniversary, so there won't be that much extra left."

"What a lovely idea," Hetta said. She turned to J.C. "Wouldn't that be romantic?"

Elaine looked at the beaming couple, who appeared to love Jan's idea. Only recently had she begun to entertain the idea of a new relationship, one with her childhood friend Nathan Culver, who had made it clear that he was interested in pursuing more than just a friendship with her.

"...So wonderful that you've restored this place," Hetta was saying as Elaine tuned back in to the conversation. "I volunteer at the Kennebec County Historical Society, and this old house must have been quite the showplace back in the 1920s."

Jan smiled at her. "Yes, we've done a little research of our own."

As Jan and Hetta continued to chat, Elaine's mind wandered to the information she and Jan had uncovered about their home. Suddenly a flash of memory assailed Elaine, and the piece she'd been trying to recall came to her with crystal clarity. A few weeks earlier, her mother's friend Richard had mentioned that the mill was sold for a pittance. To whom had it been sold?

The meeting with Hetta and J.C. concluded shortly afterward. Elaine headed for the office to record the details of the discussion in the computer and update the invoice to reflect Hetta's preferences, while Jan returned to the kitchen.

As she walked through the foyer, heading for the back of the house, a tall man stepped toward her. "Knock, knock," he said.

"Nathan." Elaine smiled with real warmth. "What are you up to this morning?" Changing course, she opened the kitchen door, indicating that he should follow.

Grinning, her friend of many years crossed the kitchen to her side, his blue eyes twinkling. "I just finished a potential sale visit. The lady has some fantastic items. I didn't inventory anything today, but on my walk-through, I noted an old oak farm table and some other really nice pieces of furniture, several slag glass table lamps, and Maine license plates dating back more than fifty years." He rubbed his hands together. "I can't wait to dig in."

Elaine laughed. "I bet. Sounds interesting." She pointed at a basket on the counter into which Jan had tossed a few broken pieces of various pastries. "Feel free to indulge. We toss the crumbs to the birds if they don't get eaten."

Nathan's eyebrows rose. "As fond as I am of birds, I'm delighted to take you up on the offer. My breakfast was rushed."

"Would you like a cup of tea?"

He shook his head. "No, thanks. I had coffee already. But a glass of water would be welcome."

As Elaine poured the water and set the glass before him, Nathan said, "Are you doing anything special for Valentine's Day?"

Elaine nodded. "We're dressing in Victorian costumes. Jan designed new ones and is sewing them herself. We also ordered a tea that tastes like chocolate-covered strawberries, and we are putting together a poster . . . "

"Elaine."

She stopped, looking inquiringly at him.

"I didn't mean Tea for Two. I meant you. Personally."

"Oh." Elaine's mind went blank. "Um, no. No, I'm not."

"Would you like to go out to dinner?" Nathan's eyes were very blue as they held hers. "I would very much enjoy having dinner with you. As a friend, if you still don't feel as if you're ready for anything more, although in the interest of fairness, you should know that I'm still hoping for 'more.'"

Elaine hesitated for a moment. She wanted to accept, she realized. She really wanted to accept. "I would like that too," she said in a rush, before she could talk herself out of it. And she was grateful when Nathan didn't push her to specify exactly in what category of relationship the dinner would be.

"Great. I'll pick you up at six thirty on Saturday." Nathan polished off the last of the broken maple croissant in his hand, took a final drink, and winked at her. "I'll probably see you before then, but I'll be looking forward to it. Catch you later."

"Later," Elaine echoed as he turned and headed out the kitchen door.

Abruptly, she plopped onto a stool. Had she really just said yes to a Valentine's Day date, of all things? True, she had begun to think that she would like to explore a more personal relationship with Nathan, but Valentine's Day, with all its hearts-and-flowers head-over-heels romance, its expectations?

Last January, she had still been reeling from her husband's death. By February, she had crafted the idea for Tea for Two and was doing her best to talk Jan into it. Last year, Valentine's Day had been nothing more than another day to get through without her husband. How much had happened since then!

She'd returned to her hometown and opened the tearoom with her cousin. They had fixed up the Victorian mansion and made it into both a business and a charming home. They had been successful beyond their modest hopes for their first year, and Elaine had begun to renew old friendships from her childhood—like Nathan Culver, with whom she shared so many memories.

Nathan and she essentially had been forced into friendship as children because their fathers spent so much time together. But Nathan, three years older than she, always had been kind. Since her return to town, he'd been more than kind. He'd shown what she could only call serious interest, although she had made it clear last spring that she wasn't ready for any new relationships. She'd still felt married to Ben when Jan and she had opened the tearoom nine months ago.

But even that had changed. Since marking one year as a widow, she'd begun to feel more open to change in her life.

More change, even, than moving and starting a new business. Proof positive was the way her mouth had opened and she'd accepted Nathan's invitation without hesitation.

Jan walked into the kitchen with a tray loaded with things to wash. "What's wrong?" she asked immediately.

Elaine smiled. For two people who had spent much of their adult lives apart, she still felt as close to her cousin as a sibling. "Nathan asked me out," she said.

Jan brightened. "Oh, that's great!" Her smiled died. "You didn't turn him down, did you?"

Elaine shook her head. "I said yes." She sighed. "And I'm looking forward to it. I guess I'm just having a moment of 'Oh my heavens, is this really a good idea?'"

Jan chuckled. She walked around the counter and placed a gentle arm around Elaine's shoulders. "I know the feeling. Actually, I don't, precisely, since I've been widowed for over ten years now without thinking much about dating until Bob came along. But dating again after losing your spouse is a big deal, and it deserves to be recognized as a major moment."

"A major moment." Elaine smiled up at her cousin. "Yes, that's exactly what it feels like."

# CHAPTER SEVEN

After dinner, Jan and Elaine were relaxing in their private sitting room upstairs when they heard someone entering the house. Jan had given keys to her children, who lived locally, and she called, "Hello?"

"Hi, Mom. Hi, Elaine." Jan's daughter Tara came up the stairs.

"Hi, honey," Jan said. "How are you?" She might be a biased mother, but Tara looked especially pretty today with her long, light-brown hair in a complicated French braid and light makeup. Only slightly taller than her mother, she was clad in navy leggings with large deep-red rhinoceroses on them and a matching cranberry sweater that hugged her slim frame. Outdoorsy and athletic, she didn't always bother with makeup, and she was attractive either way. But when she did bother, Jan thought her youngest was a knockout.

Tara was beaming as she entered the sitting room. "I'm terrific. You know Faith sold a lot of my jewelry during the Christmas season. She wants more pieces as fast as I can make them, and she's featuring my work as a local artist this week for Valentine's Day."

Faith Lanier was the owner of a local gift shop, A Little Something, who had begun carrying Tara's jewelry designs a few months ago.

"That's great," Elaine said. "Congratulations."

Jan jumped up to hug her daughter. "I'm so proud of you."

"I brought some of the things I'm working on," Tara told them. "I want your opinions."

"Opinions," Elaine said, "are one thing at which I excel."

Tara laughed as she tugged a large bag from her shoulder and withdrew a black leather jewelry roll from inside. "You're good at a lot of things, Elaine. Just look at what you and Mom have done with Tea for Two."

She untied the ribbons and laid the little organizer flat. Lined with velvet, it had a number of zippered pouches inside for bracelets or necklaces.

Carefully, Tara removed sterling silver and rose gold necklaces with beading in shades of pink, soft lavenders, and deep purples, robin's-egg blues and new-grass greens. Deep, glistening browns complimented tiger's eye, while others were webs of sparkling crystal. Matching bracelets, both dangle and stretchy elastic, came next, and earrings in varying lengths rounded out the lot.

Instinctively, Jan and Elaine each reached for one of the lovely items.

"These are beautiful," Jan told her daughter. She examined a silver chain with a polished amethyst heart dangling from it and then reached for matching dangly earrings with tiny amethyst hearts attached.

Elaine picked up a thin bracelet made of multiple strands of rose gold wire with sparkling faceted crystal beads knotted into the strands. "So is this. And all of it is going to A Little Something?"

"This and more, as soon as I get them made. Do you think this'll be appropriate for Valentine's Day?"

Elaine tilted her head and considered the jewelry. "I do. Some of it is very valentine-themed, but other pieces are good colors that people often wear, so there's a wide variety to choose from."

"And if certain colors or designs sell particularly well, you could always be prepared to make up a few more of those as soon as Faith tells you she's out," Jan suggested.

"Good idea," Tara said. "I was about to place an order for more beads, so I'll make sure I have a good range of color choices. Left to my own devices, I tend to avoid certain shades, but I try to battle my personal preferences, since everyone has individual taste."

She stopped suddenly, cocking her head, eyes flaring in alarm. "What's that noise?"

All three of them fell silent as an odd thumping, scraping noise came from overhead.

TARA'S EYES ROUNDED even more as the odd sounds from above them increased.

"We don't know," Jan said. "The game warden said he'd stop by around seven to take a look." She glanced at Elaine. "He was too busy earlier today."

Tara's eyebrows rose. "Don't you want to check it out for yourself?"

Elaine shrugged. "We already looked last night, but we didn't see anything. We assume it is some type of pest."

"Well, I want to see what's up there," Tara declared. "It sounds big enough to be a person. Doesn't it concern you that someone might be sneaking around in your attic?"

"I don't think it's a…," Jan began, but Tara was gone already.

Jan looked at Elaine. "She's always been my headstrong one."

Elaine laughed.

The doorbell rang, and Jan stood. "I bet that's Jack. Good timing."

"I'll let him in," Elaine said. "You'd better go see what Tara's up to."

As Jan nodded at Elaine's suggestion and headed to the third floor for the attic steps, Elaine walked along the hall. She turned and started down the staircase that curved around a landing midway down, running a hand lightly over the smooth wood of the banister as she went. At the bottom, she turned toward the front entry, where she could see a large shadow standing at the door.

"Nice to see you again, Jack," she said with a wry grin as she pulled open the door. "Come on in."

The game warden tugged off his black gloves and the black hat with MDIFW embroidered across the front, standing for the Maine Department of Inland Fisheries and Wildlife. Jack's role in the community encompassed a wide variety of tasks and responsibilities, as witnessed by his visit today.

"Hi again, Elaine," he said. Dimples winked in his lean cheeks and his blue eyes twinkled. "So I hear you have a guest who may not be welcome."

She grinned. "You could say that. Although at this point, we aren't even sure what species the guest is."

"Yes, we are." Jan's voice floated down from the landing of the stairs. "It's a raccoon. Looks like a young one. Tara's still up there trying to catch it."

"Catch it?" At Jan's words, Jack's grin vanished. He brushed by Elaine and sprinted up the steps two at a time. "Where's the attic and who's Tara?"

"Tara's my daughter," Jan said. "She's..." But the words were lost as Jack turned the corner at the landing and hurtled upward. A moment later, they could hear his feet pounding up the attic steps.

"Oh dear," Jan said, her eyes widening. Elaine rushed up the stairs and the two of them hurried to catch up to Jack. As they rounded the corner at the top of the stairs and turned to hurry up the third-floor steps, Jan could hear Jack's stern tones.

"Never, ever touch a wild animal, especially a raccoon. They are one of the biggest carriers of rabies in the state. Were you scratched or bitten?"

"I hadn't even touched it when you came thundering up the steps and scared the poor little thing half to death." Tara's voice was distinctly irritable. "And now it's gone back some-where behind that furniture, and I'll never catch it."

"You can't catch it." As Jan and Elaine arrived at the top of the steps, Jan thought that Jack and Tara looked like they were facing off for a quick-draw contest. "You can't touch it at all, or you risk having to get rabies shots. And the raccoon would probably have to be euthanized and tested for rabies."

Tara looked taken aback for a moment, but she quickly rallied. "That little thing didn't have rabies. It was coming right to me until you scared it."

"One of the most common behaviors of rabid animals is unusual docility and what humans perceive as tame behavior," Jack told her. "That 'Old Yeller' foaming at the mouth, snarling rage is much less common. A lot of them just get really lethargic. And since you say this one seems young, it makes me wonder what happened to the mother in the middle of winter for it to be on its own. She could have died of rabies."

Tara crossed her arms. "So if it's an orphan, then it needs help."

"And that's where I come in," Jack said. "I'll set a trap..."

"What? You'd snap a trap shut on that baby? That's awful. How inhumane are you?"

"Not a leg-hold trap," Jack said, clearly reaching for patience. "A wire cage-type trap baited with food. The door will close once the raccoon's inside. It won't be harmed, and I'll relocate it where it can't invade any more homes."

"You'll dump it out all alone in the middle of the frigid, snowy woods in February. It'll die," Tara said flatly.

"If it's as young as you say, I'll send it to a wildlife rehabilitator who will care for it until it can be released. And they are trained to watch for signs of rabies, unlike you."

Tara threw up her hands and turned away. "You have an answer for everything."

Jan cleared her throat. "Well, he is the game warden, honey. We called him because of his expertise dealing with these types of issues."

"Jack Weston." He held out a hand to Tara.

She stared at it for a moment and then took it for a brief handshake. "Tara Blake."

"When Jan said her daughter was up here trying to catch a raccoon, I was afraid there was a child up here about to get bitten," Jack said.

Jan huffed out a laugh. "Well, thank you—if that was a compliment."

"It was." Jack turned and winked at her. "I can't believe you have a grown daughter."

"Three grown children, actually," Tara said. "Of which I'm the youngest. But since you're the critter expert, I'll get out of the way and let you do your job." And with that, she very pointedly turned her back and descended the stairs.

Jan opened her mouth to apologize. What had gotten into her usually polite daughter?

But Jack prevented her from speaking when he cleared his throat and gave her a sheepish smile. "Uh, sorry about that. I guess I got off on the wrong foot with your daughter."

Jan shook her head. "I'm sorry. I don't know what got into her."

Jack grinned and switched on a high-powered flashlight. "I should probably check around up here to see how this little guy got in."

The cousins followed him. "We put a screen over the dryer vent to discourage squirrels," Jan told him. "I can't imagine where he entered the house."

Jack laughed. "Raccoons are endlessly inventive. 'If there's a will, there's a way,' probably was coined to describe them. And this old house may have some spaces in the foundation beneath the porches that will need to be sealed once spring arrives. Until then, we'll just have to trap them if you get any more in here." He looked over his shoulder at Jan. "I hope your daughter doesn't have her husband come after me for raccoon abuse."

It was such a blatant fishing expedition that Jan had to turn a giggle into a cough. "No husband," she assured Jack. "Tara's my only remaining single child."

"I have a single daughter too," Elaine said. "Unfortunately, she doesn't live around here. But I could find out when she's visiting."

Jack looked alarmed at the matchmaking tone the conversation had taken, even though he'd started it. He completely missed the grin the cousins exchanged.

"You must miss her," he said diplomatically. "I'll just go get a trap from my truck and set it up here. You could get me a little cheese or apple or pretty much anything edible to put in it as bait." And he also headed for the stairs.

Jan and Elaine looked at each other as his footsteps descended. Jan put a hand over her mouth to stifle her laughter, and Elaine snickered. There was no need for words.

Tara was in the sitting room when the cousins entered. Jan left the door open, but Tara made a point of rising and shutting it as the front door opened and closed, and Jack's footsteps started back upstairs. Jan took him the piece of cheese she had brought up from the refrigerator. When he had ascended to the attic again, Tara said, "What an insufferable man."

After a moment of silence, Elaine spoke up. "I think he's rather pleasant, actually. He deals with people and animal problems from sunup to sundown, and he handles them all courteously and kindly."

"Brown-nosing, more likely," Tara muttered. "Mom, he was flirting with you. Don't you think that's a little ridiculous?"

Jan felt the laughter bubbling up again. "He was just teasing. I found it sort of charming."

"*Hmph.*" Tara flopped back in the blue plush chair and tilted her nose in the air. "Charming-schmarming. I found him arrogant and overbearing."

After that pronouncement, there was silence in the room, until Elaine leaned forward and picked up another of the bracelets Tara had made. "So how long does it take you to make these?"

AFTER TARA DEPARTED, Jan and Elaine each returned to the projects which they had been working on for Saturday's special events. Jan was sorting vintage valentines they had picked up at a consignment sale, looking for one to mount on a vertical frame that she could place beneath a glass cloche, an upside-down bell jar on a fancy footed plate. All of the others would be scattered over the tables in the east parlor, where all of their Valentine's Day traffic would be directed, since Hetta and J.C.'s reception would be occupying the west parlor and the dining room.

Elaine, under Jan's direction, was creating a large heart-shaped floral arrangement with silk rosebuds in floral foam. Once all the roses were in, Jan intended to add a loop of white ribbon and hang it on the wall in the entry. Other projects yet to be tackled included hand-cut lacy valentines that would serve as part of the centerpieces for each table, and a display of Victorian-era costume jewelry that they had picked up for next to nothing at several yard sales and flea markets last summer. They planned to arrange the pieces on a length of black velvet.

Elaine, working rosebuds carefully into the floral foam heart, was thinking about the past twenty-four hours or so, turning everything that had happened over in her mind. "I'm wondering," she said slowly to Jan, "what possible reasons someone might have for kidnapping Gleason Wattings."

"Funny you should be thinking of that. So was I," Jan replied, placing a postcard into one smaller pile at her right. "I still can't quite wrap my mind around Joe Vennard as a kidnapper just to get back at Bud for revenge, but I suppose it's possible."

"Or maybe to get Bud to give or sell back the rental business?"

"Maybe. Or maybe to hurt or upset Bud or Shelba?"

"So those are possibilities, far-fetched as they seem." Elaine gestured with a rosebud. "What if it has nothing to do with the Wattings family? What if someone wants or needs Gleason himself to disappear?"

"I guess that's possible," Jan said, "but why?"

"Maybe he witnessed a crime, or saw something he wasn't supposed to."

Jan's forehead wrinkled as she looked over another hand-ful of postcards. "Have we been watching too many of those *Dateline* true-crime segments?"

Elaine laughed. "Maybe." Then her face sobered. "But there's got to be a reason why someone took Gleason."

"If indeed they did," Jan said. "I admit that the phone call adds a lot of weight to the kidnapping theory, but there could be a lot of other reasons for Gleason to vanish, and maybe that phone call sounding like a plea for help is sheer coincidence."

"Maybe." Elaine looked skeptical. "But let's go with that any-way. Maybe Gleason wanted to disappear or get away and thought appearing to have been kidnapped was a good way to do it."

"It would be supremely stupid," Jan pointed out, "to alarm a whole community if all you want to do is vanish. Wouldn't it be better to be as unobtrusive as possible?"

Elaine huffed out a laugh. "It would. But it's still possi-ble." She paused. "Or maybe what we saw on the lake, Gleason disappearing, and that phone call have nothing to do with each other."

"You don't believe that." Jan's voice was quiet; her hands had stilled. "Do you?"

Elaine stopped in the middle of pushing another stem through the floral foam, and their eyes met. "No. And neither do you."

JAN SPENT A happy two hours first thing on Tuesday morning baking before heading upstairs to shower and dress. As she came down the stairs again, she could hear sounds from the kitchen, and she surmised Rose had arrived. But the moment she caught sight of Rose's face, her pleasure in the day dimmed.

Something was wrong. Rose was starting the crumb cake she had decided to make for the day, but her eyes were red and puffy. She didn't look up as Jan entered although she mumbled, "Good morning."

"It doesn't look as if it was so great," Jan observed. "What's wrong?"

Rose sighed, but a sob hitched her breath halfway through. "I didn't get accepted into the Maine Institute for Culinary Excellence."

"What?" Jan was truly dumbfounded. Rose's application had been outstanding, in her estimation.

Rose shook her head. "Rejected."

"Why? Did they at least tell you why?" No wonder the young woman looked so devastated.

"There was a handwritten note from the dean," Rose said. "It said my application was outstanding, but that competition had been unusually fierce this year, and they only had a very limited number of openings."

"I'm so sorry." Jan rounded the counter and put her arms around Rose, giving her a fierce hug. "It's not the only culinary school in the world. You can apply to some others."

"It's the only one that was close enough to Lancaster to allow me to commute and still work here. Now I'll probably have to move and look for part-time work close to whatever school I get into. And I was so looking forward to learning from that pastry chef I told you about." She fought tears, but one escaped and rolled down her cheek.

Still, she continued to work, doggedly refusing to give in to her misery. "I'll figure it out somehow," she said. "This is just a setback."

Archie bustled in then, and there was no further opportunity for personal conversation. Seeing how fragile Rose's grip on her composure was, Jan determined that she would tell Archie and Elaine what had happened so Rose wouldn't have to speak of it again unless she wished. Then she resolutely set aside her concern for the young woman and went about the day's business.

But she couldn't help wondering how she was going to manage all the baking without Rose's assistance. Rose had developed into quite a baker, her skill progressing at the same pace as the tearoom's business increased. Where was she going to find another person qualified to help her with the amount of baking needed now?

# CHAPTER EIGHT

Elaine spent Tuesday morning purchasing bulk items for the next quarter and ordering some of the specialty tea stock for the next month. Tea was tricky. Various teas needed to be stored in different ways to keep it from going stale or getting too strong, so she didn't like to place orders too far in advance.

She was grabbing a cup of coffee from the kitchen when Rose returned after putting fresh linens on the tables in the parlors. Although the young woman wasn't crying, as Jan mentioned she'd been doing earlier, she was pale and hollow-eyed, and there wasn't a smile in sight.

"Hi," Elaine said to their young employee. "Jan told me about the news from the MICE school. I'm so sorry."

"Thanks," Rose said glumly. "I should have known better than to get all excited about it."

"Are you going to submit other applications?" Elaine asked.

Rose nodded. "I already completed three others and sent them out. Unfortunately, I wouldn't be able to start at any of them until the beginning of the fall semester. And none of them are the caliber of the Maine Institute."

"I know you were excited about studying with that one pastry chef in particular," Elaine said. "Maybe there will be another opportunity equally exciting."

"I doubt it." Rose shook her head. "Maine Culinary is really the only top-notch school in this area. Last night I was looking online, and I guess I'm going to apply to the Institute of Culinary Excellence, the International Culinary Center, and the Culinary Institute at Hyde Park. All three of them are in New York, and the first two are actually right in the city. Hyde Park is about ninety miles north, right along the Hudson, so it would be a tiny bit closer to home. But I certainly can't commute to any of them."

"I'm so sorry," Elaine said. "It seemed like a perfect setup for you to attend school in Maine and still be able to work her. But if it wasn't meant to be, I hope one of these other schools works out and that you love it. I know how much you want this. It'll happen in the way it's meant to."

"I hope so," Rose said. "I have no idea if I will be accepted at any of these. All I can do is try."

As Elaine went to unlock the front doors and turn over the Open sign, she felt sad, both for the disappointment Rose was suffering and for Jan and herself. They genuinely cared for the young woman, who had become both an exemplary employee and a dear friend.

She didn't have much more time to reflect on the matter though. The winter "regulars," Macy and Rue, were the first ones through the door. Though the pair didn't come in every day, Elaine suspected that they weren't about to miss any of the gossip that surely would be floating around today in the wake of Gleason Wattings's disappearance. Close on their heels were several other groups of local folks, all of who proceeded to claim tables in the east parlor where the fire was burning merrily.

Freddie Donnett also came in, but she turned and headed into the deserted west parlor.

When Elaine approached, Freddie cleared her throat. "Do you have any teas good for a sore throat?" she croaked.

Elaine nodded, wincing. "You don't sound so good."

"I caught a chill," Freddie said. "I'm hoping it doesn't turn into a full-fledged cold. And maybe bring me some of whatever I smell that's making my mouth water. Your chef is very talented."

Elaine grinned. Jan would enjoy that. "She is," she agreed.

Back in the kitchen, she prepared a peppermint tea with licorice and marshmallow root for Freddie and added some of the daily pastries. As she carried the laden tray into the west parlor, she felt something crunch underfoot.

Hurriedly, she served Freddie and went for the broom and dustpan. Although they vacuumed and mopped daily, it was difficult to keep the wood floors as clean as Elaine liked. Winter was especially difficult, with people bringing in ice melt and gravel on their shoes.

But as she swept the debris into her small dustpan, her movements slowed and stopped. Accustomed as she was to sweeping up the ice melt that they used on the sidewalks in front of Tea for Two, Elaine knew well what the small, round white or pale-blue balls looked like.

She also knew, from her childhood years before anything as sophisticated as ice melt had been created, what rock salt looked like. And the rough, irregularly shaped cloudy crystals currently tracked across the floor of the west parlor were most definitely those of rock salt.

A shiver worked its way up Elaine's spine. Slowly, she returned to her sweeping, casually following the trail of rock salt from the foyer through the west parlor to the table at which Freddie Donnett sat.

"Oh, I'm so sorry," Freddie said, noticing what Elaine was doing. "Did I track in dirt?"

"No, you're fine," Elaine replied. "I just like to keep ahead of the mess during the winter."

Retreating, she scooted into the kitchen, where Jan was loading the dishwasher. Archie and Rose must be in the east parlor, she realized.

Quickly, she crossed to her cousin with the dustpan clenched tightly in her hand. "Rock salt," she said.

Jan's eyes widened. "Where did you get that?"

"Freddie Donnett tracked it in."

"The professor?" Jan sounded incredulous.

Elaine explained how she had come to find it and tracked it to Freddie's table. "It's on her shoes," she said.

Rose came into the kitchen then. "Two pots of the special and two plates of mini maple croissants," she reported.

Elaine turned away, carrying the dustpan with her, while Jan abandoned the dishes to help Rose prepare the order. Back in Elaine's office, she emptied the contents of the dustpan into a large plastic bag and then went to return dustpan and broom to the closet where it was kept. She wasn't sure if they'd need the rock salt as evidence, but she thought it prudent to keep it for the moment.

A few minutes later, Jan popped her head into the office. "Rock salt?" she asked incredulously.

Elaine uttered a wry laugh. "I know. I was flabbergasted." She indicated the bag on the corner of the desk. "I saved it, because...you know, just in case."

Jan grinned. "I do know. About a thousand thoughts have flitted through my head in the time it took me to help Rose with that order. I mean, we can't just hand it over to the state police and tell them it came from Freddie's shoes, can we?"

Elaine shook her head. "I don't think so. Surely it's a coincidence. I'm sure Freddie Donnett has absolutely nothing to do with Gleason's disappearance. Other people around town probably still use rock salt."

"Probably," Jan said. "And really, there is no reason at all to suppose otherwise, right?"

"Right."

"But," Jan went slowly, "it might be a good idea to try to find out who around here might be using rock salt. I mean, it's not *that* common anymore. Ice melt works so much faster, and a lot of people use that pet-safe stuff like we do."

"Good idea," Elaine said. "We could ask whoever sells it around here if they have records or remember who might have purchased it."

Knuckles rapped at the open door frame of the office. "Three new tables just arrived," Archie said in his cultured tones.

"Oh, great!" Jan said. "I'll come help with the orders."

After an hour in the office, Elaine worked the front rooms while Archie grabbed a sandwich and took a short break around noon.

Jan came into the kitchen with a loaded tray of dirty dishes while Elaine was fixing a tray. "Shelba came in a little while ago with her sister. She says the police took statements from Bud and from her, and they're taking Gleason's disappearance seriously."

"Ah." Elaine nodded. "That relieves my mind." She picked up the tray she had prepared and carried it through the foyer into the east parlor where her table of customers was seated. Shelba and another woman were seated at the next table, and Shelba caught Elaine's eye as she set down the order and conversed with the customers.

As she straightened, Shelba said, "Thank you for hanging up our flier." Her eyes were red-rimmed, and she had a tissue crumpled in one hand.

"You're welcome," Elaine said.

"Gleason's Jeep is missing too," Shelba said, stifling a sob.

"I'm so sorry." Elaine patted Shelba's hand. "I am praying that Gleason is found quickly."

"The lab results on that blood found on the lake aren't back yet," Shelba said. "Trooper Benson said it was contaminated—by salt, of all things, and mud—and they were still trying to type it. But I just know it's Gleason's blood. He's a good boy. Who would want to harm my son?"

Elaine wished she knew the answer to that. She continued to move among the tables, chatting with customers and sharing information about the various teas they were serving this week. Shelba and her sister rose and left, to the accompaniment of good wishes from many people.

But as the pair left the tearoom, Alanna Nance, the wife of the electrician Elaine and Jan had used to help them get the wiring in the house up to code before they opened, said quietly, "He does seem like a nice young man."

Macy, still seated by the fire, snorted. "Maybe so, but his parents don't know nearly as much about him as they think they do."

"What's that supposed to mean?" Rue asked, raising her eyebrows at Macy's insinuation.

Macy waved a hand. "Oh, you heard Shelba yesterday, saying Gleason didn't have a steady girl, and going on and on about what a good boy he is. Gleason's a normal, red-blooded male. Zale said she's seen him with some girl over in Waterville a bunch of times. Wouldn't be surprised if he hasn't told his parents though. You know Bud and Gleason are always knocking heads."

"They are? Why?" Elaine stopped pretending not to be listening.

"Bud and Shelba think Gleason's too young for a serious relationship. Bud wants Gleason to focus on a career—and not just any career."

"Bud wants Gleason to take over the fishing rental business," Rue told Elaine. "Gleason wants to go to college—he's a history buff and he wants to teach—but Bud wouldn't pay for college because he thinks Gleason should just take over the family business."

"So Gleason works at a restaurant to put himself through school." Macy took over the conversation again. "Wouldn't be surprised if that's where he met this girl."

"If he does have a girlfriend," Rue said, "she could have been a study buddy or something. Shelba seems to think he doesn't have anyone special."

"If you were Gleason, would you want to take a girl home to meet your parents, knowing they were going to pitch a fit about her?" Macy asked.

She had a good point, Elaine had to concede, even if it was melodramatic. As she cleared Shelba's table, Freddie Donnett came into the east parlor, carrying her laptop.

"Oh no," Macy said under her breath. "Is she going to bother everyone in here about that coin?"

It appeared Freddie intended to do exactly that. Methodically, she carried her laptop around the room, speaking briefly to each group of customers. Elaine slowed, watching as person after person shook their head. "What's she doing?" she asked Macy.

"She's asking them if they've ever seen a coin like the one she found," Macy said. "I'm not sure why she thinks people in Lancaster would know anything about those doubloons. They're really rare, she says. I'd never even heard of them before she came here."

"Neither did I," Rue said, "but she acts as if she thinks someone might have."

"She's about half a bore," Macy said. "I feel like I should go around behind her apologizing to everyone."

Elaine chuckled as she picked up her tray to return to the kitchen. But she couldn't help but wonder why on earth Freddie Donnett would be asking everyone in sight about that coin she had found. And she wasn't sure how she felt about Freddie doing it in her place of business, where people were trying to relax and enjoy their company.

But by two thirty that afternoon, business had dwindled to a trickle and Freddie had long since settled into her work.

"Hey," Jan said as she and Elaine finished loading the dishwasher yet again. "We're in pretty good shape here, and Archie and Rose can close. Want to run up to the courthouse and look up those deeds for the house and the mill?"

"Oh, great idea." Elaine washed her hands thoroughly, sniffing to be sure she'd completely removed the peculiar odor that often clung to them after serving food and clearing plates for several hours. Then she depressed the top of the plastic bottle of hand lotion they kept near the sink. Between frequent wet hands, the astringent hand sanitizer that they all liberally applied, and the deep freeze outside, all four employees of Tea for Two were experiencing extreme dryness and cracking skin on their hands.

Elaine had recently purchased a pair of cotton gloves that she wore to bed at night after a liberal application of a heavy-duty skin cream. That seemed to have helped, and the deep cracks in her thumbs were healing.

Jan stopped beside her for her own handful of cream and briskly rubbed it into her abused digits. "I can't wait for spring," she said. "This was not one of the problems I anticipated when we opened the tearoom."

Elaine chuckled as they hauled out their coats, mittens, scarves, and caps. "Me neither."

They took Jan's blue Toyota. It was a beautiful, clear afternoon, the sky a deep and cloudless blue. The sun already was well on its way toward its night's slumber and long shadows feathered out from the tall evergreens that lined the road, but the cousins both donned sunglasses as a defense against the glare from the abundance of white that surrounded them. By this time of year, the small snows that fell had accumulated, one atop the last, until in some untouched places, the snow might be waist deep.

Elaine was conscious of an inner excitement curling in her tummy as they headed toward Augusta. It felt good to be taking more positive steps toward figuring out how the sapphire ring that had been stolen from Wood Woolen Mill had ended up in the wall of their lovely Victorian home.

# CHAPTER NINE

Half an hour later, they arrived at the Kennebec County Courthouse in Augusta, a utilitarian building of concrete block and glass. The registrar of deeds was quite helpful, but she laughed when Elaine asked if they could view a deed.

"Deeds are public records," the white-haired woman with smiling eyes told the cousins. "We need to have you fill out this form and then you may use one of our computers to search for the information you're seeking."

After completing the paperwork, Jan and Elaine seated themselves at the computer the registrar had indicated. With Jan feeding her the proper information where she hesitated, Elaine entered the address of the old Wood Woolen Mill. After finding the records, they were a bit taken aback by the amount of paperwork generated.

"Let's take these home," Jan suggested. "They'll be closing in half an hour or so, and I'm not all that anxious to drive back to Lancaster in the dark."

"Works for me." Elaine helped gather the papers that the efficient machine was spitting out. Thanking the registrar, they returned to the Toyota Camry and headed back home.

Jan turned into Murphy's General Store as they drove through town. "I need to fill up my tank," she said. "It'll only take a few minutes."

While Jan dealt with the gas pump, Elaine got out of the car and went into the store. Although Murphy's had a limited number of groceries, she remembered that they were running low on milk for their personal use, and she knew she could get that.

There was no one in line, but as Elaine finished paying for her purchase, Zale Atherton came up behind her. "Hi, Elaine." She plunked down two boxes of cereal and handed the clerk several bills.

"Hi, Zale. How are you?"

"Good. Busy at the tearoom today?"

"I'd say so, considering it's a weekday in the middle of February," Elaine smiled. This was a fortuitous meeting; she had been hoping for an opportunity to ask Zale about Gleason's girlfriend. "Jan's baking keeps them coming back."

Zale chuckled. "Well, that's certainly true of my mother-in-law."

Elaine cleared her throat as the clerk handed Zale her change and together they started for the door. "Macy told me that you've seen Gleason Wattings with a girl that might be his girlfriend. Do you mind telling me more about her?"

Zale looked puzzled but willing. "I don't know much. Gleason works at a restaurant called Fish 'n Fondue in Waterville. I've seen him with this girl who's a waitress there. Name's Marcy or Martha or something. I remember it reminded me of my mother-in-law's name. Once I saw them in a shoe store together, and another time, I saw them having dinner together in a little pizza place. They were holding hands across the table, so I assumed they were a couple."

The story jived with what Rose had told her. "Thanks," she said. "And thanks for bringing Freddie Donnett here for her sabbatical. She's been a great customer."

"Sabbatical?" Zale's eyebrows rose. "I heard her say that to you, but that's not the real story."

Elaine didn't enjoy gossip, but since discovering the rock salt on Freddie's shoes, she felt it was only prudent to learn as much as possible about the woman. "It's not?"

"More like a forced hiatus," Zale said. "One of my old friends on social media said he heard she was involved in a theft."

"A *theft*? From the university?" That was alarming.

Zale shrugged. "I don't know. And I wasn't really interested."

"Did you tell Macy? I mean, don't you think she should know…"

"I didn't tell Macy," Zale said, "and she doesn't need to know. It had something to do with coins that were part of the college museum's display. I don't think we're harboring a dangerous felon or anything like that."

"But if she may have stolen money, Macy really should know."

"They were ancient coins that had been found in a shipwreck," Zale said. "It's not as if she stole a bag of cash from a drawer."

Elaine nodded, trying not to let Zale see how disturbed she was. "You're probably right." Still, Zale might be right that

Macy's petty cash wasn't in danger, but wasn't it interesting that Freddie was rumored to have stolen old coins?

Bidding Azalea good-bye, Elaine headed back across the parking lot to the Toyota, where Jan appeared to have finished getting gas and was replacing the gas cap. Behind her, a pickup truck flashed its high beams and revved the engine.

Elaine saw Jan's mouth tighten. "Has he been there long?" she asked.

"Practically since the moment you walked away," Jan said with a sigh of resignation. "I couldn't have gotten gas any faster than I did."

Just then, the driver hopped out of the truck and came stomping toward them. "You two broads wanna socialize somewhere else? I got places to be, and I need gas to get there."

More than a little stunned by the man's rude attitude, the cousins turned toward him.

"I beg your pardon?" Elaine said. The man was only a few inches taller than she, on the short side, and she had no trouble staring straight at him. "There are far more polite ways to ask us to move, sir."

"I don't really care, lady. Now move it."

Jan cleared her throat. "Wait a minute. Aren't you Joe Vennard?"

"What's it to ya?" The angry eyes narrowed.

"Just wondering," Jan said airily. "I heard Bud Wattings has made a success of the business you used to own, and frankly, I'm beginning to see why."

The man's mouth fell open.

So did Elaine's. Her cousin was normally quite mild-mannered and pleasant.

"Bud's a dirty cheat." Joe's voice was loud and venomous. "He waited until he knew he could get my business dirt cheap..."

"Joe, is there a problem here?" An authoritative male voice came from the other side of the gas pumps.

All three of them turned to look at the man who had rounded the pumps and stood with his hands on his hips: Trooper Daniel Benson.

Joe's scowl grew even darker. "Yeah. I'm trying to get gas and these two are blocking my way."

"I just saw Mrs. Blake putting her gas cap back on," the officer said. "Why don't you get back in your truck, Joe? I'm sure these ladies will be moving on very soon."

There was a moment of charged silence before, with a grunt that sounded like an angry pig, Joe Vennard slammed back into his pickup.

"He's probably not a good person to antagonize," Daniel advised Jan.

"I know," Jan said ruefully. "I don't know what came over me. I just really dislike it when people forget their manners."

Elaine laughed. "We believe you." She rounded the hood, shaking her head. "Let's go. I have things to tell you, and we don't want Mr. Vennard to have an apoplexy waiting any longer."

Jan looked uncharacteristically mulish, as if she'd like to refuse. But she opened the driver's door and slid in. Elaine almost laughed out loud as she noticed how slow and deliberate her cousin's movements were. Jan ver-r-ry carefully pulled out her seat belt and buckled it. Then she sl-l-lowly put the key in the ignition and turned it, waiting until the engine caught to adjust the heat settings perfectly before she put the car in Drive.

Glancing across the pump, Elaine saw a grin on Daniel Benson's face. It probably matched her own, she decided as they pulled out and headed back toward their home.

"Just for the record," Jan said, "I don't believe for a minute that Bud waited for Joe to fail. I asked Rue about it, and she said that Bud bought Joe out after the business began to fail."

"But in Joe's mind," Elaine said, "Bud forced him out."

"That's just crazy," Jan said in exasperation.

"He struck me as pretty crazy," Elaine said frankly. "I don't think I'd want him mad at me."

"Pshaw," Jan said, dismissing Elaine's concern. "Joe's always been a grouch. He's just getting worse as he gets older."

"He's more than a grouch," Elaine informed her. "That behavior verged on serious bullying. He's a little scary. And oh! I almost forgot. I saw Zale in the store." She went on to tell Jan what Zale had said about Gleason's girlfriend Marcy or Martha, as well as sharing the odd story about Freddie Donnett's "sabbatical."

"I suppose telling people she's on sabbatical to do research is better than saying she's on administrative leave for theft or plagiarism or whatever it is she did—hey! Isn't that Marvin Bellamy?"

Elaine turned her attention to the corner where Jan was pointing. A slight young man stood in front of the open hood of his automobile. Even from a distance, Elaine could see the doubt in his face as he gazed into the engine block.

Jan slowed and rolled down her window. "Hi, Marvin. You need some help?"

The young man shook his head. "No, thank you, ma'am. I b'lieve I just flooded it. I'm waiting a few minutes for it to settle down before I try to start it again."

"All right," Jan said, "but if you can't get it started, come knock on the door of Tea for Two if you need help."

"Thank you." Marvin already was turning back to peer at his engine again.

Jan rolled up the window and released the brake, heading down the street toward their home in the tearoom.

AFTER DINNER, JAN was walking into the sewing room at the back of the second floor when movement in Elaine's bedroom caught her eye.

"Do you have a minute?" Elaine asked, just as Jan was about to turn. "I need a second opinion."

Jan changed course and entered Elaine's room across the hall. Her mouth dropped open. As she watched, Elaine held up a paisley skirt in deep blues and purples and abruptly tossed it aside.

"Purging?" Jan guessed. "Spring cleaning a couple months early?"

Elaine laughed. "No. I'm just trying to decide what to wear for my date on Valentine's evening."

Clothes were displayed across the bed and the vanity chair and more were hanging from the door frames. It was

86

as unlike the neat and tidy Elaine as could be. As Jan studied what appeared to be a mess, she realized Elaine was putting together outfits.

"What do you think of this?" Elaine asked. She held up a long navy wool dress. "With this belt and boots?"

Before Jan could reply, Elaine tossed the items aside and snatched up a pair of black fine-wale corduroy slacks. "Or maybe this with the pink turtleneck sweater? Or the white blouse under this sweater with..."

"Elaine." Jan passed by the clothing and put her hands on her taller cousin's shoulders. "You have a number of lovely outfits, any one of which will be fine. I personally love that paisley skirt with the navy cowl-neck sweater. I think you look exceptionally elegant in that one with your knee-high black boots. But truly, any of these would do."

Elaine sank down on the side of the bed, right on top of the clothes piled there. "I guess I'm still a little more anxious about this dating idea than I thought."

"Beginning to date again after having had a long and happy marriage is scary," Jan said. "I'd be more concerned if you didn't think it was a big deal."

"You're right." Elaine blew out a breath. "It would be easy to let this make me crazy."

Jan gave her a one-armed hug. "I think it's natural to have some jitters. Want some help hanging up a few of these things?"

Elaine looked around ruefully. "That would be great."

After they had picked up all the clothing, Elaine adjourned to the sitting room, while Jan went to work on their Victorian costumes for Valentine's Day.

Although the cousins each had charming Victorian dresses they had worn a number of times throughout the previous year, they had decided it was time to add another piece to their ensemble. Jan had made herself a deep wine-colored velvet fitted dress with a full skirt over crinolines. The sleeves were full at the top but fitted down the arm since she couldn't afford to have sweeping lacy sleeves trailing in people's orders, but there was lace at the cuffs. The neckline was edged in lace as well.

Elaine's dress was still in progress. Jan had found a muted antique floral fabric in rose, dusty blue, taupe, and cream for the overdress and the sleeves. A deep rose satin inset in the bodice was repeated in an inset down the front, and the sleeves were embellished with deep rose ribbon.

"This is just gorgeous," Elaine said as she entered the sewing room. She fingered the fabric of the dress Jan had just taken out from under the sewing machine's presser foot after lifting the needle.

"It's ready to hem," Jan said. "Go try it on. Also, put on whatever shoes you'll be wearing." One thing the cousins had agreed on was that comfort in their footwear was paramount. Elaine had found a pair of low, lace-up boots that looked a bit like those from the Victorian era, sans real buttons with buttonhooks, of course. But they were far more comfortable than several antique pairs she had tried, and that was what she usually wore with her costumes.

Obligingly, Elaine took the dress to her room and slipped it on with her boots, then carefully lifted it to avoid stepping on the hem as she returned to Jan.

Jan had pulled a wide wooden box from beneath her cutting table. "Here, stand on this."

Elaine stepped up and stood still, while Jan crawled around her on the floor with a pincushion on an elastic band worn over her wrist and a tape measure. "Turn," Jan told her. "This is absolutely stunning, if I do say so myself. Too bad you can't just wear this out to dinner with Nathan."

Elaine laughed. "This would certainly make a statement."

"We could pin an advertisement for Tea for Two to your back," Jan said hopefully.

"Whoa." Elaine said. "That was a joke, right?"

"Sort of." Jan chuckled. "But admit it, it was a good idea."

"I don't think we need much more business," Elaine told her cousin. "I feel silly when I think about how worried I was that we wouldn't have enough business after the tourist season ended. The local folks have really embraced us."

"They have." Jan removed a pin from the pad on her wrist and competently basted it through a section of the hem. "I admit I was nervous too."

"A lot of folks are enjoying our teas," Elaine said, "but I honestly think your pastries are what's bringing a lot of them back again and again. Those cream puffs you made yesterday with the chocolate drizzled over them and the powdered sugar were a giant hit."

"Thanks. It's one more recipe to add to our repertoire," Jan said. "After we get through our Valentine's Day events, I want to sit down with Rose and review everything we've tried and decide what to keep for the upcoming year."

"Great idea. Although honestly, I'm not sure I can think of very many recipes you've tried that haven't gone over well. You've become a bit of a creative genius with pastries."

Jan grinned. "Thanks. I like the sound of that." She paused and looked up. "Okay, another quarter turn please."

"You know," Elaine said, "I can't stop thinking about that rock salt Freddie Donnett had on her shoes."

"We can ask Macy if she uses rock salt," Jan pointed out.

"We can," Elaine said. "She will want to know why we want to know, and you know how she is with gossip. Within twenty-four hours, people would be saying Freddie conked Gleason Wattings over the head and abducted him."

Jan laughed. But then her face sobered. She sat back on her heels and looked up at Elaine. "Maybe she did."

# CHAPTER TEN

The conversation about kidnapping had suddenly taken a more serious tone. Jan thought for a minute. "We could ask around locally to see who sells rock salt, and if they recall who might have bought it."

"That sounds like a long shot," Elaine said. "But aside from asking Macy, it's probably our best option. If Freddie bought rock salt, then she's going straight to the top of my 'who-dun-it' list."

"Even though we know of no possible reason why she would have abducted Gleason?"

"Even though," Elaine said, nodding. "Or at least we start looking really hard to figure out if she did have reason."

"Turn again please," Jan said. Working quickly, she pinned the final section of the hem of Elaine's gown into place. "Okay, you can go take it off," she said.

Elaine stepped down off the stool and left the room.

A few minutes later, the cousins settled in their sitting room. Jan was placing a fast, running hemstitch around the bottom of the dress she had just pinned up. "What are you doing?" she asked Elaine, who was unpacking a box of what looked like art supplies on a tray table.

"Valentines," Elaine said. "I want to send the kids and Mom and a few friends homemade cards this year, and I need to finish them and get them in the mail tomorrow." She had a tray table before her, on which she had amassed shiny red heart stickers, white lacy heart-shaped doilies, and pink construction paper.

"What a nice idea," Jan said. "I bought valentines this year. I bet Lucy and Micah will love getting a homemade valentine from Grandma."

"I'm going to be too busy that day to even Skype with them," Elaine fretted. "I asked Jared if we could set up a Skype date for the day after Valentine's Day, so hopefully I'll get to see the kids' faces then." Being so far from her children and grandchildren was difficult sometimes. She missed seeing all the little changes and events in the children's lives, as she would be able to do if they lived nearby. Her son and his family lived in Ohio, while her daughter Sasha was even farther away in Colorado.

"That's a great idea." Jan, of course, had no idea what it was like to conduct a long-distance relationship with a family member. Her husband had been a welder and they'd never spent more than a few nights apart, and her children all lived no farther away than Augusta. Although Elaine was happy that Jan's family was so close, she often felt the sting of loneliness. Since they'd opened the tearoom, she had grown closer to Jan's family, and especially to Jan's young granddaughter Avery.

"I'm making them for your family too," Elaine said. "I thought that since we're seeing so much more of each other, I wanted them to know I was thinking of them."

Jan's eyes softened. "That's thoughtful. Avery, in particular, will be thrilled to get a valentine from you."

Elaine smiled. "We also need to finish the basket for the Valentine's Day raffle," she said. The cousins had decided to have a little drawing on Valentine's Day. Anyone who patronized the tearoom that day would be invited to put their name in, and the winner would receive a heart-shaped basket with little bags of the Valentine's Day teas, a tea ball infuser, a little stirring spoon with a charming teapot at the tip, a maple jar candle, and a small bag of chocolate bark from a Maine chocolatier.

"Oh, I'll take care of that," Jan said. "We have the basket and all the items. All I have to do is throw a little pink tissue shred in the bottom, wrap it up in cellophane, and tie it with a bow."

Elaine snorted. "You make that sound so easy. Your gifts always look so professional. I've had to work hard to learn how to make mine look like they weren't put together by monkeys."

Jan laughed at that image. "I also need to finish the poster of our customers' most romantic moments. It's absolutely adorable. I never thought we'd get so many submissions."

"I know." Elaine walked over to Jan's worktable, where the nearly finished poster in question lay. Jan had placed the photos in clear acetate corners so they would be easily removable. They didn't march in straight rows but were cleverly angled this way and that. She had printed in neat block lettering the name of the people in each picture, and drawn vines with flowers between and around them all.

Customers had brought in all manner of photos. One of Rue and Ned Maxwell had been taken on their honeymoon in the Bahamas, while others had brought in wedding photos, anniversary pictures, and photos of couples with their first baby. Eldon and Misty Carter, who had met in high school, beamed out from a photo of the two of them in caps and gowns, and Zale had brought in a print of Shane and herself from middle school, sitting side by side on bleachers at some event sharing a whoopee pie.

"It looks pretty enough to frame," Elaine said.

"We have to give the pictures back," Jan said, "or I'd do it. I've gotten kind of attached to it."

She cleared her throat. "Joe Vennard is another possibility," she said, returning to their earlier subject.

Elaine lifted her eyebrows. "He certainly fits my idea of a kidnapper's personality."

Diverted, Jan chuckled. "Do kidnappers have a certain personality?"

"You know what I mean," Elaine said.

"Maybe," Jane said. "Although I am not inclined to think that he's vicious enough to have kidnapped Gleason. But he certainly has shown that he feels strongly that he's been wronged."

"You don't just kidnap someone because you're mad," Elaine said. "If Joe did indeed kidnap Gleason, he must be planning to try to get his business back from Bud."

"You mean by ransoming Bud's son?" Jan frowned. "If I were Bud, I'd go straight to the cops if that happened."

"You might not if someone told you they'd kill your son if you did," Elaine said quietly.

Jan gaped at her. "Joe wouldn't—oh, that's horrible! I can't imagine him doing something so vile."

"You know him better than I do. It was just a theory. Is there anyone else that would have any reason to harm or kidnap Gleason?"

"We're assuming Gleason was taken," Jan reminded her. "And maybe that was what we saw happen on Sunday night. But maybe it didn't have anything to do with Gleason's disappearance. Maybe he has chosen to leave."

"Why?" Elaine asked promptly. "I mean, I know he isn't getting along well with his parents, but would that be reason enough to worry them sick by simply disappearing?"

"We don't know what may have gone on between the family members behind closed doors," Jan pointed out. "There could be far more angst than simply a little disagreement over education and dating."

"Also, do you recall how easily things get blown out of proportion when you're young?" Elaine asked. "Older people often seem less inclined to drama, which I suspect has something to do with the benefit of experience. Young people boil over really quickly sometimes."

"If he was having conflict with his parents, he'd probably talk to his friends about it," Jan said. "Maybe we should try to track down any friends or a special girl."

"Good plan," Elaine said. "Do you want to glance over those papers we printed out today?"

"Oh, I forgot about those," Jan said. "Yes, please."

Elaine went downstairs and retrieved the copies of the chains of title for their house and for the old mill that the Wood family once had owned.

As she returned to the sitting room, she said, "It occurs to me that we probably have a copy of this in our mortgage papers. Don't they have to do a title search anytime a house is sold?"

Jan laughed. "I bet you're right. I never read through every page of that. Good grief, it's inches thick."

"Oh well," Elaine said, shrugging and smiling. "Which one do you want?"

Jan shook her head. "It doesn't matter. I'll take the mill, I guess."

Fifteen minutes later, Elaine glanced up. Jan was still reading, but as Elaine watched, she finished the last page and set it down. "Well, that wasn't particularly useful," she said. "Did you find anything of interest in the transfer of ownership of the house?"

"I don't know." Elaine indicated the stack of paper before her. "On paper, everything looks fairly routine. The house changed hands from the initial builder to a second person and a third, and then the third owner owned it until the bank bought it. It was sold by the bank to the man who held the majority interest in the bank at that time. And he got it dirt-cheap. Since then, it changed hands two more times before we bought it. But I don't see anything here that raises a flag."

"So there's no way to know who might have put the ring in the wall," Jan said.

"Well, that's the odd part." Elaine held up a piece of paper that she had separated from the stack. "A sapphire ring was given to the bank to hold as collateral by Mr. Wood when he purchased the home."

"You're kidding." Jan snatched the piece of paper, reading the formal language.

"But there was nothing else in here," Elaine said, "to indicate that he ever got the ring—the collateral—back."

"It's got to be the same ring," Jan said. "But how did it end up hidden in the house?"

"I'd like to know more about the sons," Elaine told her. "This article just mentions that the father sold the property."

"What if the sons had something to do with the ring being stolen from the woolen mill?" Jan said. "We still haven't figured out why the ring would have been in the mill at all, but what if the Wood brothers—or at least one of them—knew about it?"

"That's certainly a possible scenario. So next step: finding out more about the sons," Elaine said.

Their discussion was interrupted abruptly by a thump from the attic startled them both.

"My goodness," Elaine said. "I haven't heard that sound since we set the trap."

"It was empty again this morning," Jan said. "I'd better go check it."

"I'll come with you."

The cousins rose and went up the stairs to the attic door. Jan flipped on the light and started up the steps ahead of Elaine. When her head cleared the level of the attic floor, she said, "Yes, we caught our visitor."

Elaine followed her on up until they both were standing in the attic. In the trap, which Jack had set in one corner, a smallish raccoon stared out at them from the back of the cage.

"I guess we'd better call Jack," Elaine said.

"Should we leave him up here?" Jan asked. "It's pretty cold, and he looks awfully young."

"I don't think we should move the trap," Elaine said firmly. "He has a warm fur coat. He'll be fine until we talk to Jack."

Downstairs again, Jan made the call. When she ended it, she told Elaine, "He said he's finishing dinner, and then he'll be right over. He said leave it where it is for now."

"I feel bad calling him so late like this," Elaine said. "But I would feel worse leaving that little one up there in the frigid darkness all night long."

Practically the moment she finished speaking, the sound of a key in the lock and then the front door opening and closing alerted them to the fact that someone in the family had entered the house. A moment later, footsteps bounded up the stairs and Tara's voice called, "Hello, Mom and Aunt Elaine."

"Hi, honey. We're in the sitting room," Jan called. "Come on back."

A moment later, Tara appeared in the doorway. Her navy parka was form-fitting and attractive over skinny jeans and high, fashionable boots. Her light-brown hair peeked from beneath a cute knitted cap with a large flower on one side, and a matching scarf circled her neck and spilled down the front of the parka.

"Thanks for stopping by," Jan said. "If you'll slip out of that coat, I'll take the measurements I need for this sweater."

Elaine knew she was referring to a sweater Jan was making for Tara's birthday, which was coming up on the eighteenth.

Jan held up a soft, forest-green swath of cable-knit. "I'm not sure I'll have it done in time for your birthday, but I'll try.

We've been swamped with Valentine's Day preparations, and I've gotten behind on this."

"Oh, I love that color," Tara said. "I'm excited. I don't care if it's not done by next Wednesday."

She shrugged out of her coat and laid it over a chair, doing the same with her hat, her scarf, and the bulky down vest she was wearing beneath it.

Muttering under her breath and scribbling in a small notebook she kept at hand, Jan completed her measurements. Then she smiled at her daughter. "Have a seat," she said.

The three of them watched a game show together. Jan was the only one of them who could consistently remember to phrase her responses as questions, leading to a spirited if congenial disagreement on who said what first.

Just as the show concluded, the doorbell rang.

## CHAPTER ELEVEN

Jan said, "I'll get it," and headed downstairs to let Jack Weston in.

Moments later, the heavy tread of a man's footsteps followed Jan's lighter ones up the steps.

Elaine and Tara had come out into the hallway at the sound, and Tara waved brightly at Jack. "Hi again."

Without missing a beat, Jack said, "Tara, we have to stop meeting like this."

She chuckled.

A bit startled by the marked difference in Tara's attitude from her initial meeting with Jack, both Jan and Elaine turned and stared at her.

"We had coffee this afternoon," Tara said airily. "We ran into each other in Waterville..."

"She means literally," Jack said. "I was walking down the street minding my own business when a brunette tornado blew out of that craft shop on College Avenue and nearly knocked me down."

"Ha." Tara grinned. "It felt like I a smacked into a concrete wall."

"How nice." Elaine hid a smile at this revelation.

"Okay if I head up to the attic and grab our new friend?" Jack asked.

"Oh, did you catch my raccoon?" Tara asked. "Can I see it if I promise not to touch?"

"C'mon." Jack gestured for her to precede him up the stairs.

Left alone in the hallway, Jan and Elaine looked at each other.

"They sure got chummy fast," Elaine said as she and Jan turned to troop up the attic steps after the younger pair.

Jan only smiled.

"Hi, buddy," Tara said when she saw the raccoon. "I'm pretty sure that's either the same one or one of his brothers. It's the right size."

"It looks too young to release outside during midwinter," Jack said, when he got his first look at the critter. "I'll take it home. I have cages set up in my garage for events like this, and tomorrow I'll take him to a wildlife center where he can hang out until the spring thaw starts."

"That sounds interesting," Tara said. "Could I go along with you?"

"Sure." Jack drew on the heavy gloves that protruded from his back pocket. "I'll give you a call tomorrow and let you know what time I'm heading out there."

With little fanfare, Jack carried the trap with the raccoon in it downstairs and loaded it into the back of his SUV.

"I promise I'll make sure he's taken care of," he told Jan and Elaine. "Thanks for your diligence in checking the trap."

The three women returned to the sitting room after Jack's departure. They tuned back into the game show in time for the final wager that determined the winner, and then Tara rose. "I should get going."

"Thanks for stopping for the measurements," Jan said. "Have fun with Jack tomorrow."

"He certainly works hard for this community," Elaine ventured.

"Uh-oh." Tara smiled at her mother and her aunt. "I smell matchmaking. Let me make it clear that I am not looking for a man."

"You don't have to go looking," Jan pointed out. "You ran right into this one."

Tara and Elaine both laughed out loud.

"I sure did," Tara said. "And if I said I didn't find Jack attractive, my nose would grow. But I'm much too busy for a relationship right now. We're just friends."

Tara seemed to be finished with the conversation as she donned her outer clothing and bade them good night. Silence reigned again in the sitting room as Elaine returned to her valentines and Jan to her hemming.

But after a moment, Elaine set aside her valentines and reached over to pick up her laptop which lay on the end table. "I almost forgot," she said as she booted up the machine. "I wanted to see if I could find anything online about Freddie Donnett."

"Good idea," Jan said.

Elaine tapped away at her keys as another favorite game show began. "Here she is, listed as a faculty member at URI... and here's a mention of an article she published...Oh my."

"Oh my, what?" The needle stopped flashing through the fabric as Jan's hands stopped their work.

"Here's a small article from a local newspaper about her. It's very brief, but it says she is on a mandatory leave of absence while the university looks into allegations of the theft of a coin from a museum collection."

Jan's eyes widened. "Yikes. So she really isn't as...as harmless as we assumed."

Elaine looked up, her eyes dark with concern. "Apparently not."

On Wednesday morning not long before opening, Jan was making her grocery list for the weekend's festivities. As she added *salt* to the list, her mind harked back to their odd discovery on the lake on Monday morning. On impulse, she stepped into the office, where Elaine was working.

"I wonder what happened to the rock salt scattered on the ice."

Elaine frowned. "I don't know. Why?"

Jan shrugged. "I was thinking that maybe we could compare it to the stuff from Freddie's shoes and see if it looked like the same substance."

Elaine picked up the phone. "Let me call Jack and ask him."

Without further ado, she did so. Jan waited impatiently for a moment after Elaine asked Jack several questions. When Elaine hung up, Jan raised her eyebrows. "So?"

"So no luck. Jack said that Bud swept up what was left and threw it away."

Jan snapped her fingers. "I guess if we were real detectives, we'd have done that when we found the stuff."

Rose appeared in the doorway. "Jan, you'd better add wheat flour to that grocery list. I just used almost all of it to make six pans of cinnamon rolls. I'm working on the cream cheese icing now."

"Will do." Brainstorm balloon punctured, Jan headed back to the kitchen. "Have you heard anything from your new applications?" she asked Rose's back, as the young woman preceded her.

"Just that they were received." Rose sounded dispirited, almost as if she didn't even care. Jan hoped fervently that all would work out in the end. Although she hated the notion of losing her able young worker bee, she knew the young woman had a gift and needed more schooling to hone her skills and realize her dream.

"Great," Jan said, forcing heartiness into her tone. "I can't wait to hear where you ultimately decide to go."

AN HOUR LATER, the tearoom had admitted a scant early crowd. Looking out the front window in the west parlor, Elaine could see why. The lowering clouds looked as if they might dump a few more inches of snow on the town in short order.

"Is it snowing yet?" Freddie Donnett asked. She had come in and taken a table in one corner of the west parlor, where she was sipping tea, demolishing a plate of Rose's cinnamon buns, and typing busily on her computer.

"Not yet." Elaine dropped the curtain and returned to the job she was completing, dusting and polishing the chair rail that ran around the room. It wasn't easy, given the amount of furniture in the space, but she was determined that not a speck of dust should mar the wedding reception on Saturday.

Silence fell again. A few moments later, Elaine nearly had reached the corner where Freddie was working. She was about to start from the other end, figuring she could catch that corner at the end of the day, but Freddie pushed back her chair and rose.

"I'm going to use the restroom," she said. "Go ahead and clean this corner if you like."

"Are you sure? I didn't mean to run you out."

"It's no problem. I need to take a little mental break." Freddie smiled as she stretched and then walked from the room.

Working quickly, Elaine dusted that section of chair rail and then began to go over it with some furniture polish to make it gleam. As she pushed in Freddie's chair to give herself a bit more room, she caught sight of a battered old journal partially obscured by a wire-bound notebook full of Freddie's notes.

The journal lay open, the edges of its brown leather cover frayed and stained. Interested, Elaine wondered if that was the item Freddie had found with the coin she'd gotten at the auction. It certainly looked old. And the writing she could see looked to have been done with a fountain pen, or maybe even a quill. The ink had faded to light brown, and the cursive script was flowing and elaborate. Without intending anything more than genuine interest, Elaine read the first few words on the page. It took a little work for her to interpret the unfamiliar and unusually ornate script. "...got them from..." The last word was obscured by the angle at which the modern notebook lay across the old journal. Instinctively, her eyes went to the second line. The word *Wattings* seemed to leap out at her.

Simultaneously, she heard the sound of Freddie's footsteps returning to the parlor, and she hastily faced the wall and began industriously scrubbing along the chair rail, moving past Freddie's seat and working her way farther along the wall.

Freddie smiled as she returned to her seat. "Are there any more of those cinnamon buns in the kitchen?" she asked. "I know I should stop myself, but those were delicious."

"Absolutely," Elaine said. "I'd be happy to bring you another plate." She dropped her cleaning items in the far corner and headed for the kitchen. Her mind was buzzing at her discovery.

"Jan!" She kept her voice to a piercing whisper as she burst into the kitchen.

Fortunately, her cousin was alone, Rose being occupied in the east parlor and Archie not having come in yet. "Elaine!" Jan greeted her with a similar exuberance. "What's up?" she asked, seeing the look on her cousin's face.

Quickly, Elaine told her about the journal. "I can't believe it. This lends a lot of weight to Freddie Donnett being the person who 'helped' Gleason off the ice Sunday night." She made quotes in the air around the word *helped*.

"Are you sure it was the name *Wattings*?" Jan asked.

Elaine hesitated. "I mean, no…but it can't be a coincidence, can it? That old script is really difficult to read, and I only caught a glimpse before she came back. But it almost had to be."

"So Freddie Donnett may have kidnapped Gleason Wattings to—what? Try to find out more about old coins?"

"Or maybe to ransom him in exchange for them?"

"To whom? I'm with you that she seems shady, but I can't for the life of me understand why Gleason would be a ransom for anything. But suppose she did kidnap Gleason. Where is he?" Jan asked. "She could hardly just stash him in her cottage at Green Glade. The cleaning staff comes by every day."

"I know. But it's still a possibility."

"I'm not discounting it. But I don't think we should stop looking at other options."

"Neither do I," Elaine said. "Since it's so slow, do you want to try to see if we can talk to Gleason's waitress friend in Waterville this afternoon?"

"Good idea," Jan agreed. "Rose is here until close, and Archie should be arriving any minute, so I think we could get away. Better go soon though," she added, looking out the window. "We're going to get snow, and more than a couple of inches could be a problem in either of our cars."

Elaine shook her head. "I suppose one of these days, one of us may have to break down and get some sort of SUV. Snow tires are well and good, but…"

"But not so helpful in a foot of snow," Jan added, chortling.

Archie arrived a few minutes later, and the cousins hopped into Elaine's Chevy Malibu for the short drive to Waterville.

Fish 'n Fondue was the unlikely name of the establishment, but when they arrived, Elaine was pleased to see it was a pleasant-looking little storefront establishment on a street right across from the Colby College campus. A large *F & F* was painted in lovely calligraphy on the large front window, reminding her of the elaborate script in Freddie Donnett's old journal.

"I guess we'd better order something," Jan said quietly. "We're likely to get a little more cooperation that way."

"All right." Elaine was looking at a menu on a board just inside the door. "I could go for some of that parmesan fondue."

"It's served with bread cubes, veggies, and little meatballs," Jan said, scrutinizing the menu. "Yum. Let's split it." Together, they entered the little restaurant, an informal eatery where they found seats at a booth along the wall. The booths and tables were simple dark walnut with stained-glass hanging lights above each of the booths and a larger piece with a number of globes suspended from it in the center of the room.

The midmorning clientele was light, but those who were seated varied. At one long table, a group of students appeared to be working on a group project, complete with computers, tablets, and index cards, while in a booth young lovers held hands across the table with dreamy smiles on their faces as they gazed into each other's eyes. In another booth, an earnest pair of young men appeared to be arguing over a book, which they took turns shoving across the table while stabbing at certain passages for emphasis. A solitary middle-aged man sat staring out the window, sipping coffee, while a woman and two men dressed in professional-looking dark suits exchanged comments over a meal.

Jan and Elaine shucked off their outerwear and tucked it into the corner of the benches as they slid into a booth. A fresh-faced young server with a brilliant smile came to the table promptly. "Hello, ladies. Welcome to Fish 'n Fondue. Here are some menus. Can I bring you something to drink?"

"We already know what we want," Jan told the young woman with a smile. She gave the server the order for their fondue. Elaine asked for coffee, while Jan chose lemonade. "Are you a student?"

"Yes, ma'am."

With a few more questions, Jan established that the girl, Amy, was a junior French studies major at Colby, which was a highly regarded liberal arts college. "And how long have you worked here, Amy?"

"Almost two years," Amy said. "I have some scholarship aid and student loans that I'll eventually need to start paying, but this job pays my rent and helps with expenses."

"Do you know Gleason Wattings? He's a neighbor of ours in Lancaster. We thought he worked here."

The girl's smile didn't waver, but her face froze for a second. "I know Gleason," she said noncommittally. "He's a nice guy." She glanced toward the kitchen. "Well, I'd better get this order in. It shouldn't be long." And like that, she was gone.

# CHAPTER TWELVE

W ay to chase off the waitress," Elaine said dryly.

Jan laughed. "Is it just me, or do you get the impression that she doesn't want to talk about Gleason?"

"I wonder why," Elaine said thoughtfully. "She was really friendly until we told her we're his neighbors."

"I wonder if she thinks we're friends of his parents." Jan frowned. "Remember what Macy said about Gleason butting heads with Bud and Shelba because they think he's too young to get serious. She might think we're spying for his folks."

"Good point." Elaine sat up straighter as their waitress reappeared with their drinks. The young woman set down the drinks and turned away immediately, but Elaine said, "Excuse me."

Almost visibly reluctant, the girl turned around again. "Yes?"

"We just wanted you to know that we won't tell Gleason's parents anything you say to us." Elaine hesitated. Was that a fair statement? Probably, she reassured herself, unless the girl gave them a bombshell that they could not, in good conscience, withhold from the police. And even then, they would not be telling Bud and Shelba Wattings. The police would decide what, if anything, was necessary to share with them.

"I don't really have much to say about Gleason," the girl said hurriedly. "He works here, but it's not like we're close or anything."

And before either cousin could utter another word, she was gone again.

Elaine and Jan watched as she headed for the counter at the front. Two other servers met her there and while none of them glanced at the cousins' table, Elaine felt certain they were being briefed on the nosy women from Lancaster.

She imagined that the other servers were avoiding them, taking different routes to the tables around them so as not to come too close. When their waitress appeared with their fondue, she was smiling pleasantly, professionally, but her lips were pressed tightly together. Elaine glanced at Jan, who promptly winked at her.

After the young woman walked away, Jan said, "They've taken an oath. They'll submit to torture rather than talk to us about Gleason."

Elaine chuckled. "It does appear that way. Really makes me wonder what they're hiding."

The rest of their visit was uneventful. Their waitress presented them with their check and returned with the credit card, leaving it to be signed with, "Thanks for visiting F 'n' F. Please come back soon." She escaped before they could even thank her for her prompt service.

After sliding out of the booth, each of them donned the knee-length down coats they wore, wound scarves around their necks, adjusted woolen caps, and dug mittens from their pockets. But as they walked to the door, a waitress filling salt and pepper shakers at a table nearby backed up suddenly, knocking heavily into Elaine. The shakers scattered across the floor. Fortunately they were plastic. Both cousins knelt to help the waitress pick them up.

As they did so, the girl discreetly tucked a napkin into Elaine's palm. "This is Gleason's girlfriend Marlene's next shift. You might be able to talk to her then."

"So you don't think they ran off together?" Elaine asked hurriedly.

The girl shook her head, fumbling with the shakers. "They've talked about eloping, but she's still here, and she's worried sick. So are the rest of us. No one's heard from him since Sunday."

"Are you about finished?" An autocratic feminine voice made all three of them jump.

"Almost. Just dropped a couple of these things," the young woman called back.

Jan handed her one final shaker that had rolled some distance away. "Thank you."

"Talk to Marlene," the girl whispered as she hurried away.

Jan and Elaine scrambled to their feet, donning their mittens as they pushed through the door into the small vestibule and then moved on out into the early afternoon.

They climbed into Elaine's car and secured their seat belts. As Elaine started the ignition, Jan said, "So I guess we have to go back to Fish 'n Fondue. When?"

Elaine unfolded the crumpled napkin the girl had given her. "Marlene Hanlen. 8:00 a.m.–2:00 p.m. Thursday. That's tomorrow."

Jan grinned. "If we went just before two, we might be able to catch her right after her shift."

"Okay." Elaine made a thumbs-up gesture.

As they headed back into Lancaster, Jan said, "Hey, let's stop and ask Tag about the rock salt. He's the only one in town that might even sell it, and if he doesn't, he might know where else it's sold."

Obligingly, Elaine drove to the motorcycle and snowmobile sales and repair shop owned by Taggert King. An open, metal-roofed shed along one side of the building was filled with pieces of snowmobiles and motorcycles, many of which were scattered outside during better weather. The cement parking lot had a covering of snow embedded with sand and gravel.

Stepping inside the front door, the cousins entered the paneled office with its small waiting area. Tag was behind the register at the counter, invoicing a customer. "Be with you in a minute," he told them, smiling in welcome.

When the customer hurried out, Tag turned to Jan and Elaine. "Hey, ladies. How ya doin'? I bet you're here to buy snowmobiles."

Jan laughed. "I wouldn't put any money on that bet, Tag."

He chuckled too, enjoying the banter. "What can I do for you?"

"Rock salt," Elaine said. "Do you sell it here?"

"Sure do," Tag said.

"Is there anyone else in the area that sells it?"

Tag thought for a moment. "Murphy's used to but they stopped about five years ago. There's nobody in Waterville that carries it, but I imagine you could get it at a couple of the hardware stores in Augusta."

Elaine felt a bit of her excitement fade at this statement. The big chain stores like Ace, Home Depot, and Lowe's all had a presence in Augusta, and there had been at least two other local ones in her youth. Anyone thinking of covering their metaphorical tracks would not have purchased rock salt in town if they were planning to use it for a nefarious purpose. Still... "Would you happen to have a list of customers who bought rock salt this year?"

Tag's eyebrows rose and his blue eyes widened. "Um, not offhand. But I could maybe put one together for you in a day or so. Would that work for you to stop back by on Friday?"

To Elaine, that seemed an eternity when Gleason Wattings was missing and she and Jan may well have seen the person who kidnapped him. But she didn't suppose they had any choice.

"Friday would be fine," Jan said, exchanging a look with Elaine that indicated she was thinking along the same lines. "We'll stop in then. Thanks, Tag."

They returned to the car. As they fastened their seat belts, Elaine asked. "Do we have some time?"

"Sure. What did you have in mind?"

"I thought it might be a good idea to run over to the newspaper office in Penzance."

"Why? We already searched them at the library," Jan reminded her.

"I know, but don't you remember there were a few issues missing?" Elaine pulled a sheet of paper from her handbag. "I have a list of the missing issues here. I think we should check the *Courier* files to see if we can find any more information about the Wood family."

Jan's eyes widened. "Those old papers aren't on computer. We'd have to find and read through each one."

"I know, but there are only a couple dozen, and it would be a quick scan," Elaine said. "The older papers were very predictable. Remember when we were kids? Local news was either on page one—if it was a really big deal—or in the "local news" section on page two. I'm betting a similar setup existed back in the thirties, and I'm also betting that any news regarding one of the area's wealthiest families would make page one."

Jan nodded thoughtfully. "All right. I'm in."

They drove the five miles around the lake to Penzance, the small town at the far end of the lake from Lancaster, where the daily newspaper, *The Penzance Courier,* was published. The landscape was a white blur, everything except the dark trunks of the trees around the lake covered in snow. To their left, the lake was snow-covered as well.

You wouldn't even know the lake was there if you weren't local, Elaine thought, save for the one small spot just past a bridge about halfway along the stretch of road where it never froze.

A few minutes later, they drove into Penzance. *The Penzance Courier* was located on a side street just a hundred yards or so from the main street that ran through the town. It was housed in a brick storefront, alongside a charming array of shops, including a bakery.

Elaine parked in the lot, and she and Jan walked around to the front of the building on a sidewalk that flanked it.

The front double doors opened into a foyer through which one entered the business area of the paper through an old-fashioned revolving door.

Jan greeted the receptionist, and Elaine realized with surprise that they had been classmates "back in the day." "Hello, Cookie. Remember me?"

"Elaine Willard. I sure do." Cookie smiled and stood, reaching over the counter to hug Elaine. "Heard you had come back and started a tea place. I'm sorry about your husband. It's hard to lose your spouse."

"It is," Elaine agreed. Something in Cookie's tone alerted her, and she said, "You married Harry Thome, didn't you?"

Cookie smiled. "I did. We had twenty-seven years together before he passed." Her smile dimmed. "It was so fast. One day he was fine, six months later he was gone."

"I'm so sorry."

"It was the heart with your husband, wasn't it? Military man?"

Elaine nodded. "Yes. Ben had just retired. He'd had some heart issues before, but you never think the worst is really going to happen."

"Until it does," Cookie said softly. "I'm sorry for your loss. If it helps any, I was sure my life was over." She looked at Jan. "I bet you felt the same way at the time."

Jan nodded. "Thank goodness for family. It was all that kept me going for a while."

"Me too." Cookie shook her head. "I had kids and grandkids which helped me get past the worst of the grief, but I thought I'd spend the rest of my life alone. And then I met Arne."

"Arne?"

"Arne Svenson. He came here from Minnesota with a surveying company when they were putting in the new highway, and he decided to stay after we met."

"I met him last summer at the state fair," Jan recalled. "He seems like a lovely man."

"He is." Cookie beamed.

"That's wonderful," Elaine said sincerely. "How long have you been married?" What she really wanted to know was, "How long was it after your husband died?"

As if she'd read Elaine's mind, Cookie said, "Harry was gone eighteen months when I met Arne, and we got married about six months after that." She smiled. "You just know when it feels right." The statement was quite similar to what Hetta Fishburn had said: *Sometimes you just know.*

A few months ago, Elaine would never have believed it. But now she could almost imagine how Cookie had gently moved on. "Congratulations," she said to her classmate. "I'm glad you're happy."

"Thanks. What can I help you with today?"

Elaine explained that they wanted to look through some of the old papers from around 1930.

Cookie directed them to the morgue in the basement where decades of past newspapers were stored. They hung their handbags over the backs of a couple of chairs and draped their down coats atop them. The room was temperature-controlled to preserve the papers, which were stored in long drawers from which they were able to withdraw them, and it didn't take them long to locate the first of the editions on Elaine's list. Protected by acid-free sleeves, the papers still seemed very fragile, and both cousins were as careful as they could be.

As Elaine knew, the paper was very small back then. A fast reader, she found that it took practically no time to scan each one for articles about the Woods.

In twenty minutes of looking, they found a couple of articles about Wood Woolen Mill, one description of how Mrs. Wood had donated a brooch for a charity event, and another in which Mr. Wood had been a judge at a local festival where he taste-tested entrants' pies and declared a Mrs. H. G. Aubrey the winner. There was nothing particularly revealing.

"Elaine. I think I found it," Jan said, just as Elaine rose to put away that edition.

# CHAPTER THIRTEEN

Quickly, Elaine crossed to the chair where her cousin was hovering over an above-the-fold article that declared: Area Families Lose Everything. The reporter mentioned a number of families who lost their homes, their land, and their livelihoods. The Woods were mentioned as a once-prosperous family whose ruin was made final thanks to the Crash of 1929.

"Oh my," she said softly. "It's really sad to think of what the Depression did to this country."

"And all the families who lost everything in the Depression," Jan agreed. "It's hard to imagine, isn't it?"

Elaine was reading the article, and Jan bent to do the same. Quiet reigned for a short time.

Then Jan said, "Elmer and Frank were the sons' names."

Elaine nodded. "It gives Elmer's age as twenty-two, and it says Frank was twenty. It also says Frank was a resident of Augusta."

"But look—it doesn't say anything about where Elmer lived." Elaine was thoughtful as she pointed her finger at the appropriate line in the article.

Elaine drummed her fingers on the table. "How else can we find out more about those brothers? The library?"

"I think we have time," Jan said. "Archie and Rose are prepared to close, so we don't have a specific time to be back."

"And the library is still open..."

Returning to the car, they skirted the lake again and arrived back in Lancaster. Since the library was so close, Elaine parked at home, and she and Jan walked to the Lancaster Public Library, a small brick building almost directly across Main Street from Tea for Two.

Jan was hailed by her friend Bettina, so Elaine went on into the library to get started.

Priscilla Gates was behind the desk scanning something into a desktop computer when she entered. "Hello, Elaine," Priscilla said. "How may I help you?"

"Hi, Priscilla," she said. "How are you?"

"Fine," the librarian said. "Are you just going to browse or will you need help?"

"I need help," she said. "I'd like to look up some people who were born in Lancaster in the early twentieth century, to see where they lived as adults and when they passed away."

"The Social Security Death Index might be helpful if the people about whom you're inquiring passed away after 1961. Ancestry.com also has helpful information in some cases, particularly if family members have done genealogical research and entered the results. Both of the sites are fee-based. Fortunately for you, our library maintains subscriptions to those." She turned and beckoned as she walked to the area where the computers for the public's use were located. "Here," she said, pointing to a laminated card, "are the websites to which we maintain subscriptions, their passwords, and any other information you need. Let me know if you require further assistance."

"Thank you," Elaine said as the librarian turned and headed back toward the front desk where she'd been working.

Jan entered a moment later. Elaine heard her warm tones addressing Priscilla, and what sounded like an animated conversation followed. The two women were in a book club together. Then Jan slid into the seat beside her and shucked her coat.

Elaine greeted her and explained what she was doing.

"Okay." Jan looked at the page of the Social Security Death Index that Elaine had pulled up. "So we need to enter each brother and see if we can find out when and where he died, and maybe we also can see if he had any descendants."

"Sounds good. Let's start with Frank. We know he lived in Augusta at the time of the Depression."

It took some time and some looking into several different indices the library subscribed to, but eventually they unearthed the information they were searching for. "So Frank married at the age of nineteen and was twenty years old, living in Augusta during the period we're interested in," Jan said. "He died young, in Augusta."

"And here's the older brother," Elaine murmured in satisfaction. "Elmer Wood, born in Lancaster in 1908."

"No record of any marriages or offspring on any of the genealogy sites," Jan reported from the next computer.

"Look here," Jan said. She had gone on to another site. "I found a 1932 address for him." Her voice trailed away. "Well, that's odd."

"What? What's odd?" Elaine repeated it when Jan didn't answer immediately.

"He's listed at our address," Jan said.

Elaine cocked her head, confused. "Why on earth would he have been living there?" She turned and looked at Jan. "Do you suppose he became a boarder too?"

"Wow." Jan looked stunned.

Elaine made a motion to open a new tab on the computer so she could pull up the same information Jan was seeing, but she inadvertently hit a different spot.

Immediately, another window on the monitor popped open.

It was a site on which someone had blogged about local ghosts in the Lancaster area. Elaine couldn't help but find it of interest, and she took a moment to read through it.

"Jan," she said a moment later. "Have you ever heard about tire tracks that disappeared into the lake in the fifties?"

Jan lifted her head from the monitor she was studying. It took a moment for her gaze to focus. "Um, a little," she said absently. "Don't you remember the kids on the bus saying that spot by the bridge over Milkweed Creek was haunted?"

"Oh, I do." A sudden memory of the bigger kids on the bus scaring the daylights out of Jan and her surfaced. The creek was a modest stream that emptied into the lake about halfway between Penzance and Lancaster. "You mean it wasn't just a joke? It really happened?"

"I think so," Jan said. "Why?"

"Someone had pulled up this post," Elaine said, "that talks about tire tracks. Supposedly a single set of tracks went into the lake but there's no record of anyone being saved from a car."

"Really? I guess I always thought it was just an urban legend," Jan said. She came over to Elaine's monitor and read over her shoulder. "Wow, that's kind of creepy. So the tire tracks went into the lake right after a winter storm."

"And there was no sign of anyone coming out of the lake," Elaine read. "They assume whoever was in the car drowned..."

"But they were never able to find anyone missing."

"Well," Jan said, "that was before computer technology, so the local law enforcement's methods of investigation would have been limited."

Elaine agreed. Back then, visiting in person, sending a letter, or making tedious, time-consuming phone calls would have been the only investigative options available. A visit or phone call might or might not yield results, depending entirely upon whom one spoke with, and a letter was easy to ignore or set aside if a department was busy or understaffed. So essentially, nothing had been learned by those methods of investigation.

That didn't mean that a car hadn't gone into Chickadee Lake. But what had happened to the driver? The thought gave her the shivers.

"I wonder," she said, "who was looking at this."

"That should be easy enough to find out." Jan rose and walked toward the circulation desk, where Priscilla was industriously organizing books to return to the stacks. They spoke for a moment, and the Jan returned, an odd look on her face.

"What?" Elaine asked.

"The last person Priscilla saw use that computer came in during the lunch hour. It was Freddie Donnett."

"Freddie Donnett?" Elaine gaped. "Maybe someone before her opened this tab. She's not even local."

But Jan shook her head. "Priscilla said they had a short power blackout around eleven today, and all the computers went down. When the power was restored, she had to shut them down properly and reboot."

"So there would have been no old tabs open before Freddie arrived," Elaine concluded. "But why would Freddie be researching an old incident like this?"

"I don't know," Jan said slowly, "but given that she's rented an ice shanty *and* we are wondering if the person we saw 'helping' Gleason Wattings off the lake was Freddie, I think we have to consider the possibility that it could be connected."

"Connected how? You think a car going into the lake way back when has something to do with Gleason's disappearance?"

"It could be entirely unrelated," Jan said, "if Freddie is not the person involved with whatever has happened to Gleason. But if she is, it means we might have to figure out what Gleason could possibly have to do with these old tire tracks disappearing into the lake."

ELAINE AND JAN arrived back at Tea for Two a few minutes after four. All the customers had left except for Freddie, who appeared to be reluctantly packing up her things as Archie vacuumed the foyer, and Rose moved from table to table checking to see that the sugar bowls were full.

Elaine hid a grin as she and Jan hung up their outdoor gear and headed for the kitchen. Since Monday, Freddie had stayed until they had loudly indicated they were closing each day. She had a computer right in front of her; she knew what time it was.

Rose returned to the kitchen, moments after they did, and Archie was right behind her.

"I wish that woman would take a hint," Rose said. "Yesterday she stayed until Archie vacuumed right up to her table."

"I didn't want to be rude, so I didn't ask her to move." Archie broke into a broad grin. "I just vacuumed all around her."

The others all chuckled.

"She was going to do some ice fishing," Jan said. "But she's been in here all day every day since Monday. I'm a little surprised she hasn't spent any time on the lake in her rental."

"She may have rented a shanty, but she didn't rent any equipment," Rose said. "People are talking about how weird it is."

"Perhaps she brought her own," Elaine said.

But Rose shook her head. "Macy said not, and she should know. And no one's ever seen her with fishing gear."

"Maybe she changed her mind about fishing after she'd already paid the rental for the shanty." Jan was usually the first to give someone the benefit of the doubt. "She should talk to Bud. I bet he'd give her a refund."

"Maybe," Rose agreed.

THAT EVENING, JAN and Elaine made paper flowers. Having decided that real flowers would be far too costly for their

Valentine decorating, Jan had found a fabulous idea on Pinterest for large, lavish flowers made of tissue paper. To that end, she and Elaine sat down with scissors, large sheets of tissue, and long green stems of pipe cleaner.

Following Jan's directions, Elaine folded her pieces of tissue in eight equal parts and rounded the corners of the unfolded edge. Then she unfolded the sheet again, showing scallops where she had trimmed the edges. After pleating the sheet in the center, she gathered it until she could wrap one end of the pipe cleaner around the middle.

Fluffing out the "flower," she exclaimed in delight. "Oh, this is pretty!"

Jan laughed. "I know. With a whole big multicolored bunch in a vase, they are going to be glorious."

"How many do we need?"

Jan pursed her lips, thinking. "Four dozen, maybe?"

"Whew. Okay." Elaine picked up another pipe cleaner. "Thankfully, Hetta and J.C. are providing fresh flowers for their reception. Making eight dozen of these might be a bit much."

Jan laughed as she walked over to the table where the poster of photographs lay. "I guess I'll go ahead and nail these down now that the entry deadline has passed."

The cousins worked in silence for a time.

Elaine couldn't keep her thoughts from returning to the unsolved issues that had been mounting all week. "One thing I don't understand," she said, "is why Freddie would rent an ice shanty if she isn't going to fish. That just makes no sense."

Jan looked up from the photo in her hand. "I know. Maybe she goes out there to think?"

"When?" It was a practical question. Freddie had spent nearly all day every day at the tearoom.

"First thing in the morning?" Jan suggested.

Elaine grinned. "To watch the sunrise over the lake, maybe?"

Jan gestured helplessly. "I have no idea, honestly. That's just weird."

One more "weird" thing to do with Freddie Donnett, Elaine thought, her own smile fading. *Stop it,* she thought, admonishing herself. "Maybe Freddie's strange habits are purely harmless coincidence," she said out loud.

"I suppose," Jan said, "that those old coins she's obsessed with could have something to do with it, although for the life of me, I can't imagine what." She paused, as if in thought. "And if not," Jan continued, "that means either Gleason chose to take off and make it look like an abduction, or someone else truly did kidnap him."

"Someone like Joe Vennard, you mean?"

"Possibly. Really, all we know about Joe is that he has an ugly temper and a nasty attitude toward the Wattings family."

"He's the right size," Elaine said abruptly, thinking of Joe's stature from their unfortunate exchange at the gas pump. "He could have been the person leading Gleason Wattings off the ice Sunday night."

Jan nodded. "It's possible—if indeed it was Gleason that we saw being helped off the ice." She went to the window of the sitting room, looking out at the darkened lake contemplatively. Although it was at the side of the house, one could see part of the lake from the window. "Hey," she said, "there's someone coming off the lake right now."

# CHAPTER FOURTEEN

W hat?" Elaine was startled. "How can you see that?"
"They're carrying a flashlight," Jan said.

"Why would anyone be on the ice at this time of night?" Elaine asked. She rose and came to the window beside Jan. "Where's the light?"

Jan lifted a hand to point, but she froze in midair. "It's gone!"

ON THURSDAY MORNING, Rose was off, so Jan was even busier than she normally was trying to get all her baking done for the morning crowd. In addition to her miniature maple croissants, which were a house specialty, today she had made danishes with lemon curd filling that gave the sweet pastry a distinctive zing, apple strudel, and *bossche bol*, a Dutch pastry that literally translated to "chocolate ball," a pastry shell about four and a half inches in diameter filled with whipped cream and dipped in dark chocolate.

She and Archie taste-tested one of the first ones she'd finished. It tasted fabulous to her, but Jan watched Archie anxiously for his reaction. When he had fastidiously cleaned the remains of the chocolate from his spoon, he said, "You should be right chuffed with that, love."

Jan stared at him. "What? Is that good or bad?"

Their British employee laughed. "You should be pleased with yourself. Can't think of anything much more delicious than what I just tasted."

"Oh, that's good." Jan smiled and relaxed as she began transferring the first batches of pastries to serving dishes. A few minutes later, she carried a tray of pastries and tea into the dining room, where Archie was pulling tables together to seat a large group of women from the hospital auxiliary of Maine General in Waterville. She was delighted that people from points outside their own little town were beginning to learn about Tea for Two and were willing to drive over and try out the tearoom. She hoped the tea selections and pastries would convert them into return customers.

Freddie had come in on the dot of ten, as she had all week, and had ordered tea and pastries while she set up her workspace in the west parlor. Elaine, who had gone to wait on her, came back into the kitchen with a speculative look on her face.

"You look like Earl Grey might if he got into the cream," Jan observed as she prepared an order. "What's that expression for?"

Elaine shrugged. "I just told Freddie I heard she wasn't fishing. I casually suggested that if she had rented the ice shanty and then decided not to use it, she should ask Bud Wattings for a refund."

Jan was fascinated. "And she said...?"

"First, she asked how I knew she wasn't using it," Elaine said. "I explained that this is a very small community, and it's the dead of winter. We have nothing better to do than observe each other and the few tourists that come to town."

Jan laughed. "Sad but true."

"She didn't know how to respond to that," Elaine said. "Her face got red, and she fumbled around for an answer. Finally, she just said it wasn't worth bothering Bud about. Which implies that she does regret renting the shanty, but I don't know—there was something in her expression that made me think there is more to it than that. She's hiding something. Maybe it has nothing to do with Gleason Wattings, and maybe it does, but that woman is definitely hiding something."

Jan picked up her tray with a teapot, several saucers, and a large plate of pastries. "Now all we have to do is figure out what."

As Jan returned to the kitchen a few minutes later, she saw Max, the man who made their food and supply deliveries, angling a box onto the kitchen counter. "Hi, Max," she called.

"Hi, Jan. It smells great in here."

"Thanks." Jan pointed to a plate on the counter that held some broken pastries they couldn't serve the customers. "Help yourself to a taste."

"Thanks." Max hitched a thumb toward the back door. "Do you know what's going on out at the lake?"

"At the lake?" Automatically, Jan turned to look out the windows at the back of the house, where the lake could be seen through the screened porch, which wasn't being used in February. There was a small knot of people on the ice not far from the dock over by Wattings Rentals. "I don't know." She and Max peered through the window.

Elaine came into the kitchen. "I just heard one of the ice fishing huts was broken into," she announced.

Jan and Max turned from the windows.

"What? Who told you that?" Jan asked. She thought of the light she'd seen coming off the lake last night. Had it been connected to the break-in?

"Whose was it?" Max asked.

"I don't know whose it was," Elaine said. "Macy just came in and said Jack Weston was on his way down to the lake to investigate a report of vandalism."

"Not again," Max said. "That's the third time this winter it's happened. I think it's just kids, but it's threatening to give Lancaster a bad reputation." He turned and opened the door. "Have a good day."

"Was anything stolen?" Jan asked Elaine.

Elaine shrugged. "I don't know. Do you think you'd better mention the light you saw on the lake last night to the police?"

"I guess so," Jan said, "although with absolutely no detail I can't imagine that's going to be of much help."

"It might establish a timeline," Elaine offered. "I'll leave Daniel Benson a message."

"Why don't you go out there and see what's going on?" Jan suggested. "I've got these buns in the oven and more pastry to make, so I can't leave. But we really should tell them I saw someone on the ice last night."

"And you want me to get the skinny on the break-in," Elaine said, grinning.

"That too," Jan said, grinning back.

Elaine put on her boots and bundled up. After leaving the house, she made her way along Main Street and over to the Wattings Rentals parking lot. Bud Wattings removed snow from the ice so that he could run his business, and the marina did as well, for those who chose to erect their own ice shanties and had no need to rent. Consequently, there were two clusters of ice huts on the Lancaster end of the lake. One along the west side that was accessed from the marina, and the other to the east, closer to Green Glade Cottages, that were the ones Bud rented out.

Trooper Benson's SUV was in the parking lot, Elaine saw as she neared the edge of the ice. So was Jack Weston's big SUV with the Maine Department of Inland Fisheries and Wildlife logo on the sides.

Carefully, she stepped on to the ice. She wasn't wearing any form of ice grippers on her shoes, but the ice was rough and bumpy where the snow had adhered, and she had little trouble walking.

She followed the path plowed by a snowmobile out to the area where the ice shanties were. The one where the blood had been discovered stood at the right edge of the cluster. Another, perhaps fifty yards behind it, was the one where a small cluster of men stood, including Bud Wattings, who was shaking his head gloomily.

"Hi, Elaine," said Jack in surprise as she approached. "What's up?"

"I have some information for you," she said. She looked beyond him to the ice shanty from which the door hung open. A broken padlock lay on the ice nearby. But far more interestingly, a scuba diver's wetsuit lay halfway out the door. "What on earth is that doing here?" she asked.

Jack shook his head. "We're not sure. The lock was sawed off. We've had two similar robberies in the past month on the ice, but in those cases, expensive fishing rods and gear were taken. We haven't interviewed the person who rents this shanty yet, so we don't know what may have been taken, but there's a full set of cold-weather diving gear in there that they left behind. There's also a really large ice hole," he added.

"Man-size?"

Jack nodded.

"Do you mean someone's been diving in the lake?"

"I don't know yet, but it sure looks like it," Jack said. "But there's only one set of scuba gear, and nobody I know is crazy enough to dive alone this time of year. It's far too dangerous." He seemed to recall her words. "So what's this you wanted to tell me?"

Elaine quickly recounted what Jan had seen from the window last night, little as it had been.

"Dan." Jack beckoned to the state trooper who was talking to two other people near the door of the shanty. "Elaine has something."

"Not very much," she said as Daniel approached. She repeated her information, being sure to note the time.

Daniel Benson scratched his head. "Thanks," he said. "That's about the same time we think the other two break-ins happened. Guess I'll go talk to the owner of the equipment now and see if anything's missing." He turned to Jack. "The scuba gear appears to be complete. I imagine that would be a lot harder to fence or sell than fishing gear, so maybe they didn't get anything this time."

Seeing that she would be in the way if she lingered any longer, Elaine turned to head back to the tearoom.

"Hey, Elaine, wait up." It was Daniel. "I'll walk with you."

"Sure," she said.

As they made their way back to shore, Elaine asked after Daniel's wife, Charlotte, and their children. The Benson family attended Lancaster Community Church, as Elaine did, and she knew both children had gotten the flu that was going around in January. Thankfully, Daniel indicated that they were on the mend.

To her surprise, he didn't stop at his SUV but kept walking with her.

"I'm heading back to the tearoom," she informed him.

"So am I," he said. "The person who rented the ice shanty is staying in a cottage at Green Glade, and when I called, Macy said I'd find her at Tea for Two."

Icy fingers tickled the fine hairs at the back of Elaine's neck. "Are you talking about Freddie Donnett? She's the one with the scuba gear?"

"Yeah. That's kind of weird, isn't it?" Daniel chuckled. "What could anyone possibly expect to find in Chickadee Lake in the middle of winter, other than fish or an old shoe?" He sobered. "But I am going to have a talk with her about diving solo. That's really dangerous."

"But that's just it," Elaine said. "She spends practically all day at the tearoom. I can't imagine when she'd have time to dive."

"That's what I want to find out," Daniel said. "Oh, and I also wanted to tell you something else. Our follow-up of the phone call Jan got from Gleason was a dead end. The number was blocked. Without an order from a judge, we can't pursue it, and we need to have more evidence of wrongdoing for a judge to approve that."

Back at the tearoom, Elaine showed Daniel Benson into the west parlor where Freddie sat, head bent over her computer. She desperately wanted to linger and hear what Freddie had to say about the scuba gear, but she couldn't think of any good excuse to hover within earshot. Reluctantly, she withdrew to the kitchen.

Quickly, she told an incredulous Jan about the scuba gear.

Jan's forehead wrinkled in astonishment. "Do you think she's been diving at night?"

Elaine shook her head. "I don't know. Macy says she walks to the office around eight o'clock each morning to get a paper, and she's here by ten, so I don't think she'd have time then. And it doesn't get light out until almost seven this time of year."

"Then she's here until we pretty much kick her out at four," Jan commented wryly. "And sunset right now is before five. So if she's diving, she's diving in the dark." She shivered. "How creepy would that be?"

"Not just creepy," Elaine amended. "Stupid. One of the cardinal rules of scuba diving is that you have a buddy. Even highly experienced divers don't recommend diving alone. Too many things can go wrong. Especially at night."

Jan nodded. "I would think diving in the lake could be really dangerous. I know branches have fallen in there during storms. Who knows where they end up? Get tangled up in one of those and you might never get free. Why would she do that?"

Elaine lifted her shoulders helplessly. "I can't imagine. Practicing for cold-water dives? Maybe she just goes under the ice and doesn't swim around?" But that sounded as ridiculous as Elaine felt suggesting it. "What would make you take a risk like that?" she asked Jan.

Her cousin blinked. She frowned. Finally, she said, "I would only do something that crazy if there was some reason of very great importance to me."

"So what would be of such importance that Freddie would take a chance like that?" Elaine pressed.

"I don't know," Jan said slowly. "I was thinking more along the lines of if someone I loved was endangered and could only be saved or cured...but I suppose it could be something less ephemeral and more tangible."

"Like money," Elaine said flatly. "Like those gold doubloons she's shown us. I looked them up online, and she's right. There are only about a half dozen of the real gold ones in existence. Finding another would make the finder richer than you and I can even imagine."

"Could this have anything to do with the research Freddie was doing at the library?" Elaine asked.

Jan threw up her hands. "Who knows? I feel as if we have all these threads hanging but none of them weave together in any way that makes sense."

"Yet," Elaine said.

The cousins looked at each other.

Finally, Jan said quietly, "Do you suppose the Wattings family knows something about Brasher doubloons?"

# CHAPTER FIFTEEN

An hour later, Elaine had gotten into the swing of the morning routine at the tearoom. The sun was shining and the temperature was in the low twenties—practically balmy. And it showed in the number of patrons who had poured into the tearoom during the morning rush.

Still, Elaine hadn't been able to quit thinking about Freddie Donnett and those gold doubloons. And her scuba gear. In the kitchen again, she went to the window and looked out at the lake. There were two fishermen trudging off the lake, each with a bucket in hand, and over by Wattings Rentals, she could see Bud tinkering with a snowmobile. The sun shone with blinding brightness on the lake, highlighting the tiny ice shanties that dotted it here and there.

Automatically, her gaze went to the one behind which they had found the small puddle of blood. Next, she sought out Freddie's—and her eyes narrowed. "Hey, Jan," she said over her shoulder as her cousin came into the kitchen. "Do you think there's any significance to the fact that Freddie Donnett's ice shanty is nearest to the one where we found the blood?"

Jan's gaze followed Elaine's to the lake, and she sucked in a sharp breath. "I think we need to find out if there is," she said simply. Then she shifted her shoulders, recalling herself to the work at hand. "Rue Maxell just brought Shelba Wattings in," she said. "I was trying to think of a polite way to ask her if she knows anything about Brasher doubloons."

Elaine smiled, appreciating the thought. "Great idea. Want me to take their table?"

Jan nodded. "You'd better. Archie and I are both tied up."

Accordingly, Elaine went into the east parlor where Shelba and her sister had come in with Rue.

"Elaine," Rue said, beckoning her over, "why don't you let us know what the specials are today? I told Shelba a good cup of tea is just what she needs to help her get through another day."

"Of course," Elaine said. "But first, I've been praying for you, Shelba...Do you have any news on Gleason?"

Shelba immediately teared up. "No," she said, dabbing at her eyes. "The police don't really have many leads. They keep saying maybe the blood on the lake is unrelated, and he went off of his own accord because of his Jeep being missing. But I know my son. He would never just disappear and worry us like this."

"I'm so sorry," Elaine said. As requested, she went on to share the day's specials with them and hurried to get the order prepared. A cup of tea was a small thing, but she suspected it did Shelba some good to sit with her friends for a time.

She hated seeing the distress in the poor woman's eyes. She could imagine how distraught she would be if Sasha or Jared vanished without a trace. How, she wondered, could she introduce the topic of the old coins to Shelba? It might amount to nothing, but if there was the slightest chance that the Wattings family was connected to the Brasher doubloons, she had to try to find out. If there was, she promised herself, she and Jan would turn the information over to the police. But if they went to Trooper Benson now with the unlikely suspicions they harbored, he would—at best—gently tell them to leave the investigating to the police.

Ironically, it turned out that Elaine didn't have to do a single thing to determine whether or not Shelba Wattings knew anything about the Brasher doubloons. Elaine had just set down a pot of tea, tea cups, and pastries at a table beside Shelba's when she noticed Freddie Donnett approaching the table.

"Hello," Freddie said. "May I interrupt for a moment?"

"Oh, not those old coins again," Rue said. "Don't you ever think of anything else?"

But Shelba's sister spoke at the same moment. "Certainly," she said, although Shelba barely appeared to notice Freddie.

Freddie had her little notebook computer with her. As Elaine had noticed before, the professor seemed to have no qualms about interrupting others. It was a good thing she wasn't teaching etiquette classes.

In a flash, Freddie had flipped it open to display the shining golden coin she'd shown Elaine the first day she'd come to Tea for Two. "Have either of you ever seen anything like this? It's called a Brasher doubloon."

Shelba's sister shook her head. "No, but I'm not much into coin collecting. It's very pretty. Is it yours?" It was clear the woman was just making conversation to pass the time. Shelba herself could not have been less interested in the coin.

"I do have one similar to this." Freddie angled her computer toward Shelba. "How about you, ma'am? Ever seen anything like this?"

Shelba just shook her head apathetically. "No."

Rue appeared to have had enough. She took Freddie firmly by the arm and dragged her away, saying, "I'd like to see that." Elaine knew Rue had already seen the image, but she appreciated the motive behind it. Clearly, Rue was trying to protect Shelba Wattings.

As she watched, Rue reached out and snapped the computer shut. Freddie's head came up at that, but Rue spoke rapidly, gesturing once at Shelba, and Freddie looked surprised, then chagrined. She nodded and turned away, heading back to her table in the west parlor. Elaine could only assume that Rue had told Freddie about Shelba's son being missing and adjured her not to pester the poor woman.

As it had yesterday, the morning's business dwindled to almost nothing over the lunch hour and didn't really pick up again in the afternoon. Jan did not appear the least bit perturbed by this as she untied the large work apron that had covered her clothing. "Ready to go?" she asked Elaine.

With no further delay, the pair climbed into Jan's Camry and headed for Fish 'n Fondue in Waterville again. Gleason's girlfriend, Marlene, was supposed to be getting off at two, and they hoped to catch her.

"Should we go in?" Jan asked as she parked the car down the street from the little eatery.

Elaine hesitated. "I think we're going to have to. How will we know who Marlene is if we don't?"

"And she could leave by a back entrance," Jan said, "and we'd miss her altogether."

Unlike before, they felt no need to patronize the restaurant. A young woman they hadn't seen before approached as they entered and waved at the room. "Have a seat anywhere," she said, "and I'll be with you in a minute."

"Actually," Elaine said, "we'd like to talk to Marlene. Is she still here?"

"Oh, she's just about to clock out. Let me get her." The girl eyed them speculatively. "Can I tell her who's asking?"

"Elaine and Jan," Elaine said firmly, knowing this would mean absolutely nothing to Marlene or any of the other servers.

A moment later, a slender young woman with long blonde hair caught up in a twisty sort of do came through the swinging doors that led to the kitchen. She carried a brown down coat with a fur-trimmed hood over one arm, and she smiled quizzically as she walked toward them. "Elaine and Jan?"

"Hello, Marlene." Elaine stepped forward and offered her hand. "I'm Elaine Cook and this is my cousin Jan Blake. We're from Lancaster and we're friends of Gleason Wattings's family."

"Oh." The young woman looked nonplussed and then almost instantly distressed. "So Gleason's parents know about me now?"

"Actually, no. Not to our knowledge," Elaine said, attempting to reassure her. "We're not here on their behalf. We've sort of been unofficially trying to figure out what happened to Gleason."

"Very unofficially," Jan put in, offering her hand as well. "On Sunday night, we saw a tall person being helped off the ice by someone, and we think it was Gleason."

Marlene's eyes rounded. "I just got off. Would you like to take a little walk and talk with me?"

"That would be perfect," Jan said, and the three of them pushed through the vestibule and out on to the sidewalk. It still felt fairly mild out, and when Marlene turned and headed on to the Colby College campus, the cousins made no demur.

"How did you find me?" Marlene asked.

Elaine was amused at the naiveté of the young woman, although she was careful not to show it. "Lancaster and Waterville are very small towns. Everyone knows everyone else's business."

"But Gleason's parents don't know about me?" She sounded quite concerned about that.

"No," Jan assured her. "One of our employees saw you together, and another friend of ours also saw you having a meal together somewhere."

Marlene's face twisted. "And we thought we were being so discreet."

"So you and Gleason have been dating for a while?"

"It'll be a year in April," the girl said.

Jan nodded. "So it's serious."

The girl's head jerked up at that. "On my part, it is," she said. "It is for Gleason too. But he respects his parents," she said softly.

"And they don't want him to get serious with anyone yet." Elaine nodded.

"They think he's too young," Marlene said. "I still have two years of school left, and going part-time, Gleason's going to take even longer to get his degree, so we're in no hurry."

"We understand his parents aren't thrilled about him getting a degree," Elaine said, trying to be delicate.

"No, his dad wants him to take over the rental business in a few years," Marlene said, her face troubled. "Gleason is determined not to do that, but he also doesn't want to cause a permanent rift with his parents." She looked unhappy. "My mother and dad divorced, and my mom's folks couldn't stand my father. It made my childhood difficult, and Gleason and I really don't want to set a bad precedent for our family dynamics, you know?"

"That's very sensible," Elaine said.

"Tell Gleason that," Marlene said, trying to smile. "He wants to introduce me to them, but I said I thought we ought to hold off on that until they're more reconciled to his career choice."

"What, exactly, does Gleason want to do?" Jan asked.

"He wants to be a history teacher," the young woman said promptly. "And I think he'll be a really good one," she added with pride. "He just started a night course on the American Revolution right now, and you should hear him go on about it. He can really make it come alive."

Elaine felt an odd tingle of premonition. She cleared her throat. "Do you by any chance know who his professor is?"

Marlene hesitated. "Professor Donner? Donnegan? Something like that. She's only here for one semester."

"What?" Jan looked startled, but she quickly attempted to cover her shock. "We've met her. She's staying in Lancaster."

Marlene nodded, but didn't appear to have much else to say about the professor. "Gleason and I were supposed to have dinner before his class on Monday. I hadn't heard from him all day, which was unusual. He texts all the time, but he hadn't texted me back. And then he didn't show for dinner. First, I was annoyed, but then I got worried. And then on Tuesday, I found out his parents had told the police he went missing Sunday night." She sniffled, holding back tears, and Jan put a consoling arm around her. "Gleason would never have stayed out all night; he's a thoughtful person."

A SHORT WHILE later, the cousins took their leave of the distraught young woman and headed back to Lancaster.

"Even if he chose to disappear on his own," Elaine said as she buckled her seat belt, "I don't think Marlene knows anything about it. She's genuinely upset and worried."

"Do you really think there's a chance Gleason took off?" As Jan put the car in gear, she sent Elaine a skeptical look. "After that odd phone call and the blood on the ice, I think it's much more likely that he was kidnapped."

"I know. I'm just trying to keep myself from focusing too much on one theory," Elaine said. "I don't want to miss something because we have tunnel vision."

"Fair," Jan said. "Let's ask ourselves this: if Gleason wasn't involved in any altercation on the ice, whose blood is that?"

"Remember when we thought the guy might be drunk? That's still a possibility."

Jan smiled. "It is. Except it doesn't explain the blood. Or the rock salt. That's just weird."

"I know. And then you add in the idea of Gleason trying to make a phone call, maybe from an unfamiliar phone and hitting a wrong number and getting us instead of his folks..."

"And then having the phone apparently taken from him, don't forget," Jan added.

Elaine sighed. "I guess I don't really believe he just walked away. I just think we need to try to keep an open mind." She tapped a package that they had brought along. "Hey, don't forget to stop at the post office so I can mail this."

"No problem." Jan drove to the post office, waiting in the car while Elaine ran in to mail her package.

Elaine walked through the vestibule and passed the small room where the post office boxes were located. As she reached for the handle of the glass door that led to the post office proper, a man slammed through it, crashing it back against the wall.

"That ain't right," he snarled. "I'm gonna talk to the cops about this, you wait and see."

As the fellow bulled his way past Elaine, she scrambled to one side, her mouth open. It was Joe Vennard.

Elaine looked at the door as it began to close on its pneumatic hinge. It appeared to be undamaged, so she walked to the desk where the postmistress stood, her eyes wide.

"Are you all right?" Elaine asked.

The woman nodded, appearing to recover herself. "I'm fine," she said. "He's all bluster. He's done this before."

Elaine raised her eyebrows in question but didn't comment.

"He comes in here to pick up packages that are postage-due," the woman said, "and then gets mad when he can't claim them. He loses his post office box because he doesn't pay the rent on time and then gets mad." She sighed. "I think he enjoys making other people miserable."

"I'm sorry," Elaine said.

"Not your fault." The postmistress smiled. "I appreciate your patience. How can I help you?"

When Elaine returned to the car, Jan immediately said, "I assume you saw Joe Vennard in there? He came stomping out and took off like his pants were on fire."

"I did," Elaine said. "He was mad at the postal employee."

"He really needs—hold on. What's that?" Before Elaine could answer, Jan was out of the car, picking something up off the ground from the next parking space over.

When she got back in the car, she had a very strange look on her face. "Why would Joe Vennard have this in his possession?"

She was carefully holding Gleason Wattings's driver's license by the edges.

# CHAPTER SIXTEEN

Elaine called Daniel Benson. He said he'd meet them at the tearoom.

When they arrived, he was already waiting in the kitchen. Rose and Archie were finishing the day's cleanup, giving him curious glances as he nibbled on a pastry.

"Hi, Daniel. Come on into the office." Elaine didn't even pause to remove her coat. Jan and the trooper followed her.

In the office, Jan carefully held up the license, still holding it with her fingers bracketing the edges so that she didn't leave any prints on it. "I found this in the parking lot of the post office," she said without preamble. "Joe Vennard was parked in the space next to me, and after he left, I saw this lying on the ground."

"Joe Vennard." Daniel nodded, not looking particularly surprised. "Do you have a baggie I could keep this in?"

"Sure." Elaine slipped into the kitchen and grabbed a small baggie. "Here you go."

Daniel held it open and Jan dropped the license into the bag, which he promptly sealed. "Guess I'll have this checked for fingerprints and then go talk to Joe."

"But he won't tell you if he dropped it," Jan said.

"Probably not," Daniel said. "But I know Joe. He's a terrible liar. And if his fingerprints are on it, well, that's going to make him very nervous."

"If they are, will you arrest him in Gleason's disappearance?" Elaine asked.

"Not necessarily." Daniel scratched his head. "There could be a lot of reasons why someone would have another person's license. He could have found it somewhere and was planning to give it back."

"Occam's razor," Jan said.

Daniel lifted an eyebrow in inquiry.

"A philosophy principle," Jan explained, "which holds that the simplest explanation is usually correct."

That made Daniel smile. "True," he said.

"But perhaps not, in this case," Elaine said. "You know Joe doesn't particularly care for Bud Wattings."

Daniel snorted. "And there's the understatement of the year. But not liking someone and kidnapping his kid are two giant leaps in opposite directions."

Elaine agreed. "Will you let us know what Joe says about the license?" she asked.

Daniel shrugged. "Sure. Thanks for turning this in right away."

Once the trooper had taken his leave, Elaine peeled off her coat and flopped down in the office chair. "This changes everything."

"Not necessarily." Jan took off her coat as well. "You're the one who said we need to keep open minds." She snapped her fingers. "And I almost forgot to tell you. I invited Bob for dinner on Sunday evening. I was wondering if you'd like to ask Nathan to join us."

"Right on the heels of our Valentine's Day date?" Elaine made a face. "What if it doesn't go well?"

Jan chuckled. "Can you honestly imagine that you aren't going to enjoy yourself Saturday night?"

Elaine smiled. "No. Nathan and I know each other too well for that to be a concern. I just wouldn't want him to think..."

"Well, keep it in mind. You can invite him at the end of the evening if you feel like it."

"All right." Elaine was relieved not to have to make that decision right now. "What's on the menu?"

"I hadn't thought that far ahead," Jan admitted. "But I guess I'd better, since it's only three days away. What do you think we should serve?"

Elaine drew a blank. "I don't know. Pasta? Beef?"

"Let's go traditional," Jan said. "I've been hungry for pork loin for weeks now. How do you feel about that?"

"With mashed potatoes, biscuits, and maybe grilled asparagus? I would feel really, really good about that," she said, grinning.

"Sounds good. We could serve some of that applesauce I made and froze last fall too."

"And dessert. I'll even help you make it."

Jan waved away that suggestion with a laugh. "I'll make an angel food cake, and we can drizzle chocolate over it. That'll take no time at all."

FRIDAY WAS THE day before Valentine's Day. From the moment Elaine stepped into the kitchen that morning, the pace was beyond hectic at Tea for Two. In addition to all the preparation for their daily customers, the cousins were determined to make sure that everything would be perfect for Hetta and J.C.'s wedding reception the following afternoon.

Rose had come in early to do much of the day's baking, freeing Jan up to bake and decorate the cake and cupcakes for the reception. When Elaine zipped into the kitchen at seven, Jan already had two dozen red buttercream rosebuds created and was starting on pink ones.

"I'm going to lay out the linens and get the napkins folded," Elaine said, "and then I'll get out the large rosebud china platters we picked up last summer at that estate sale. They'll be perfect for the buffet. Speaking of which, I'll check the silver and make sure nothing needs to be polished, and I'll set up the chafing dishes and make sure we have full cans of Sterno ready."

She went into the dining room and pulled out a snowy white lace tablecloth, which she whipped over the dining table. A second pretty lace table runner draped the top of the side buffet. The cake and finger foods would be set up in both those locations, while tea and beverages would be served at the tables.

Next, she pulled out a stack of red cloth napkins. She had found a pretty, if complicated, folded napkin pattern, and she sat at one of the tables in the west parlor, quickly and efficiently forming them into stunningly pretty rose shapes. One would be set in the center of each place setting.

After placing them on a tray, she moved them to a side table and covered each of the square pine tables with pink or white tablecloths. At the last minute, she left one uncovered so that Freddie would have a place to work for the morning. She placed the pink candles Hetta had provided in the hurricane globes on unfolded red napkins laid in the center of each table and then put the rose napkins at each place.

Empty crystal vases went on accent tables and the buffet in the dining room. They would be filled with flowers tomorrow morning when the florist arrived. According to Hetta, the florist would take care of arranging the flowers around each of the hurricane globes and in the vases, so that would be one less thing for her to worry over.

She covered an additional table just inside the west parlor door with a snowy white tablecloth and placed a silver plate-framed engagement photo of Hetta and J.C. on it. The table would be used to collect any gifts brought by guests.

Once the actual decorating was as done as it could be, she placed a velvet rope across the entrance to the west parlor so that customers would enter the east parlor. Next, she turned her attention to the serving dishes they would need. They had two sets of chafing dishes for warm foods, which she placed on the side buffet. Opening one of its doors, she found the cans of Sterno they stored for such occasions and placed one beneath each dish.

The rose-festooned platters came next. Jan was making finger sandwiches, deviled eggs, and arrays of fruit and vegetables with accompanying dips. Opening another drawer, she pulled out a velvet-lined case and opened it. They had collected a number of badly tarnished silver serving utensils at sales for next to nothing. With a little elbow grease and liberal applications of silver polish with toothbrushes, the pieces now gleamed in the morning light. They would lend an elegant touch to the display.

Jan, who had taken a break after completing her pink roses and gone in to glance over the arrangements in the dining room, halted before the photo of the happy couple on the gift table.

"Oh, isn't that lovely!" she said. "They look so happy. I think it's wonderful that they've found love a second time."

"It is," Elaine said softly. "It really is."

After they opened at ten, the tearoom was busy. As she greeted and seated customers, recited the menu, and took and prepared orders, Elaine still found a corner of her mind occupied by puzzling over the odds and ends of information she and Jan had amassed that might—or might not—help to solve the mystery of what had happened to Gleason Wattings.

Freddie Donnett came in at ten, just as she had all week, and commandeered the table in the west parlor where she spread out her notebooks and laptop. She thanked Elaine for letting her use the room in the morning.

Elaine smiled as she responded, wondering if she could get another look at that journal that had contained the name "Wattings."

"Good morning, Freddie," she said, approaching the table. "Today we're featuring a blueberry Rooibos tea called True

Blue. It's caffeine-free and chock full of antioxidants, and both the flavor and the aroma are berry-filled and gently tart with an earthy undertone."

"That sounds terrific," Freddie said. "What sort of pastries has your kitchen whipped up today?"

"Well, of course we have our mini maple croissants as always. They're sort of a house specialty. But today we also have mini blueberry galettes to complement the tea. They're a sort of small tart. And there's also cheese danish and a braided Nutella bread."

"They all sound wonderful," Freddie said, smiling. "How about a plate with one of each, and I'll call it breakfast and lunch?"

Elaine laughed. "Sure thing." She paused. "I was sorry to hear about the break-in out at your ice shanty. Was anything stolen?"

Freddie shook her head. "No." She frowned. "They said they think it might have been a bunch of kids."

"You're lucky you didn't have any fishing rods," Elaine said. Might as well let Freddie know that the whole town now knew about her scuba gear. "When the other shanties were broken into, they stole some very valuable rods, reels, and other stuff. I'm surprised they didn't want your scuba equipment."

"Yes, well, I was lucky." Freddie looked uncomfortable, pressing her lips together.

"I'm too curious to resist being nosy," Elaine said cheerfully, determined to get an answer. "Why on earth did you have scuba gear in your hut? The game warden thinks you must have been diving in the lake."

Freddie's lips pressed into an even thinner line. "It's not illegal."

"Just ill-advised," Elaine said with some asperity, noting that wasn't an answer to her question. "Here in Lancaster, we would take it poorly if we lost a guest in the lake in February."

"I've realized it's too dangerous to dive alone," Freddie said very stiffly.

"Indeed it is," Elaine said. "At any rate, I'm glad none of your equipment was stolen and equally glad you didn't meet with misadventure. I'll be right back with your order."

Back in the kitchen, she told Jan about the conversation. Or interrogation, perhaps, she decided. Freddie had looked far less than comfortable answering her questions. "And she totally fell back and punted the question of why there was gear in her hut. We still don't know if she actually ever did dive in the lake."

"Brr." Jan wrapped her arms around herself and panto-mimed shivering. "Can you even imagine?"

"No. I really can't."

Just then, the sound of a loud voice from the front hallway interrupted their frigid exchange.

"I can't believe you don't even remember him!" And the speaker began to weep noisily.

Both Jan and Elaine barged through the kitchen door into the foyer. The voice belonged to Shelba Wattings, who was standing in the doorway to the west parlor. Macy was on one side of her and her sister was on the other, both urging her away.

Freddie stood frozen by the table where she had been sitting. "I'm sorry," she said. "I see a lot of students—I don't remember them all. And it's only a few weeks into the spring semester. They don't usually distinguish themselves until after the first exam."

Macy mimed a zipper across her mouth, silently telling Freddie to stop speaking. Freddie, looking affronted and annoyed, stomped back to her table in the west parlor, pointedly taking a seat and not looking at any of them.

Shelba's sister led her out the front door as the poor woman continued to sob loudly.

"What's going on?" Elaine asked Macy.

"Shelba found out Gleason's history class is being taught by Freddie," Macy said. "When she said she'd like to speak to his professor, I said that would be easy since she's a guest at Green Glade and she spends all day every day here at the tearoom." Macy rolled her eyes. "How was I to know Freddie didn't even remember him? You saw how well that went over."

Oh dear.

Back in the kitchen, she grabbed Freddie's order, which she'd nearly prepared before the hullabaloo, and went into the west parlor. "Here you go," she said, setting the teapot, saucer, and pastries on the table. "Are you all right?"

Freddie looked a bit shaken. She blew out a long breath. "Yes," she said. "I feel bad. My mother used to fuss at me for being so involved in my research that I didn't hear her when she spoke to me. That's how I feel now. I should have recognized the name when I heard that boy was missing. He was in my class, for pity's sake."

She sounded completely sincere. If she had something to do with Gleason's disappearance, she was quite an actress, Elaine thought. "Do you have any impression of him at all?" she asked. "Maybe it would be helpful for you to talk to the police."

"I doubt it." Freddie dropped her head and speared both hands into her thick, dark hair. "I can't even bring his face to mind."

# CHAPTER SEVENTEEN

The real question is whether or not you believed her." Jan looked at Elaine as they walked the short distance to Tag King's shop later that afternoon.

Both women were tired. It had been a busy morning, and they were a little tense and nervous, albeit excited, about tomorrow, their first Valentine's Day at Tea for Two. It felt good to be out in the crisp, cold air with the late-day sunshine gently touching the buildings around them as it traveled toward the horizon.

"She seemed genuine," Elaine said thoughtfully. "You know, I keep wondering why Freddie is so obsessed with that doubloon she's showing everyone. Did you hear Macy say that?"

"I've seen her do it," Jan said. "It's almost as if she expects to get a reaction from someone."

"But not any particular someone," Elaine interjected. "She's an equal-opportunity show-er."

Jan laughed. "That she is. Although I can't imagine why she would think someone in Lancaster would know anything about Brasher doubloons."

"Have you forgotten the journal?"

"Oh, right." Jan snapped her fingers. "With the name *Wattings* in it. But you said she showed the picture of the doubloon to Shelba, and Shelba didn't seem to recognize anything about it."

Elaine nodded. "Then again, Shelba is carrying the weight of the world on her shoulders right now, worrying about Gleason."

When the cousins entered Tag's little office a short time later, Tag glanced up and saw them, waving a hand to indicate that he would be there in a minute.

It was more like five, but he was smiling warmly when he entered the office. "Hey, I've got what you wanted," he announced. Reaching behind the counter, he plucked a small sheet of lined paper from a stack and waved it in the air. "Only got three people who bought rock salt since September," he said. "We really don't have much call for it, and it's hard to keep. The stuff clumps up something awful if it gets the least little bit damp."

Jan accepted the slip of paper, and they both beamed at him. "Thanks, Tag," Jan said.

"We really appreciate your time," Elaine told him.

"No problem." He was already heading back to his work. "Have a good day."

By mutual accord, the cousins walked back outside before Jan unfolded the little sheet of paper. "Number one," she said, reading the list out loud. "Joe Vennard."

"Aha!" Elaine said.

"Number two: Macy Atherton."

"Macy? But she's not on our list of suspects."

"Maybe not, but she owns Green Glade and guess who is staying in one of her cottages?" Jan reminded Elaine.

"And number three," Jan said, "Mickey and Marvin Bellamy."

"Who probably don't know that ice melt works faster and better," Elaine said. "I bet their folks used rock salt, so that's what they still do."

As they stopped to wait for a car to pass at the corner where Pine Ridge Road met Main Street, Elaine noticed a solitary figure trudging back and forth with a shovel in front of Oldies But Goodies, removing the two or so inches of snow that had fallen earlier in the day.

"Hey, isn't that Marvin Bellamy? I wonder if his ears are burning."

Jan laughed. "Alone again," she commented sotto voce. She lifted a hand and waved, raising her voice. "Hi, Marvin. Where's your brother?"

The young man stopped. "You're the third person to ask me that today," he said, sounding aggravated. "I do stuff on my own sometimes."

Jan was taken aback. "I'm sorry," she said gently as they drew near. "I was concerned that maybe Mickey was ill or something, since I've seen you without him several times this week. I didn't mean to be insulting."

"Mick ain't sick," Marvin said sullenly. "I can do stuff by myself."

"Yes, I know you can. And you're doing a good job too." Giving Elaine an expressive glance, Jan walked on. The cousins crossed the street to the tearoom.

"He's really touchy about that," Elaine said.

"I didn't realize it bothered him so much to be one half of a duo," Jan said. "I wonder if Mickey feels the same way."

"Where do you suppose Mickey is?" Elaine asked. "Marvin said he's not sick, but he didn't say why suddenly he's on his own this week."

"Maybe he found a girlfriend," Jan suggested. "That might account for Marvin being a little annoyed at constantly being asked about him."

Elaine grinned. "Wow. I'd like to meet the girl that would take on either of those two."

Jan cleared her throat as they approached the porch of their own home. "Do you think we have time to run over to Penzance to the newspaper again?"

Elaine was surprised. Checking the time, she said, "I think so. They're still open. Why?"

Jan shrugged. "I can't stop thinking about those vanishing tire tracks that Freddie Donnett was reading about. What interest could she possibly have had in that incident?"

"Maybe she heard the story and found it fascinating," Elaine offered. "But given how obsessed she appears to be with that brass coin she has, I'd think it more likely that there's some particular reason she looked that incident up."

"I agree," Jan said. "Maybe the *Courier* article will have more details." The blog they had discovered at the library had mentioned the event in question only in the most general sense, along with a number of other supposedly "ghostly" things that had occurred in the Kennebec County area.

Cookie Svenson glanced up in surprise as Elaine and Jan came through the door again. "Hello, ladies. Back so soon?"

Elaine smiled. "We're finding all kinds of interesting things in your archives. Is it all right if we go on down there again?"

"Absolutely." Her former classmate made a note of her name and the time on the log she kept.

The cousins headed down to the basement of the building and entered the records room once again.

"That blog only said the tire tracks were discovered in the early 1950s," Elaine said, "so I suppose we are going to have to start with 1950 and read forward from there."

"At least we know we can skip the summer months," Jan said, "because it said the lake was frozen."

Carefully, the cousins withdrew the first set of old newspapers from the drawer in which they were kept and began skimming the headlines.

It was tedious work. 1950 passed and they moved into 1951, but they found nothing.

"This is making me hungry," Jan murmured. "Ads for Coca-Cola, fresh fish..."

"I've got Libby's corn and peas, something called Pot o' Gold noodles and hand-dipped ice cream," Elaine told her, grinning. "And, oh, look. Here's one for coffee. 'Give yourself a Coffee-break! Coffee always gives you a break,'" she proclaimed. "Oh, what I wouldn't give for a cup of coffee right now."

Jan made a face but declined to comment. She was well aware of Elaine's not-so-secret love for coffee.

Recalling herself to the task at hand, she continued reading. The circus came to town, complete with a bearded lady, a sword swallower, man-eating lions, and a family of "death-defying acrobats." A local beauty pageant was won by Miss Esther Edmonds, making Elaine wonder if the young woman had been a fore-bear of Russell Edmonds, the marine postman. There were a surprising number of advertisements for Coca-Cola and cars, and many more for movies, plays, and other live entertainment.

With a start, she realized she was wasting far too much time perusing the ads. She rose. "I'm going to start 1952."

Silence fell again, punctuated only by the turn of the pages, or by one of the cousins rising to replace an old newspaper and get out the next.

"I found it!" Jan crowed suddenly, startling Elaine.

Elaine hurried over to read the article, although Jan was reading the salient points out loud already. "In late January 1952, the school bus driver who picked up students along the west side of the lake saw tire tracks leading from the edge of the road into the lake. The sheriff later confirmed there were no footprints anywhere around." Jan looked up. "Apparently, the bus driver had the good sense to keep the children on his bus."

"The tire tracks diverged from the road at Loon Point," Elaine said. "Where's Loon Point?" It sounded familiar, but she couldn't place it immediately.

"If you drive out the west road toward Penzance, you pass a stone dam on your right," Jan said. "Then you pass over a little bridge that's over a stream. That stream makes its way into the lake about fifty yards farther on—just about where Loon Point is. Of all the places around the lake, that's the one that freezes last, and even in winter the ice is rarely frozen there."

Elaine mentally pulled up her view of the lake from the windows of Tea for Two, but Loon Point was far enough away that a person would need binoculars to see it well. "Come to think of it, I've never seen skaters around Loon Point," she said. "Or ice fishing shacks or snowmobiles either."

Jan nodded. "They'd get a dunking if they tried. A lot of years, the water doesn't ever freeze completely over there."

"Oh yes, I remember! When we were kids, we always skated close to the shore near this end of the lake. Do you remember your mom and mine both insisting that we stay at this end of the lake? Now I realize why."

They were both silent for a moment, staring at the article Jan had found. Elaine couldn't stop thinking of what it would be like to plunge into an icy lake on a pitch-dark night. She shuddered and shook herself.

"The sheriff said they would pursue all leads," Jan read, quoting the last line of the article.

"So we need to look through at least another month or two and see if there are any additional mentions of it," Elaine said.

Doggedly, the cousins returned to their scanning.

Almost immediately, Elaine found a follow-up article in the next week's paper. Unfortunately, it simply stated that no one from anywhere around the county was reported missing, and they never figured out for certain if a car really did go into the lake. "I wonder if that was the end of it," she said to Jan.

"I wouldn't be surprised," Jan said. "I mean, if you have no one missing, why would you pursue it? Back then, I imagine they probably put it aside and waited to see if anyone from outside the area ever came looking for someone."

Still, they agreed to read through the summer just to be sure no effort was made to find the vehicle. There were no more mentions of anything to do with the tire tracks though.

After climbing the stairs from the archives, they said farewell to Cookie and drove home. Tomorrow was going to be a big day.

ON VALENTINE'S DAY, Elaine was too excited and nervous to sleep until her usual time. Not only did they have a huge day of business ahead of them, but tonight was her dinner date with Nathan.

She was wide awake at five thirty, so she got up, took her Bible and the devotional book she was currently working her way through, and sneaked down to the kitchen, hoping to have a quiet breakfast without waking Jan.

She laid the valentine she had made for her cousin at Jan's place at the table and then treated herself to coffee and a pastry left over from yesterday, along with a dish of blueberries and strawberries. Seating herself at the old chestnut table, she then enjoyed twenty minutes immersed in the Word. The author drew inspiration from the first chapter of Paul's letter to the Corinthians, and Elaine found that she enjoyed the contemporary perspective applied to the Scripture.

Jan wandered into the kitchen, yawning, just as Elaine concluded her devotions. "Wow! You beat me downstairs." She extended an envelope she held to Elaine. "Happy Valentine's Day. I was going to leave this at your place at the table."

"Great minds think alike," Elaine said. She picked up her card for Jan and rose to hug her cousin. "Happy Valentine's Day. It's our first one at Tea for Two. Almost seems like a dream sometimes, doesn't it?"

"It does," Jan said. She smiled as she headed over to light the stove to put on the teakettle. "I know I've said it before, but I am so happy we're living together."

"Me too. Especially on a holiday." Elaine had been alone on holidays when Ben was deployed and the kids had moved out, but last year, after his passing only months before, everything had been exceptionally difficult. Holidays had been miserable. It suddenly struck her that living with Jan had been good for both of them in ways that neither probably had really understood when they'd decided to open Tea for Two. "Thanks for being willing to take this leap with me."

"So far, it's exceeding my wildest dreams," Jan said. "I was hoping for a modest Valentine's Day business for our first year, but instead, I fear we're going to have standing room only in the east parlor since the wedding reception is using the west."

"What if we moved the tables in the east parlor closer together, just for today," Elaine asked, "and borrowed maybe three more of those little square folding tables from the church?"

"Oh, that's a great idea," Jan said. "I lay awake last night worrying about what we'd do if we didn't have room for everyone."

"There's no way we could have waited until lunchtime to get set up in the west parlor," Elaine said. "It would have been just our luck to have patrons settle in there for a several-hour chat."

Jan laughed. "I reminded Freddie Donnett yesterday that her usual room would not be available today. She seemed a little surprised, although I know you already mentioned it to her. I don't know if we'll see her today."

"The florist arrives at nine thirty," Elaine said. "So I've got to be ready to work with her for a bit. I'm going to get in costume first, since I doubt I'll have time to change before we open, and I expect we'll be busy first thing. Two more couples in the last week made reservations for the dot of ten o'clock."

"I'll call the pastor and send Archie over for the tables as soon as he gets here," Jan offered.

"Great. Thanks."

Jan looked thoughtful. "I'm going to put this cake together now. Rose will be here by seven to start the daily baking, and Archie is also coming in early since you've got the flower thing happening."

"Great. I never worry about the pastries. You always have that end of things well under control."

Jan nodded. "We have plenty for all those who made reservations and that many again, and if it looks like it's going too fast, we'll whip up a few more things."

"I'm really hoping we're not overwhelmed," Elaine said with a nervous laugh. "Busy is good. Insanely busy, not so much."

# CHAPTER EIGHTEEN

J an and Rose outdid themselves with the day's pastries as the morning rolled on. Rose had baked and iced heart-shaped sugar cookies to look like candy hearts with beautiful freehand love messages on them. Jan made heart-shaped chocolate brownies stuffed with chunks of Ferrero Rocher chocolate and iced with a Nutella icing recipe she had found. Even Archie got involved, hand-dipping plump, juicy strawberries in chocolate glaze under Jan's supervision.

Rose, who taste-tested the first one of Jan's brownies, swooned dramatically over a chair after her first mouthful, making Archie, Jan, and Elaine all laugh. Elaine didn't like to ask about Rose's plans because it invariably made the young woman droop a little, but she hoped to hear soon that she'd heard back from the other culinary schools to which she'd applied.

In addition to the iced cookies, the Nutella brownies, and the chocolate-covered strawberries, they had made individual cheesecake tarts with cherries on top, cream puffs with pink-tinted filling, tiny red velvet tortes, and as always, Jan's miniature maple croissants.

They were serving several special teas in honor of the special day. One was called Valentine Tea, a black tea that tasted of chocolate and strawberries, while another, Hint of Roses, was an intensely floral tea with the scents of roses, jasmine, and cardamom. It even had tiny dried pink roses in the loose-leaf mix. A third called Love Tea was an organic herbal tea with floral accents and a crisp aftertaste.

Elaine also had spent some time Googling new ways to fold cloth napkins, and she'd found a gorgeous rosette fold that fit inside a teacup and looked for all the world like a rose on the verge of unfurling into full bloom. For their Valentine's Day event, she had ordered some new cloth napkins in two shades of pink, and they had placed the rose-folded napkins in every teacup. Elaine couldn't believe how professional they looked.

After the florist had left and just before ten, Elaine picked up the poster of their customers' most romantic moments and carried it into the hall, setting it on an easel in a place of honor front and center as guests entered.

In a basket in the kitchen were the little heart-shaped tins of tea tied with pink ribbon that they planned to present to those who had made reservations in advance. The last thing Elaine did before she went to unlock the doors was to place a list beside the basket and remind her coworkers to be sure to check off the names as patrons received their tins of tea.

"Okay." Elaine drew in a deep, bracing breath. "Let's get this party started."

The morning flew by. Elaine felt like a princess floating around in the beautiful satin Victorian dress Jan had made. Every single person who came through the door complimented the cousins on their charming costumes. Everyone loved the "Most Romantic Moments" poster, and Elaine noticed that the rose-colored glass jar she'd set out for the raffle had entries piling up in it almost as fast as folks arrived.

All nine of the tables crowded into the east parlor were full ten minutes after they opened, making Elaine very thankful she had scheduled the flower delivery before opening. As she put in the CD of 1940s love songs and Doris Day began to croon "Sentimental Journey" accompanied by the Les Brown & His Orchestra, Elaine caught herself humming along with the music.

There was no lunchtime lull to speak of, as there often was, with customers coming before or after the noon hour. Today, every table in the place was occupied every minute.

Shortly after twelve, a florist's deliveryman arrived, bearing a tall vase crammed with yellow, pink, and red roses.

"Is Jan Blake here?" he asked, standing in the front hallway.

"I'll take them," Elaine said. "She's in the kitchen."

She carried the lovely flowers back to the kitchen and pushed open the door.

Rose sighed. "Oh, how pretty. I know they're not for me, but I wish they were."

"Wow," Jan said. "Those are gorgeous. From Nathan?"

"Nope," Elaine told her, extending the bouquet. "The card is addressed to Jan Blake of Tea for Two."

"For me?" Jan's eyes rounded. She fumbled with the card, pulling it out of the flowers and opening the little envelope. "Wish I could be there to give you these in person. Thinking of you, sweetheart ~ Robert," she read out loud.

"*Ohhhh.*" Rose and Elaine both sighed the word together.

"That's so romantic," Rose said.

"It is, isn't it?" Jan's face lit up, and her eyes glowed with warmth. "He's out of town in Baltimore until late tonight. I didn't expect to hear from him today," she said, her voice wavering. A moment later, she found her composure and placed the flowers safely on the kitchen table to carry upstairs later.

At one, Freddie Donnett came in with Macy and Zale, who had made a reservation for two. "The west parlor isn't even being used," she said. "I thought you said you were busy today."

"We have a wedding party coming in shortly," Elaine said. "It wasn't possible to decorate today, so we had to get it prepared ahead of time."

"I still think I could have sat in one single seat for a few hours," Freddie said in a rather petulant tone.

Elaine was a bit surprised. The woman had been civil and, more to the point, congenial every other time she'd been in.

"Oh, get over it," Macy said. "We're here to sample all the Valentine goodies. You can go right back to the cottage and work to your heart's content as soon as we're done." To Elaine, she said, "We're adding her to our reservation."

Elaine almost laughed out loud at the look on Freddie's face. She might be a guest, but she wasn't getting any special treatment from Macy.

"Come on," Zale said, obviously trying to placate both women. "I can't wait to see what Jan and Elaine have cooked up for Valentine's Day."

Elaine led them to their table. "We have three special blends today." She recited her rehearsed information about the properties of each of the different teas. "Why don't I bring you a pot of each?" she suggested. "You can share and taste-test and order the one you like best."

"That sounds like a deal to me," Macy said. She was always happy to think she was getting special treatment. "And bring us a plate of all the pastries you've got back there. I didn't eat lunch, so I can eat as much as I want."

"Right away," Elaine promised, hurrying to the back of the house as she chuckled to herself.

In the kitchen, she prepared the teas. She placed a final cream puff in an empty spot on the platter and balanced two brownies in strategic locations. "I'll follow you in with this," she told Rose.

They had finished serving Macy's crew and were seating two other new tables when the front door opened again. Elaine glanced into the hallway to see Hetta and J.C. and a large number of other guests filling the hallway.

"Excuse me," she said to Rose. "Please tell Jan the wedding party is here already."

"Oh boy. It's about to get crazy." Rose skedaddled off to the kitchen.

"Welcome and congratulations," Elaine said as she stepped into the hall, holding out her hands to Hetta and J.C. "That was some short ceremony."

"We didn't need to say much more than 'I do,'" J.C. informed her, his eyes twinkling.

"And now we're here for our little reception," Hetta said.

Elaine indicated the west parlor. "Your place settings are just as you requested."

Hetta stopped in the doorway, clasping her hands beneath her chin. "Oh, it's beautiful!"

"Look at the napkins, Mama," said a pretty thirty-something woman in navy lace. "They look like roses."

"And, oh, look at the cake, honey." Hetta tugged on J.C.'s sleeve and pointed to the stunningly decorated cake, surrounded by a cascade of cupcakes and roses, in the center of the dining table through the door at the end of the room. Turning to Elaine, Hetta said, "You did a wonderful decorating job. Thank you."

"We aim to please," Elaine assured her, smiling. "Once everyone is seated, your pastor can offer a blessing and then we'll begin serving."

She hung up the newlyweds' coats and rushed back to the kitchen. "Time to get the food on the buffet," she said to Jan.

"We're already on it," Jan said. "It'll be ready by the time they all get their coats put away and sit down."

Perry Como's "Till the End of Time" was playing, which Elaine thought was quite appropriate, as she began to carry in the tea, hot chocolate, water, and fruit punch that Hetta had requested for the wedding guests. The rest of the work day passed in a blur. Archie and Rose worked with the late afternoon crowd in the east parlor while Elaine and Jan focused on the wedding party.

One memory stood out, when Elaine looked back on the reception later. She and Jan were standing off to one side, waiting to begin serving. The minister who had married the couple rose and offered a simple but heartfelt prayer.

Then, as they stood for a toast, J.C. slipped his arm around Hetta's waist, looking down at her with such pure love in his eyes that Elaine had to look away. Hetta, she thought, was a very lucky woman to have gotten a second chance at love with someone who so adored her.

"OH, MY ACHING tootsies." Upstairs at the end of the work day, Elaine took off her boots and stretched her toes. "What a day."

Jan removed her own boots with a grateful groan. "You can say that again. I think we made more money today than we did all last week."

"The wedding reception skews it a bit," Elaine admitted, "but even without that, you're probably right." She picked up her boots as she stood to leave the sitting room. "I am going to lie down for thirty minutes before I start getting ready for my date tonight. I'm beginning to wish I'd suggested postponing it a day."

"You'll have a good time once you get your second wind," Jan assured her. "Go rest now. You'll feel like a new woman after you've gotten off those poor tired piglets for a bit."

"I'm going to Skype with the kids and then take a nap," Elaine said. Her spirits revived at the thought of seeing her grandchildren's faces.

"Oh, that will be fun," Jan said. "Tell them I said 'Happy Valentine's Day.'"

DESPITE HER NAP, Elaine was a bundle of nerves as she descended the steps two hours later. She was a few minutes early, but she hadn't wanted to risk being late. After assuring her that the paisley skirt and cowl-neck sweater was a lovely combination, Jan had gone to her daughter Amy's to babysit her twin grandsons so that Amy and her husband could go out for dinner. Bob was out of town, so Jan didn't have any big plans for the evening other than her double date with six-year-olds Max and Riley.

Elaine laid her long black wool dress coat over a chair with her pink cashmere scarf, a nod to the holiday. Crossing to the ornate gilt mirror on one wall that was often used by patrons checking their lipstick or hair, she took a quick glance. Her short brunette hair with its strands of silver glinting here and there looked exactly as it had upstairs two minutes ago.

Hearing footsteps on the porch, she went to the door. At the firm knock, she took a deep breath and turned the knob.

"Hello, Nathan."

"Happy Valentine's Day, Elaine." To her relief, he hadn't brought flowers but instead handed her a small bag of nonpareils tied with red ribbon. She chuckled, recalling how when they were young, Nathan's father sometimes bought them each a little paper bag of nonpareils while he and Elaine's father had discussed the merits of a certain location for the next hunting trip.

"Oh, thank you. I've always had a weakness for these."

"I remember." He grinned, then mimicked a little girl's voice. "If you don't want those, Nathan, I'll take them."

"You never gave in though," she said, laughing.

He reached into his pocket and pulled out a second, half-empty bag of nonpareils. "I like them pretty well too."

Delighted and completely at ease again, Elaine let him help her into her coat. Wrapping her scarf around her neck, she pulled a black cloche hat down over her ears and donned her gloves before preceding Nathan out to his car.

"Where are we going?" she asked as he helped her into the car.

He came around and settled himself behind the wheel, fastening his seat belt before he replied. "A new place in Waterville called Amanda's. The owner is the daughter of an old friend, and she just opened last summer. Everything is farm— or boat—to table, and everyone says it's terrific."

On the drive to Waterville, he quizzed her about her day. He shook his head when she mentioned juggling the wedding reception and the special holiday. "Wow. You should have told me you had all that going on. I thought the tearoom was just going to be serving a few special things for tea. I bet you're tired."

"Not too tired for a pleasant meal with you," she said, mentally thanking Jan for encouraging her to take that catnap. It had really helped.

In Waterville, they parked and entered the little restaurant. It had a cozy feel, with candles on the small square tables and low lighting. Crystal and silver gleamed on the tables and the chairs were comfortable captain's-style seats. There were five other tables occupied by couples already, and the hostess directed them to the sixth.

Nathan helped her out of her coat and seated her. It was lovely to have a man observe small courtesies that seemed to have all but disappeared from daily life.

Nathan had taken the liberty of preordering their meal. They enjoyed large chilled shrimp cocktail and tasty spinach salads tossed with dried cranberries, toasted almonds, and a sprinkle of feta cheese with a tangy cranberry-pomegranate dressing. The entrée, two decadent crab-stuffed filet mignon cuts wrapped in bacon and smothered in sliced mushrooms beneath a peppercorn sauce, simply melted in her mouth.

As they ate, they chatted. Nathan kept her entertained with stories of recent antique finds he had made.

"Did you make some good finds in that house you were looking at last week?" she asked.

He nodded. "Oh yes. I think I told you about the license plates and some of the other things. But one of the best finds was a wooden milk crate with metal milk bottle dividers from Landry's Dairy, which was down near Biddeford."

Elaine told him about some of the photographs that had come in for the Valentine's Day "most romantic" display.

"Did you have a favorite?" he asked.

She thought for a moment. "Anita Picard brought in one of her and her husband as children. They were next-door neighbors, and it's a picture of them sitting on a stoop eating drippy ice cream cones side by side. It was especially amusing given that they grew up to own and operate the I Scream Ice Cream stand."

Nathan chuckled. "Is the poster still there? I'd like to see that."

The comment jogged her memory, and she thought of tomorrow evening's dinner. *Yes,* she thought. "It is," she said.

"We plan to start returning the photos to the owners next week, but if you'd like to come for dinner tomorrow evening, I could show it to you then. Jan and Bob will be there," she added, suddenly feeling anxious and gauche.

To her relief, Nathan smiled immediately. "I'd love that," he said. "Can I bring anything?"

"Just yourself," Elaine said. "We're not having anything special. We just thought it might be fun."

"And you can show me the poster then," he said, grinning.

"Perfect." Something else occurred to her. Nathan had lived in Waterville his whole life. He probably knew a great deal about the town. "Nathan, have you heard about Gleason Wattings's disappearance?"

Nathan's smile disappeared. "I have. It sounds a little suspicious to me, even though I know he's a young man and it's quite possible he took off to sow some wild oats."

"It is possible, but I actually don't think so," she said. She told him about Shelba and Bud's desire to see Gleason take over Bud's business, and Gleason's own stated desire to study and teach history. She went on to explain that she and Jan had located Gleason's girlfriend, and that in her opinion, there was no good reason for Gleason to have run off.

"But the most important thing," she said, "was that we think we saw Gleason being helped off the ice, possibly after suffering some injury, last Sunday night."

"What?" Nathan sat up straight in his chair.

She told him about the two men they'd seen, and about the blood and rock salt they'd found on the ice the following morning.

"That wasn't in the paper," Nathan said. "All it said was that Gleason Wattings's whereabouts were unknown and the police were investigating."

Elaine nodded. "I think they want to keep it quiet, possibly for fear of alarming his folks."

"Was it Gleason's blood?"

"They sent it to a lab, but if they know, the state police haven't shared that with us. But I'm glad all the details haven't gotten out because whoever did it probably thinks no one knows."

"But you and your crack sleuth cousin know." He smiled. "You'll probably have found him by tomorrow."

"Very funny," she said. "But we'd be thrilled if that was the case. Do you know a man named Joe Vennard?"

Nathan immediately made a face as if he'd smelled something very unpleasant. "Indeed I do."

"We know he blames Bud Wattings for stealing his business."

Nathan gave a short, unamused laugh. "Yeah. He talks about it to anyone who will listen. But do you think he really had something to do with Gleason's disappearance?"

"I don't know," she said honestly. "I'm just fishing. But here's something else. Have you ever heard of a Brasher doubloon?"

Nathan paused to nod to the waitress who inquired if she could remove their plates.

After their dishes were cleared away, the server brought a tray full of several fresh desserts from which they could choose their favorite.

Elaine chose a white chocolate cheesecake with a chocolate cherry sauce, while Nathan picked an "éclair cake" with chocolate ganache topping. It was actually baked in an oven rather than having the éclair filling piped into the shell, the server explained. Along with the desserts, she added a bowl of chocolate-covered strawberries.

Elaine moaned. "I can't possibly eat all this."

"I'll take care of anything you can't finish," Nathan promised her with a wide grin.

Both declined coffee.

As they ate, Nathan said, "You asked me about some sort of doubloon. I know a little about some of the most commonly found coins, but not that one."

"It's hardly common," Elaine said. "I'm told there are only a few authentic Brasher doubloons in existence, although there must be any number of reproductions."

"And what does this have to do with Gleason?"

"Maybe nothing," Elaine admitted. "One more question. Did you ever hear about the tire tracks that led into Chickadee Lake? It would have happened in the early fifties, before we were born."

"Oh yes." Nathan smiled. "There's a guy in Augusta who makes a living investigating ghosts, and he wrote a book that references it. Although it's barely a mention, because I don't think anyone ever found out much about it. Why?"

"Jan and I recently saw something about it, and we were curious. Did they ever find out what happened?"

"Not that I'm aware of. I believe there was talk some years back—maybe twenty years ago—of sending a diver down to see if there was really a car there. But who would pay for it? I can tell you now the local government won't. And the police really have no reason to reopen an investigation into a possible accident that's over sixty years old. No one was ever reported missing."

Elaine felt a small *zing* when she heard the word "diver." Could Freddie Donnett be looking for that car? But why? Especially at night? It was probably just a coincidence that Nathan had mentioned that. But she still intended to share Nathan's comments with Jan.

They finally left the restaurant and headed out into the dark night. It was clear and still, with no clouds anywhere, and the stars seemed dense and brilliant. Elaine felt content. Very content, and she had no wish to analyze it. She was just going to enjoy it.

"Penny for your thoughts," Nathan said, pulling into the driveway beside the big old Victorian tearoom, and she realized she'd been quiet the whole way home.

"They're not worth that much," she demurred.

"I thought maybe you were falling asleep over there," he told her. "Not that I could blame you after a day like you had today."

"It was pretty frantic," Elaine agreed. "I was just enjoying the peacefulness of the evening and thinking of how delightful our meal was."

Nathan parked the car in the driveway. After coming around to her side, he opened her door and put an arm beneath her elbow. Then he slipped his hand around her waist as together, they walked up the steps to the front door.

"I had a good time tonight," he said. "Thank you for coming out with me."

"It was lovely," she agreed. "Thank you for dinner. Amanda's was a wonderful choice." Nerves took over as she realized

Nathan was cupping her elbows and leaning in toward her. He was going to kiss her!

Panic struck Elaine, pure and simple. At the last second, she averted her face so that his lips struck her cheek.

Time froze. His lips lingered, and she could feel his breath caress her. Finally, he chuckled. "Good night, Elaine," he said, and stepped back.

"Nathan, wait." Instinctively, she reached out a hand and clasped his forearm. "I had a wonderful time. Come over at around six tomorrow evening?"

"I'll look forward to it," he said, and she could see the gleam of his teeth as he smiled and stepped away.

"Good night." She fumbled her key into the lock and opened the door without looking back. A moment later, his footsteps receded, moving down the steps and back to his car.

# CHAPTER NINETEEN

Elaine slipped inside and closed the door, leaning back against it with a groan. "You're an idiot!" she said to herself.

"Why?" asked a voice from the darkness at the back of the hall.

Elaine shrieked and slapped a hand to her heart. "Jan! What are you doing? You scared the life out of me."

"Sorry." Jan moved closer. As she stepped into the tiny pool of light cast by the small lamp on the half-circular piecrust table inside the door, Elaine could see that she carried a steaming mug in her hand. "Hot chocolate," she said, gesturing to her cup. "Want some?"

"No." Elaine held up a hand in a "stop" gesture. "I am so full from dinner I couldn't eat or drink a thing."

"I didn't mean to startle you," Jan said. "I had a yen for hot chocolate. I had just turned off the kitchen lights and started to head back upstairs when you came in. How was your date?"

"It was lovely." Elaine began to remove her outerwear and unbutton her coat, trying not to sound as shaken as she still felt. "We went to Amanda's in Waterville."

"Oh, I've heard it's terrific."

Elaine regaled Jan with a complete description of both Nathan's and her meals as they headed upstairs. Her nerves settled as she did so, and by the time she joined Jan in the sitting room a few minutes after changing into comfortable flannel pajama pants and a Henley shirt beneath a long, warm robe, she felt much more herself.

Then Jan asked again, "So why are you an idiot?"

Elaine sighed. "I was hoping you'd forgotten that."

Instantly contrite, Jan looked down at her hot drink. "I'm sorry. If you don't want to talk about it, consider the question withdrawn."

"It's okay," Elaine said. "It's just that, well, Nathan made a move to kiss me outside the door, and before his lips touched mine, I turned my head. I honestly didn't even have time to think about it. It just happened."

"Oh." Jan smiled into her drink. "Cold feet."

"Only for a moment," Elaine said, "but by then the moment was gone. He's coming for dinner tomorrow though."

"Oh, great. Bob called. He just got home. I'm looking forward to seeing him tomorrow." Jan stifled a yawn. "I'm thinking about going over to the Maple Sugar Fete in Penzance after church. Want to join me?"

"Oh, I'd love to," Elaine said. "After lunch?"

Jan nodded. "I believe it runs from noon to five."

"Sounds good. I'm heading for bed now," Elaine said. "What a day. I'm exhausted."

"I'm wiped out too." Jan indicated her mug. "Heading for bed myself as soon as this is gone. 'Night."

On Sunday, Jan and Elaine attended Lancaster Community Church together as they usually did. As was usual in the winter months, the congregation was a more modest size with fewer tourist visitors to swell the crowd. In fact, Elaine noted that she knew every single person in the church today, including Freddie Donnett, who had arrived with Macy. Elaine was amused to see the ubiquitous notebook computer tucked into the large bag Freddie had slung over her shoulder.

Pastor Mike's sermon was based on verses selected from Psalm 119 and from the fifth chapter of Matthew, known as the Sermon on the Mount. The children of the church, during the children's message, passed out cut-out hearts they had made during Sunday school to share their love with members of the congregation, and Elaine was thrilled when Kit and Russell Edmonds's little girl, Marcella, made a beeline for her with a wide smile and a hug and handed her a valentine.

"This is for you, Mrs. Cook!" Elaine had substituted in the six- and seven-year-old class in Sunday school in January, and Marcella had stuck to her like glue every Sunday. When she glanced across the sanctuary at Marcella's parents, Kit smiled and winked at her.

On their way out of the sanctuary afterward, Elaine waved to Macy and her family, Shane and Zale. Freddie was looking around at everyone and everything. She hoped the professor had enjoyed herself and perhaps been inspired by the sermon, but she feared that the woman's true motive in attending might be to continue to ask unsuspecting local folks about the Brasher doubloon and see if anyone had ever known of one. Again, she wondered why Freddie was so determined to see who in Lancaster might know something about a Brasher doubloon. They weren't common, so it would be quite unusual for anyone to recognize it. Especially here.

Obviously, Freddie suspected someone in town already was familiar with the coin. And given that Elaine had seen the name *Wattings* in Freddie's notebook, it was possibly the Wattings family. But Shelba hadn't appeared to recognize it at all. Then again, Shelba had been considerably distracted.

Suddenly, she remembered the rock salt. "Hey," she said to Jan, "want to distract the younger Athertons and Freddie so I can ask Macy about the rock salt?"

Jan's eyes crinkled. "On it," she said, wheeling and heading for the group. Elaine moved around the far side where Macy was standing.

"Hi, folks," Jan said. "Are you going to the fete this afternoon?"

"What fete?" Freddie was instantly intrigued.

Jan began to speak in an animated voice, and Elaine used the opportunity to touch Macy's elbow. "Can I talk to you for a moment?" she asked.

Macy shrugged. "Good morning to you too."

Elaine laughed at the woman's taciturn expression. "Peace be with you, my friend."

That made Macy laugh, and she said, "And also with you. What do you want?"

"Do you keep rock salt on hand?"

"Sure." Macy spoke easily, without any hint that the question was unusual. "But you probably don't want to use that for your sidewalks or an asphalt driveway. It'll ruin them."

"Then why do you have it?" Elaine asked. "I'd think ice melt would be a better option for you too."

"It is, everywhere but that pebbled path that leads down to the cabins. Those little round pieces get down between the pebbles and the path stays slippery. Rock salt works better." Her face closed. "Why are you asking?"

Elaine shrugged. "Oh, just curious about what you prefer."

Macy, clearly flattered by Elaine's interest in her opinion, lifted her chin. "Oh. Well, I'd recommend ice melt first if it works. It melts ice faster than the rock salt. Only thing is, you have to keep it really dry, or you wind up with a huge clump of salt as hard as concrete. I keep mine in a sealed can in my mudroom. Don't even leave it outdoors."

"Thank you," Elaine said gravely. She lifted her gaze to find Jan staring at her with lifted eyebrows. Giving a tiny nod, she said, "Hope to see you at the Maple Sugar Fete this afternoon."

"Never miss it," Macy said. "See you there."

It began to snow as they headed for home.

"Oh dear," Jan said. "I hope it won't snow too hard. I really wanted to go to the fete this afternoon."

"I don't think it's supposed to amount to much," Elaine said, echoing several assessments she had heard at church. "We could probably get a ride down to the other end of the lake with someone who has four-wheel-drive, but I think we'll be fine."

She told Jan what Macy had said about the rock salt.

"*Hmm.* So there's a good reason Freddie had that on her shoes." Jan looked frustrated. "And given that guests don't have access to the house, she probably had no way of getting her hands on it."

"And she couldn't have scooped up enough from the path to account for the amount we saw on the ice," Elaine said. "That was fresh, no dirt or pebbles in it."

Jan sighed. "Okay, so Freddie probably didn't sprinkle rock salt on the ice—but that doesn't mean she's not involved in some other way." Her eyes widened. "Could there be two bad guys? Freddie and someone else who was out on the ice?"

"We only saw one," Elaine pointed out. "But certainly there could have been someone else still in the car."

"And we still have to consider Joe Vennard a suspect," Jan said. "I think his attitude about the Wattings family probably gives him enough motive, and we know he bought rock salt."

"But that's not enough," Jan objected. "If he kidnapped Gleason, we also need to figure out where he is keeping him, and why he wouldn't have made a ransom demand by now."

# CHAPTER TWENTY

Maybe Joe did make a ransom demand," Jan said, "and the police are asking the Wattings family to keep it quiet." Then she snorted. "Oh, who are we kidding?" she said to herself and to Elaine. "Can either of us honestly imagine Shelba Wattings keeping that quiet?"

Elaine shook her head. "I think she'd have a really hard time not sharing it."

On that note, both of them went upstairs to change out of church clothes and put on warm, practical pants for the afternoon.

Elaine got back downstairs first. Giving Jan a break from the kitchen, she whipped up two BLT-grilled-cheese sandwiches, a combination of two popular recipes she'd begun making years ago for her own family. She thawed and heated some of the tomato soup Jan had made last summer, and the cousins enjoyed a tasty lunch before they hopped into Jan's Camry and headed around the lake to Penzance.

As they crossed the little bridge over the stream and passed Loon Point, both women fell silent, looking at the dark water that contrasted so starkly with most of the frozen, snow-covered lake. Elaine couldn't help but think of what Jan had said about that spot, about how it hardly ever froze over.

"A car really could have gone into the water there without leaving any trace other than the tire tracks," Elaine said thoughtfully. The thought literally sent a chill down Elaine's spine as they drove on.

The Penzance Maple Sugar Fete was bustling despite the weather. Not much kept Mainers from going about their lives, and the light snow currently falling certainly wasn't enough to disrupt anything. Ice sculptors were carving giant blocks of ice outside the community center, where vendors and displays were set up. One had set his chain saw aside after carving the basic shape with it, and now he had begun finer work. Elaine studied it for a moment before she realized it was going to be a bear. Another had carved a wishing well with pennies embedded in the ice—she was going to have to come early some year and see how that was done—and yet another carving was Cupid shooting an arrow into a heart.

The fete was as magical as she remembered from her childhood. In a timber-frame sugar house, maple sap was being boiled over a wood-fired evaporator the traditional way, while clouds of steam billowed into the air.

"Hi, Grandma. Hi, Elaine!" Jan's granddaughter Avery rushed up and threw her arms around Jan, then turned to Elaine and repeated the gesture, lingering to hug her waist.

"I thought we might see you here." Jan turned to see her son, Brian, and his wife approaching. "Hi, guys."

"Elaine?" Avery drew back and looked up at her. "Are you going to come to my spring concert? I have a solo."

"A solo?" Elaine infused her tones with appropriate admiration. Avery played the cello and did so beautifully; she had made first cello in her school orchestra. "Of course I'll be there, and I'm sure your grandma will too."

Tourists and locals alike were climbing into horse-drawn wagons for tours of the "sugar bush," the stand of forest to the south of Penzance composed mainly of sugar maple and black maple trees from which they could see the sap being "tapped" or collected from the trees. A moment later, Avery had dragged her parents and younger sister, Kelly, for one of the tours, while Jan and Elaine continued on.

Inside the community center, maple goods and other Maine items were being sold. The cousins took a turn churning maple butter as well as maple ice cream. A local Wabanaki woman was stretching birch bark over black ash splints to make baskets like those made in earlier centuries, while another booth featured an opportunity to try hand-dipping candles. Some distance away, a man showed off a collection of birch bark canoes and lectured on large laminated photographs of the process. Beaded jewelry was sold, as was Maine honey, handmade furniture, carved decoys, hand-tanned leather goods, and much more.

Licking a cone of maple ice cream, Elaine was studying a display of laser-cut wood wall art when she heard a scuffle behind her. Turning, she saw that Freddie Donnett was standing a short distance away. She had an annoyed expression on her face as she attempted to untangle the big shoulder bag she carried from another fete-goer, a teenage boy who, inadvisably, had a large gym bag slung over his shoulder with an ice hockey stick protruding from it.

The hockey stick had caught on Freddie's bag, and half the contents of the bag were strewn across the floor.

"Oh, gracious," exclaimed Jan. Both of the cousins rushed to help Freddie retrieve her belongings from the flustered young man, who, in his efforts to help pick up the scattered items, kept turning and twisting Freddie's bag even more upside down.

"Stand still," Jan finally barked at him.

The boy, hearing the note of command only teachers and mothers seemed to be able to inject into their voices, stopped moving and stood still as a tree trunk.

Jan was grabbing an array of small items—Chapstick, a small bottle of painkillers, a brush and hair ties—while Elaine grabbed for a small notebook that had fallen open. As she picked it up, she realized it was the stained leather journal she'd seen before. It automatically fell open to a page marked with a paper clip, the same page Elaine had seen before—the page on which the word *Wattings* had been hard to miss.

"Thank you." Freddie carefully reached around and began to untangle her strap from the hockey stick.

Elaine scanned the page, feeling the bottom drop out of her stomach, just as Freddie turned and knelt beside her.

"What a mess," she said. "Thank you both." She began taking items from both cousins and stuffing them back into her bag. "I really appreciate the help."

"No problem." Elaine handed back the journal and got to her feet. Jan joined her a moment later, and as soon as Freddie was on her feet, they walked away.

"Was that the journal?" Jan asked in a low voice.

"It was." Elaine spoke in an equally low tone. "But it's not what we thought. What *I* thought," she clarified. "I'll tell you later."

"All right." Jan smiled. "I'm about ready to go anyway. Are you?"

"Yes. I'd like some quiet time before we start our dinner preparations."

As one, the cousins made for the door of the community center and headed for the car. They got in, fastened their seat belts, and Jan got them headed back to Lancaster before Elaine spoke again.

"It's not *Wattings*."

"What?" Jan looked startled. "You picked up that journal, didn't you? You mean the name you saw isn't *Wattings?*"

"Correct." Elaine shook her head slowly in disbelief and perhaps disappointment. She'd been so sure... "It does mention Lancaster, but the name is *Watkins*. W-A-T-K-I-N-S. So does Freddie have any motive for kidnapping Gleason Wattings? Maybe the rock salt truly was just chance."

"Maybe," Jan said. "But we know she's Gleason's professor, and we know she was scuba diving on the lake. We also know from Zale that she's had some shady dealings recently..."

"Which is suspicious, even if we can't figure out her motive yet." Elaine felt as if all the information they had learned was whirling in a cyclone above her head, odd snippets descending for a moment only to vanish again.

"Wait a minute." There was an odd note in Jan's voice. "Are you positive it said *Watkins?*"

"Absolutely," Elaine said. "I had time for a much longer look at it this time." She closed her eyes, thinking of how she would feel were it one of her own children who was missing. "I really thought we were on the right track," she whispered.

Jan cleared her throat. "Do you recall the couple named Watkins in town when we were kids?"

Elaine shook her head. "Were there kids our age?"

Jan shook her head. "No. They lived in that big house down past Green Glade Cottages."

"Oh, now I remember," Elaine said. She grinned. "Everyone said the old guy that lived there would 'get' you if you went into their yard, right?"

"That's the one," Jan said. "Read that plaque on the wall of the library sometime. I guess his wife predeceased him, and when the old guy died, he willed everything he had to the library, which is why we have that lovely, remodeled building with all the modern technology."

Elaine didn't know what to say. Watkins. Not Wattings. So still there was a connection to Lancaster in that journal. There was something about this place that had drawn Freddie here, that much was clear.

Thirty minutes later, Elaine sat in the sitting room upstairs, propped up her feet, and opened her laptop computer.

"Whatcha doing?" Jan asked, entering the room.

"Looking up information about Brasher doubloons," Elaine said. "Freddie seems so intent on finding a connection to them in Lancaster and I want to learn more about them. Why are they so important to her?"

"She said she might write a scholarly paper on them, remember?" Jan didn't sound as if she thought it was too odd.

"True. But does that justify her intensity about them?"

"Maybe. She's a bit of an intense personality, so it could fit. But you're right—looking into the doubloons is still a good idea."

Googling "Brasher doubloons," Elaine was soon lost in history. Ephraim Brasher, which apparently was pronounced similarly to *brazier*, she informed Jan as she read, had been a well-known silver- and goldsmith in New York City. In addition, he was a neighbor of George Washington, who was known to be a customer. In 1787, the New York State Assembly turned down Brasher's petition to produce copper coins for the state.

"Why did they turn down Brasher's petition?" Jan asked.

"This article says it wasn't personal," Elaine reported. "The state turned down all such petitions and decided not to produce copper coins."

After that, Brasher's gold coins began to circulate. There was no law against producing gold, and quite a bit of foreign money was being circulated as well. Approximately equal in weight to a Spanish doubloon, the Brasher was also called a doubloon.

There were only seven known examples in the world today. An additional unique half-doubloon was owned by the Smithsonian. Many modern copies, sold at places like Colonial

Williamsburg in Virginia, existed, but were valued at only about a dollar. The electrotypes such as the one Freddie had found were worth about fifty dollars.

"And listen to this," Elaine went on. "A true gold Brasher doubloon from 1787 would be worth between half a million and a million dollars, depending on its condition and a number of special attributes some of the coins had that others did not."

"A million dollars!" Jan looked stunned. The amount was breathtaking. "For one little coin?"

Elaine nodded. She thought of Freddie's evasiveness early on when she had asked whether there had been other coins. "I think Freddie may believe there are other doubloons. What if one of them isn't an electrotype but the real McCoy?"

Jan looked up from Tara's sweater, which appeared to Elaine's untutored eye to be nearly finished. "So perhaps Freddie's strange behavior has nothing to do with Gleason going missing but rather a totally different motive?" Jan sighed. "Which leaves us with two probable options: either Gleason decided to abscond on his own, or Joe Vennard did it. And we have no way of proving either of those things."

"Yet," Elaine said. "Besides, what if Freddie believes Gleason knows something about the coins?"

Arrested by this new wrinkle, Jan froze. "This is all getting too confusing," she said. With great precision, she set her knitting aside and got to her feet. "Time to start this evening's dinner."

"Already?" Startled, Elaine looked up. "I'll set the table and prep for you. Just tell me how I can help."

"We don't have to do much yet," Jan said. "I just need to get that angel food cake in the oven so it has plenty of time to cool."

"You know," Elaine said, trailing her cousin to the kitchen. "It's not even three o'clock. I was thinking of calling Pearl and seeing where her mother's old friend Nan Colchester lives. Remember her? The little lady Pearl brought in about a week ago?"

Jan nodded. "What for?"

Elaine shrugged. "I can't stop thinking about those tire tracks and I can't shake the suspicion that they're somehow relevant. Nan would have been a youngish woman then. Maybe she recalls something that wasn't in the paper."

"It's worth a try," Jan agreed. "I'll get the meal organized if you want to try to visit her."

Quickly, Elaine called Pearl.

"Good morning," came Pearl's cheery voice over the phone. "This is Pearl."

Elaine identified herself and explained what she wanted.

"Oh, Nan would love some company," Pearl said. "She lives at Lakeside Retirement Home over in Penzance. You know where that is?"

Elaine did. The home fronted a small street just off Penzance's main street. She had noticed it any number of times because it was a big, handsome Victorian much like Tea for Two. "Thank you," she said to Pearl. "Do you think I should call first?"

"Go on ahead," Pearl said. "I'll give her a call right now and tell her you're coming."

Grabbing her handbag, Elaine stomped into her boots and zipped her parka.

After bidding Jan a hasty farewell, Elaine drove her red Chevrolet carefully through town and around the frozen lake to the retirement home. Obeying some instinct she couldn't really identify, she once again took the west road, crossing over the bridge and passing Loon Point, where the dark patch of water still showed despite the snow that continued to fall.

There was a small parking lot just across from Loon Point, near where the creek met the lake, and she pulled into it without planning the move. Sitting quietly in the car, engine idling, she contemplated the dark spot of water at the edge of the lake. She thought about the tire tracks, and the near-certainty she felt that someone had lost their life in the lake fifty years ago during a freezing January winter.

# CHAPTER TWENTY-ONE

Driving the rest of the way to Penzance, she soon arrived at the retirement home. Lakeside was a charming old Victorian to which single-story wings had been added much more recently. A small parking lot fronted the property, and there was more parking in front of each wing.

The front of the house had been preserved, and discreet handicapped ramps flanked each side of the house, leading to the wraparound porch. With its pale-pink paint and gray-and-white trim enhanced by the drifts all around and light snow gently falling, the place looked more like a postcard photo than a home for the aged.

The parking lot, walkways, and front steps were well cleared of snow and liberally sprinkled with ice-melt, so the walk to the door was easy. Inside, a woman sat behind a counter to one side of the door.

"Welcome to Lakeside. How may I help you today?" she asked pleasantly.

"I'm here to visit Nan Colchester if she's available."

"And who may I tell her has arrived?"

"I'm Elaine Cook. I'm a friend of Pearl Trexler's. Pearl said she would call ahead and ask Nan..."

"Oh yes. You're the one. Nan told me about you."

"How's she doing?" Elaine asked. Nan had seemed very alert, brimming with personality the day they first had met.

"Wonderful. She's one of our most capable seniors." The woman stepped out from behind a desk, turning over a little placard that read *Please wait. We'll return in a minute.* "I believe she's in the sunroom. I'll show you the way."

As Elaine followed her down a hallway, the woman explained over her shoulder, "This living option is for seniors who need a bit of help with daily tasks but are able to care for themselves and live mostly independently. They take their meals together, but they are not confined to their rooms or even to the house if they choose to go out. We do ask that they let us know when and where they're going and how long before they expect to return. We also have a full-time nurse who visits each patient weekly or more frequently if needed to make sure they are not having any physical issues or medication confusion."

"How nice," Elaine said. "What happens if someone falls ill? Do you have other levels of care?"

The woman shook her head. "No, this is a small, independent facility. If someone needs full-time supervision or nursing care, they go somewhere like Millpond over in Augusta, which has a unit that offers more specialized care." She stopped on the threshold of an open set of french doors. "This is the sunroom. Nan?" She raised her voice. "You have a visitor."

The tiny woman whom Elaine recalled from last week rose from a chair at the far end of the room in the Lakeview Retirement Home.

"Mrs. Colchester," Elaine said, moving forward. "It's nice to see you again. Thanks for agreeing to talk to me." As she took the woman's extended hand in hers, she was very careful with the fragile skin and bones in her clasp.

"Call me Nan." The woman's eyes twinkled up at Elaine from behind thick glasses that made her resemble a wide-eyed sprite. "I'm not old enough yet to be 'Mrs.' to someone your age."

Elaine grinned. "Well, we can't be more than a decade apart."

The old woman laughed out loud. "I like you. Now tell me why you're taking time out of your day to visit me."

Elaine smiled again. "I like you too. I have some questions about an incident that occurred in town when you were a younger adult. The tire tracks that went into the lake in the winter of 1952. Do you remember anything about that?"

"Oh my. The tire tracks that went into the lake. I haven't thought about that in years," Nan said. "What on earth made you ask about them?"

"Just curious," Elaine said easily. "Someone mentioned them to me, and I looked up what little information I could find in the old newspapers, but it never said if they figured out what happened. Do you remember?"

Nan shook her head slowly. "Nobody ever went missing, as far as I know. People talked about it for a while, and then it was just forgotten."

"Can you tell me anything you remember about it?"

"I lived in Lancaster back then, you see," Nan said, gesturing. "I was married, and we had three kids. They'd have been...well, let's see. The whole reason I was on the road and saw the tracks was because Jimmy was sick, and I was takin' him to a doctor down in Penzance because the doctor in Lancaster was sick himself."

"Wait. You saw the tire tracks?" Elaine was riveted.

"Indeed I did." Nan's gaze was unfocused as she looked back into the past. "I was right behind the school bus, which only went to Loon Point and then turned around. See, the kids that lived closer to Lancaster went to school in Lancaster and the other half from closer to Penzance got picked up by a Penzance bus."

"I see."

"The bus had to stop because the game warden's truck was parked in the road. So while he was moving it, and I was stuck in the road right behind the bus, I got out of the car to see what was happening." Nan fell silent, still absorbed in her memories.

"And what did you see?"

"Not much." Nan smiled wryly, raising one shaky hand. "There was just a set of tire tracks that veered off the road and went straight into the water. A bunch of men were standing around scratching their heads, figuratively speaking. As far as I know, they never figured out a thing, and nobody ever turned up missing."

"Do you know how long they searched for anyone missing, or how far away they looked?"

Nan shook her head. "I think they probably sent word to all the local towns and asked the state fellas to look into it, but nothing ever came of it. I think in the end they decided it might have been a hoax."

"Is that what you think?"

Nan paused, the good humor draining from her faded eyes, magnified by the strong lenses of her glasses. "No. I saw those tracks. It stuck in my mind over the years. There was no sign of another vehicle—you know, like if a truck with a chain pulled a car back from the edge? Just one set of crisp, clear tire tracks going right off the road into the lake." She shuddered. "I fear some poor soul has been at the bottom of the lake for a long time now."

Elaine sat back. "How sad that would be."

"Is that all you want to know?" Nan asked. "I'm a treasure trove of historical information."

Elaine chuckled. "I'm sure you are."

"Priscilla over at the library comes to visit once a month, or if I'm feeling good, Pearl takes me over there. Priscilla asks me all kinds of questions about my growing-up years and about life in Lancaster, and she records everything I say on a movie." The old woman smiled widely, showing a very nice set of dentures. "It's fun."

Elaine wished she had time to sit and listen to Nan for a couple of hours. She imagined she'd get quite an education. "You know," she said as something else occurred to her, something that had been superseded by all the other information clamoring for attention in her brain. "I do have one more question."

"What's that, dear?"

"It's about the Great Depression. Do you recall a family named Wood who lived in the area when you were young?"

"Oh yes," Nan said. "Indeed I do. When I was a teenage girl, I had quite a crush on Frank, the younger one. Those Wood boys both were good-looking fellas. What do you want to know?"

Elaine felt a surge of excitement. "The older brother Elmer—I'd like to know what happened to him."

"Let's see. Elmer stayed in town after he graduated. I believe he got work for one of the sugar men and after your house was turned into a boarding house, Elmer was one of the boarders, along with Arthur Murphy and some others." She shook her head, clearly thinking of the days of the Depression. "Times sure were tough then."

The woman's recollections confirmed the suspicion Elaine and Jan had harbored ever since their foray into research began. Although they temporarily had shunted aside their questions about the ring for the more urgent matter of Gleason's disappearance, Elaine could hardly wait to share this confirmation of Elmer Wood's presence as a boarder in the house with her cousin. She and Jan would not be satisfied until they had figured out how that sapphire ring wound up in the wall of the house and to whom it really belonged.

JAN HAD ONLY two potatoes left. It was ridiculous. She was usually meticulous about her grocery purchases. But with the Valentine madness and the wedding reception, she'd completely forgotten to add them to her shopping list before Sunday afternoon's dinner. Since mashed potatoes were on the menu, she was going to have to make a quick trip to Murphy's General Store.

After grabbing her keys and donning her outerwear, she locked the house and headed out the front door. Murphy's was just a short walk east along the other side of Main Street.

The general store only had three aisles devoted to groceries, along with a few refrigerator and freezer units along one wall. As she grabbed a five-pound bag of potatoes from the shelf and turned to walk back to the front, a small, dignified older woman smiled at her in passing.

"Hello, Jan," she said. "It's nice to see you, dear."

"Hi, Mrs. Vennard," Jan said. The older woman had been her teacher in fourth grade. Jan had liked fourth grade a lot, and much of it was due to this teacher. "How have you been?"

"Just fine, dear. I hear that tearoom you started is gaining quite a good reputation. I'll have to try to get over there one of these days."

"Say the word, and I'll come pick you up myself," Jan said warmly. "Really. I'd be delighted."

"Oh, I'm sure Joe could bring me," Mrs. Vennard said. "We have dinner every Sunday evening. I'll ask him tonight. That's why I'm at the store. I always like to have ice cream for him. I'm cutting it a little close today."

"Oh? He'll be arriving soon?"

"He comes over at four," his mother said, "and helps me with laundry and some of those chores that are getting a little more troublesome, and then we sit down together and have ice cream after the meal. He's such a good boy."

Jan immediately thought of the suspicions she and Elaine shared. "So he's there until well after dark this time of year, I'm guessing?" she asked lightly. "I believe we're supposed to get another inch or more of snow, and it might get slippery later. He should be careful."

"Oh yes. He's with me every Sunday evening until it's time for me to go to bed. We enjoy watching true-crime shows together. And, between you and me"—she smiled conspiratorially— "I try to stay up later when he's around."

"I won't tell a soul," Jan whispered.

So Joe could not have been the smaller person walking Gleason Wattings off the ice—if indeed it *had* even been Gleason—because he was, of all places, at his mother's eating ice cream.

"And I'll tell him about the snow," the retired teacher promised. "But he bought me some rock salt last fall, and he always scatters it over the porch and walk so I won't fall." Her eyes twinkled. "I think he's afraid if I'm incapacitated, I might want to move in with him."

Jan chuckled with her. "I'll help you out to the car after we pay for these things," she said, indicating her potatoes and Mrs. Vennard's ice cream. "I wouldn't want you to be incapacitated."

After helping Mrs. Vennard get into her car safely, Jan walked back to the house. Elaine was just hanging up her coat when she walked in, and Jan held up the sack sheepishly. "Forgot I wanted to make mashed potatoes. But get this." She proceeded to share her unexpected chat with Mrs. Vennard with Elaine.

"So Joe really must have found that driver's license," she said.

"But where? That would be a pretty big coincidence," Elaine said.

"It would," Jan agreed. "But I'm not sure Joe's our man."

"And if he is, he's not in it on his own," Elaine said. "If he's at his mother's from four until after dark, he couldn't have been on the ice at five, when we saw those two people. And while I suppose he could have scattered rock salt on the ice, at least now we know he had a valid reason—other than putting it on the lake, I mean—for his purchase." She stopped to take a breath. "So how did you make out with Nan?"

Elaine shared the information she had gleaned from the visit. Then she said, "And I asked her about the boarding house too. She says Elmer Wood lived there at the same time Arthur Murphy did."

"Arthur Murphy?" Jan looked taken aback. "You mean Des's grandfather and Elmer Wood both lived there at the time the ring was stolen from Wood Woolen Mill?"

THE DOORBELL RANG just as Elaine finished setting the table ninety minutes later. She gave the table one final satisfied glance before she headed for the door. She knew it couldn't be Bob, because he was already in the kitchen with Jan, and her heart beat a little faster.

Nathan stood on the other side. "Hello," she said. "Come on in."

"Something smells good," Nathan said, sniffing the air as Elaine took his coat. "Anyone else joining us?"

She smiled, shaking her head. "Just the four of us."

Conversation at dinner was lively and free-ranging, with everything under discussion from the latest Star Trek movie to the best recipe for fried chicken. The pork loin was so tender it almost melted in the mouth, as did the mashed potatoes. Everyone seemed to be relaxing and enjoying themselves, and both men took second helpings of meat and potatoes.

Nathan fit right in with Bob and Jan, and Elaine felt a little glow of happiness. She was dating...and what's more, she was dating and enjoying herself. Something must have shown on her face, because Nathan winked at her, smiling, and she hastily lowered her gaze to her plate before she made a complete idiot of herself.

As Elaine and Jan rose to clear the dinner dishes, Robert's cell phone rang.

"Oh, I'm sorry," he said ruefully. "I've been waiting for an important call from Baltimore. I meant to silence the ringer, and I forgot." The phone rang again. "Excuse me. I need to take this."

"Go right ahead," Jan said. "Just don't be too long, or you might miss dessert."

"Which means more for me," Nathan said, grinning.

Robert sent him a mock glare as he moved out of the room. But privately, Elaine couldn't help but wonder. What *was* so important that the man had to take a call in the middle of a dinner party on a Sunday evening?

# CHAPTER TWENTY-TWO

Elaine rose early, enjoyed a leisurely devotional period, and finished breakfast well before Rose arrived to give Jan an assist with the day's baking on Monday. As per her usual morning routine, she went about setting up tea trays, preparing pots, filling little pitchers with cream, setting honey pots and maple sweeteners out, and making sure the airtight containers with all the teas most commonly ordered were full. Today's special was a low-caffeine white tea called Snowflakes, particularly appropriate given the forecast calling for yet another couple of inches throughout the day. Elaine couldn't wait to see how the customers liked it.

Jan and Elaine were both in the kitchen when Rose burst in for her shift at nine.

"Guess what?" The young woman's words were practically a shriek.

"What?" the cousins demanded in unison.

"I got another letter from the Maine Institute of Culinary Excellence!" Rose paused for breath, and Jan practically sprinted around the table.

"What did it say?"

"It said," Rose proclaimed, unfolding a letter and flourishing it, "they have received a grant allowing them to offer an additional spot to one student—and I was chosen. I'll be starting at MICE in May."

Jan whooped and dragged Rose into a hug, while Elaine hurried around the counter with an enthusiastic exclamation to offer her own embrace.

"Oh, Rose, that's fabulous. Congratulations!"

"You won't have to leave us!" Jan had tears in her eyes, and Elaine felt close to tears herself. They had grown close to their young employee; this was wonderful news.

Archie, who also had just arrived and had been adding fresh water to the flower arrangements in the parlors that had just been delivered, came into the kitchen. "What am I missing?"

Rose shared her good news again, and they all touched their tea mugs in a toast. "To Rose's success at culinary school," Jan proclaimed before everyone took a sip. "May she learn to make many more unique and outstanding treats!"

"And test them all on us first," Elaine said with a grin.

All of them turned back to their individual tasks. Elaine was about to head into the office when Jan gasped.

"What on earth is going on out there?" She was at the back window, gaping out at the lake. Within seconds, she had whipped open the back door and stepped right out on to the unheated screened porch. Rose, Elaine, and Archie all poured out of the house after her, Archie, at least, having the good sense to pull the kitchen door closed to prevent the warmth in the kitchen from escaping.

All four of them looked down the lake. "The sheriff's car and a bunch of others are parking at Loon Point," Archie said, squinting. "Aren't they?"

"There's some kind of van too," Rose said.

Shivering in the frigid air, the cousins and their employees could see two other law enforcement vehicles as well as a truck with some kind of emblem on it and two cars that she thought were probably those of members of the local fire department.

"An accident?" Jan wondered as they trooped back inside.

"Or something similar," Elaine agreed, picking up the cloth napkins to fold into intricate shapes. "That's a lot of law enforcement."

The tearoom opened less than ten minutes later. Macy was the first one through the door.

"Macy," Elaine said, greeting her in the foyer, "do you know what's going on over at Loon Point?"

"This morning when I was sweeping off the back deck, I saw a car go into the water down at Loon Point. I ran right inside and called 911, and they had a rescue team there within half an hour. But they didn't find any sign of anyone on shore." She paused for breath. "So now they've called in a team of police divers and they're going down to look for a body!"

"Oh no," Jan said softly from behind Elaine. The cousins retreated to the kitchen as soon as Macy had placed her order.

"Let's pray," Elaine said immediately. She and Jan joined hands with Rose and Archie, and the four of them spent a moment praying for anyone who might have been in whatever vehicle had gone into the lake.

Straightening, Jan said, "Maybe you should take hot drinks and pastries down." Although both cousins were aware that visiting the site would be a likely way to get more information, Elaine knew that Jan's primary motivation was to support the rescue—or recovery—personnel over at the site.

She nodded. "Why don't you and Rose get some hot drinks and things together. Archie can handle the front for a short time."

Jan nodded, and she and Rose immediately began preparations, their faces grim.

Meanwhile Elaine went in search of her warm clothing. It was a little too cold out to walk the nearly two miles around West Cottage Road to Loon Point. She'd have to drive and hope there was a safe place to park where the snow wasn't too deep. The next time she bought a vehicle, she vowed she'd be smarter and buy something easier to navigate Maine winters than a Chevy sedan.

Archie carried the heavy basket out to the car for her, and Elaine carefully drove the short distance around West Cottage Road to where all the vehicles were parked at Loon Point. The road was double-wide the whole way from Lancaster to Penzance, and there was a small parking lot near Loon Point now, which hadn't been there during her childhood. Then the lake road had been little more than a bumpy single lane with tall grasses and wildflowers leading down to the lake on one side and forest on the other.

She was relieved to see that there was a space left in the parking lot. Deciding to leave the heavy basket in the car until she knew where it would be most useful, she got out and headed across the road toward the lake, where several people stood. As she did so, she realized the white police van was running. She supposed that made sense, as the divers probably stored extra gear in there and also would need a warm place to go as soon as they came out of the lake.

"Hey, Elaine." Trooper Daniel Benson waved at her. He stood with Jack Weston, Arnie Sheffield, Russell Edmonds, Waterville Detective Floyd Adams, and two men she didn't know. Although they were chatting among themselves, Elaine noted that no one was looking away from the lake very long, so the divers must be down there now.

She waved as she approached the group. "I brought hot drinks and some of Jan's pastries for you if you're interested. Standing around in the cold is no fun."

"That sounds great," Jack said. "Need help bringing the goods down here?"

"Please." Elaine nodded gratefully. "Jan packed the basket so full it weighs a ton."

"We can help lighten the load for your return trip," Russell said, smiling a little despite the general sober air.

"I'll get it," Jack volunteered. "In your car or your trunk?"

"Car. Backseat. Not locked."

"Elaine," Trooper Benson said, "this is Detective Chevalier. He's overseeing the retrieval of the vehicle."

Elaine shook hands with the detective. "It doesn't seem quite right to say 'nice to meet you,' in this situation," she said. "But thank you for coming."

She looked out at the lake. As she and Jan had noted, there was indeed a patch of open water, much larger than she had previously thought from the safe viewing distance of the road. A good-size fast-moving stream, thinly skimmed over with ice in some places, emptied into Chickadee Lake at the point where the open water was.

Just then, everyone's attention was diverted by a shout from Russell. "They're coming up," he said.

Elaine could see a big burst of bubbles disturbing the surface of the water. Simultaneously, excitement and dread gripped her. She could see from the sudden tension in the faces of the men around her that they shared the mixed feelings.

Suddenly, a man's head appeared. He gave a thumbs-up gesture, and Daniel sucked in a breath. "That's a positive. They found something."

Then a second man surfaced, and both quickly swam to shore. Covered completely in black neoprene dry suits, the men looked disturbingly, to Elaine's mind, like monsters emerging from the water.

Tubes ran around their bodies, regulating the air they breathed and the amount of air inside the dry suit. On their backs they carried canisters of oxygen, and weights, dive knives, and other paraphernalia hung from belts at their waists. Hoods, gloved mitts, and long black booties covered their bodies almost completely. The large masks and regulators covered the little exposed skin. As they emerged from the shallows, she could see each man was carrying a large set of black fins.

"Man, that's cold," were the first words out of one man's mouth the minute he removed his regulator.

"We've got hot drinks and food waiting," Jack said.

"Cool."

"Report?" asked the detective.

The second diver answered. "We need the tow truck. We've got a Jeep in about fifty feet of water down there."

A Jeep. Elaine's heart sank. Gleason Wattings drove a Jeep. Her mind worked feverishly. But Gleason had been missing for a week. So why...?

"Then you'd better call a flatbed for the other car," the second man said. "You're not going to be able to tow that one away."

"What?" Daniel's eyes widened. An electric tension gripped the entire group.

"Yep," said the first diver. "You heard him. There's a second car beneath the Jeep. It's kind of in a hole, settled on a slant with the back end lower than the front, and it's really buried in the mud. Been there a long time. But the tow should be able to pull it out."

There was a long moment of silence as everyone considered the implications.

"Fifty feet. I didn't even know the lake was that deep," Russell said.

"Most of it's not." Jack knew the lake like the back of his hand. "But I know the spot they're talking about. I think it's probably eroded from the constant current here."

"Better call the coroner too," added the first man. "We may find remains when it comes up. We didn't see anything when we looked into the Jeep, the one that just went in this morning, but you never know."

Another car pulled up in the little parking area across the road. As River White got out of his car and pulled the hood of his parka firmly up around his head, Elaine rolled her eyes. She should have known the *Penzance Courier* reporter would somehow find out about the diving exploration.

"Hello, local folks," he said with a charming smile. "And hello, Detective Chevalier. Fancy meeting you here. What's going on?"

Everyone looked at River, but no one spoke. Finally, Daniel Benson said, "Come with me and I'll tell you what we're doing." It was clear that he didn't want River interviewing the divers or anyone else.

River smiled pleasantly. "Thank you. I'm always happy to get the story so that the public can be informed about what's going on in the area."

As the trooper led the reporter away, the two divers accepted thermoses and food from Elaine's basket and hurried back to their van to keep warm until they were needed again. Detective Chevalier called his captain and updated him, and authorization was given for the tow and the coroner, who would be called immediately. Even so, Elaine realized it could be quite some time before they arrived, so after distributing all the items she'd brought, she extended an invitation to all the men to wait for the arrivals at the tearoom. Then she returned to her car and headed home.

When she arrived, Jan and Archie were serving and Rose was in the kitchen preparing another tea order. Elaine gave her a brief rundown of the events out on the lake, and then Rose asked, "Can you take that to the couple in the west parlor? I've got to bake some more maple croissants before we run out."

"Sure."

Elaine picked up the order and carried it through the hall and into the west parlor, where Freddie Donnett had her things spread out at her usual table.

Two other tables also were occupied. Jan was with one, three women who were just giving her their order, so Elaine carried the tea order to the remaining couple.

"Hello," she said. "I'm Elaine, one of the co-owners of Tea for Two. I've got the Peach Blossom oolong here..."

"That's mine," said the young woman.

"And yours must be the Darjeeling First Flush," Elaine said to the man, setting his before him. She added a plate of assorted pastries. "And here are your goodies to go with the tea. Is there anything else I can bring you?"

The woman shook her head. "Don't think so. Thanks."

As Elaine moved away from the table, she saw Jan stop by Freddie's table, so she headed over there.

"You're back," Jan said with obvious relief. "Freddie was just asking me what was going on out at the lake."

"Haven't you seen Macy this morning?" Elaine asked.

Freddie shook her head, looking blank. "No, why?"

"The state police brought in divers to retrieve a car that went off the road and into the lake this morning," Elaine explained to Freddie. "And the divers have found another car beneath it."

"What?" Freddie stared at them, clearly aghast. Then she dragged a hand through her hair and started stuffing her things into her backpack with rough haste. "I've got to go," she said, grabbing her coat. Before either of the cousins could ask what was wrong, Freddie was out of the dining room. As she opened the front door and took off, she still was struggling to get one arm in her coat sleeve while fighting with her backpack.

JACK, TROOPER BENSON, and Detective Chevalier came into Tea for Two just before lunch. The tearoom was practically empty, with only one table in the west parlor still occupied.

Elaine hurried to greet them. "Hi. Come on in. Would you like hot drinks and a bite to eat?"

"That would be great," Jack said. "It's freezing out there."

"Coffee?" Elaine asked.

All three men smiled. "If you wouldn't mind," the detective said. "Do you serve coffee here?"

"Normally, no," Elaine said, grinning. "But I'll make an exception in your case. And we might even be able to rustle up some lunch."

She hurried back to the kitchen to find Jan hurriedly putting together a large plate of grilled-cheese sandwiches and a big pot of tomato soup. Archie had left already, and Rose was tidying up from the morning's business.

As soon as the coffee was ready, the cousins carried everything, including generous slices of blueberry pie, into the east parlor, where the three men had settled as close to the fire as they could get.

"Sit down," invited Daniel. "You two deserve an update, since you were the ones who saw Gleason Wattings—or at least we assume at this point it was Gleason—being kidnapped."

"Thank you." Elaine pulled up a chair from a nearby table, as did Jan. Anxiety warred with anticipation inside her. What could the law enforcement officer have to tell them?

"First," Daniel said, "it was Gleason's Jeep we pulled from the lake, but there is no indication he was in it.

Elaine nodded, impatient for him to go on.

"We think someone deliberately ran the Jeep into the lake," Daniel said. "We found footprints near the road that could be from the person who wedged a brick in there to hold down the accelerator."

"So Gleason isn't...deceased?" Jan asked.

"We hope not," the detective said. "We know he was alive when you got that phone call last Monday, and we have no reason to believe that he isn't still alive at this time."

"Then what about the other vehicle?" Jan asked. "Were you able to bring that one up?"

"The mud was reluctant to let it go," Jack said, "but yeah, we got it."

"The tire tracks," Elaine said. "Is it an old car?"

Daniel nodded. "An old Dodge sedan. And yes, we believe it's probably the car whose tracks led into the lake in 1952."

Jan and Elaine looked at each other.

"There were no human remains found inside the vehicle," Chevalier said, "nor did the divers find any, but the windows on one side were broken. Moving the vehicle stirred up a tremendous amount of silt, and the currents in that area limit visibility somewhat. Those same currents also could be responsible for moving things out of the immediate area."

"We did find something else," Jack said.

"What?" Elaine asked. Both cousins sat forward on the edges of their chairs.

"We found an old Marbles matchbox."

"You mean one of those waterproof containers?" Jan asked.

He nodded. "Nickel-plated brass with a rubber gasket. It was wrapped in an oilskin cloth that was partially caught on a spring in the seat, which in turn prevented it from opening or from being swept out of the car as it filled with water."

"Waterproof." Jan clasped her hands together. "Was it intact? Did you find something inside?"

"We did." Detective Chevalier nodded. "We've sent it to the crime lab since they have the necessary materials to handle it properly without damaging it. I just heard a preliminary report. They found a note and two coins inside."

The sound of a gasp registered dimly with Elaine in the wake of Daniel's confirmation.

"No." The voice was loud and hoarse, and all five of them startled. They'd been so engrossed that no one had seen the woman in the doorway.

Freddie Donnett advanced into the room. "Those are *my* coins," she said.

# CHAPTER TWENTY-THREE

D o you want to explain that comment?" Detective Chevalier asked. Although it was a question, it was clear that he didn't expect her to decline.

"I found a journal that mentioned Preston Watkins finding them." Freddie took a deep breath. "I tracked him to Lancaster, where his brother and his wife lived. I don't know exactly what happened to her, but I believe he was going to leave town and never made it to his destination."

"So why didn't the police figure this out way back when?" Elaine asked.

Benson shrugged. "If he wasn't reported missing on the other end, there wouldn't have been a search initiated. Remember, this was a long time ago before technology made it much easier to find people."

Freddie took over again. "When I learned about the tire tracks, the time frame made it possible that he'd driven into the lake. And if he did, some of the coins might have gone in with him. Those are *my* coins," she repeated angrily.

"Please state your full name and address," Trooper Benson said.

Freddie gaped at him for a moment, but then she gathered herself and complied.

"How did you figure out where the car was?" the trooper asked after Freddie had given him her information.

"I'm a researcher." Freddie's nostrils flared. "Preston's brother must have gotten rid of the old box I bought without realizing it had a journal and one coin inside. When I got here and started researching, I found that Preston Watkins supposedly left town right around the same time the tire tracks were found leading into the lake."

But that didn't mean the things in the lake were hers, Elaine thought. Freddie's reasoning might make sense to her, but it certainly wasn't going to hold water, so to speak, with anyone else.

"So you were scuba diving in the lake trying to find the car," Jack said. "Even knowing how dangerous it was."

"I thought it would be easier than it was," she said sullenly. "And I thought some of the Watkins family would still be living. Who knew they would die out?"

"Freddie," Elaine asked gently, "do you have any reason to believe one of the coins is a real Brasher doubloon?"

The professor blinked. "Not specifically," she said, "but it might be. Why else would Preston Watkins have kept them?"

"They look like gold," Jan said, "so maybe he thought they were. But I imagine the chances are good that they are simply brass-covered lead like yours."

Freddie dismissed that with a blink, turning her head away. "So," she said to the law enforcement officers, "when can I get my hands on the coins when you're done with them?"

Both the game warden and the trooper looked a little stunned at the brazen request. Both recovered quickly. "No."

"Miss," Daniel continued, "they're in the custody of the state of Maine now, and will be disposed of accordingly if no living family members can be located."

SHORTLY AFTER THAT, the men got up, thanking Elaine and Jan for the food before retrieving hats, coats, and gloves. Daniel motioned the cousins aside for a moment as he shrugged on his jacket. "I wanted to let you know I talked to Joe Vennard about that license."

"Gleason's driver's license?" Jan asked.

Daniel nodded. "He says he found it in the Wattings Rentals parking lot early Monday morning. He said he was going to give it to the police, but he was nervous. He said he was afraid since there's bad blood between Bud and him we'd suspect him. Which I did."

"Why was he in the parking lot?" Elaine asked.

"He said he wanted to count how many ice shanties Bud had rented out. He's still pretty unhappy about losing the business."

"But you don't think he kidnapped Gleason?"

Daniel shrugged. "I haven't taken him off my suspect list."

Jan and Elaine followed the men on to the front porch and simply stood there in the chilly air as the trooper, Jack, and Detective Chevalier all drove away.

Recovering themselves, they hurried back inside. Freddie had remained, now slumped in a chair and morosely staring at the tabletop. "Well," she said as Jan and Elaine approached, "I guess that's the end of that. No early retirement for me."

"I'm sorry," Elaine said. "Were you really thinking that might be a possibility?"

The professor sighed. "I had talked myself into believing it was, but in hindsight, it wasn't much of a likelihood." She looked up at Elaine. "Was it?"

Elaine shook her head gently. "I don't think so. It's extremely unlikely that the coins would have turned out to be real Brasher doubloons rather than copies, given the few that have ever been identified."

"Yeah. I know."

"Will you go back to Rhode Island at the end of the semester?"

Freddie's mouth twisted. "I don't know. I didn't tell you this, but they think I had something to do with the theft of two old coins from one of their exhibits. I'm on administrative leave now."

Elaine didn't know what to say. *Did you?* sounded rather crass. And she really didn't want to tell Freddie she already knew because she'd investigated her.

"I didn't steal those coins," Freddie said, "but I don't know if I want to go back there, given the way they have treated me."

"Maybe they'll have figured out who really did it by the end of the semester," Elaine said, "and your name will be cleared."

"Maybe." Freddie didn't sound convinced. "Even if it is, I think I might get out of education. I've enjoyed this research on the Brasher doubloons." Her mouth twisted a bit at one corner, but she went on. "I'm thinking of writing a book." She tried to smile. "Who knows? Maybe I'll spend another winter here working on some project."

"You're always welcome at Tea for Two," Elaine said.

"So all that time we found Freddie's actions suspicious, she was only searching for more doubloons," Elaine said when the tearoom was finally closed for the day and they were replacing the soiled table linens with crisp, freshly ironed ones.

Jan gave a dry chuckle. "That sums it up."

"If Freddie didn't kidnap Gleason, and Joe Vennard didn't kidnap Gleason," Elaine said, "what on earth actually happened to him?"

Jan was quiet for a moment, then finally spoke. "There was one other person—people, really—who bought rock salt from Tag King," Jan said slowly.

"The Bellamy brothers," Elaine said.

Jan looked away, then did a double take. "Hey, look."

Elaine looked in the direction her cousin pointed out the front window. "Well, what do you know?"

The young man was standing uncertainly on the sidewalk in front of Murphy's, looking in the window. After a moment, he appeared to square his shoulders, draw in a deep breath and exhale it, then enter the store.

Jan nudged Elaine in the ribs. "Let's go."

Elaine looked startled. Then she nodded. "I suppose we'd better see what he's up to." Quickly they abandoned the tablecloths, grabbed coats and handbags from the hall closet, and locked the house behind them.

They crossed the street and entered the general store. Marvin was disappearing down an aisle near the far end that displayed assorted clothing, boots, shoes, gloves, and outerwear.

Jan and Elaine hesitated, not wanting to walk right up to their quarry.

The cousins moved down one of the grocery aisles. "I need bran flakes," Jan said. "Keep your eyes open. If he goes up to the checkout counter, we'll go up right behind him."

"And then what?" Elaine asked. "We can't just ask him flat out if he kidnapped Gleason."

"We'll go with the flow," Jan said. "If we can't think of anything to say, then we won't. But if he and Mickey really have kidnapped Gleason for some crazy reason, you can bet Marvin will be back in town on his own again tomorrow or the next day."

"He just walked up to the counter!" Elaine hissed. "Come on."

Quickly, Jan grabbed the box of bran, and they headed for the front of the store. Marvin Bellamy was indeed at the checkout counter. He had a large box with a pair of sneakers in it, and he was fumbling to open the box.

"I just need one," he was saying to Jo Murphy as the cousins approached.

"Marv," Jo said patiently, "you can't buy one shoe. You have to buy them both."

"But I only need one," he said doggedly.

"Then buy them both and just use one," Jo said. She pinched the bridge of her nose and looked skyward, giving Jan the impression that she had been forced into several of these types of conversations with Marvin recently.

"Okay," Marvin said. "How much?"

Jo took the box and rung up the sale. "Nineteen dollars and sixty-seven cents."

Marvin dug into his coat pocket. Carefully, he pulled out a small wad of bills, and a shower of coins came along with them, merrily dinging everywhere as they hit the floors, the shelving, and the counter.

"Hold on," Jo said. "Let's do the bills first." Clearly she had dealt with Marvin before. The young man opened his stack of bills and spread them out in his hands. "Nineteen," he said.

"I still need sixty-seven cents."

In reply, the young man simply held out a handful of change so that Jo could pick out two quarters, a dime, a nickel, and two pennies, totting up the amount as she went.

Marvin dumped the rest back into his pocket and methodically began picking up the extra coins he had scattered.

Elaine, who had knelt and picked up the ones on the floor, said, "You dropped these," and he turned with an air of surprise.

"Thank you, ma'am."

"You're welcome," she said, dropping the money into his palm.

Jo and the cousins watched as Marvin picked up his shoe box and walked out of the store, stopping to say, "Thank you, Miss Jo."

"You're welcome, Marv." She waved as he headed out into the street. Then she picked up Jan's box of bran. "Can you even imagine him trying to run a business?" she asked. It was clearly a rhetorical question.

But as Jan paid for the bran and replaced her wallet in the bag slung over her shoulder, Elaine snapped her fingers. "That's it," she said.

"That's what?" Jan asked.

Elaine gripped Jan's elbow and propelled her out of the store before she spoke again. As they headed back to the house, she said, "The Bellamys kidnapped Gleason. And I can tell you why."

# CHAPTER TWENTY-FOUR

O kay," Jan said as they walked. "Why?"

"Remember what Rose said last week? The brothers tried to start a rental business. I bet you they planned to try to force Bud to get out of business by kidnapping his son."

"That's a lousy plan," Jan said critically. "Didn't they realize they'd surely get caught?" Then she shook her head. "Never mind. I forgot who I was talking about. You might be right."

A look of deep worry crossed Elaine's face. "But there's been no ransom demand. I would have expected them to approach Bud and tell him he'd get Gleason back if he'd get out of business, or sell to them, or something like that."

Jan sucked in a breath as an unpleasant thought occurred to her. "Oh, I hope they didn't accidentally harm Gleason. But I can imagine something awful happening by accident, can't you?"

Elaine nodded. "We have to find him fast. Where on earth might they have put him?"

Jan stopped dead. "That's an easy one."

"What?" Elaine looked at her as if she'd lost her mind.

"We just need to follow Marvin," Jan said. "Those shoes he bought were a size thirteen. Marvin's a small guy. I'd estimate that his feet couldn't possibly be bigger than a size ten. He was buying a shoe for Gleason."

"You're right! I totally missed that," Elaine said. "We've got to follow him. That's why his brother hasn't been with him all week—he's holding Gleason hostage."

The cousins hurried across the street, keeping an eye on Marvin Bellamy, who appeared to be walking toward a beat-up old car parked a little farther down Main Street.

Jan stayed in the shadow of some tall shrubs on the sidewalk, keeping Marvin in sight, while Elaine dashed into the garage and pulled her car out.

"Perfect timing," Jan said as Elaine came to a stop beside her. "Marvin just pulled away. He's headed out East Cottage Road. I bet he's going home."

"Do you know where they live?"

"Same place they've lived since before their grandpa and their folks passed away. It's a little house about a mile back from the lake on Granite Road."

Granite Road turned off East Cottage Road about halfway between Penzance and Lancaster, winding its way east. "So we'd better drop back to be sure he doesn't see us following him."

Jan nodded. "I don't know that it would occur to him, frankly. But since we're pretty sure he's heading home, we can pull off at Green Glade and wait for a minute."

After a tense sixty seconds, Elaine cautiously pulled back on to the road and drove slowly along the lake. She turned left on Granite Road and continued at her slow pace.

"It's right up here," Jan said. "Keep driving, and I'll check it out."

Elaine did so. The house was on the right side of the road, the head of a drunken mailbox sticking out of a drift at the edge of the gravel drive. The building itself was a small frame two-story Cape Cod style with a saggy front porch stretched across the front and dormers above. A separate garage stood just to the right of it at the end of a short driveway in which two cars were parked. The one closest to the road was the battered old Ford Marvin had driven away from town.

"Look," Jan hissed as they went on past. "Tire tracks leading from behind the house. Recent tire tracks, meaning they had to have been made today, since they're not covered by snow."

"Maybe they just moved one of the cars," Elaine said, keeping a slow but steady pace as they continued down the road.

"No way would a car have driven through snow that deep," Jan said. "The two cars in the driveway are a Ford Escort and a little Honda. Those tire tracks had to have been made by something with four-wheel-drive capability."

"Like a Jeep Wrangler, which is what Gleason drove and what was pulled out of the lake this morning."

"Exactly."

"We need to call Daniel Benson," Elaine said. "Where do you want me to go?"

"There's a picnic ground about another mile farther," Jan said. "Pull in there and let's see what Daniel says." She immediately yanked her phone out of her handbag and made the call. She put the trooper on speaker so Elaine could hear what he said.

"Daniel," Jan said after she identified herself, "the Bellamy brothers bought shoes for a large man this afternoon. Remember how they wanted to start a fishing rental business? Elaine and I think they've cooked up some plot to kidnap Gleason and force Bud out of business."

"That would never work," Daniel said.

"You and I know that," Jan said, "but the Bellamys might not have thought it through. We just followed Marvin out of town to their home on Granite Road and there are fresh tire tracks from an off-road vehicle coming from behind the house. We think they may have driven the Jeep over to Loon Point and ditched it this morning."

"And you think they are keeping Gleason at their house?"

"Mickey hasn't been seen in public all week long," Jan told him, "and you know they're nearly always together. Also, they bought rock salt from Tag King not too long ago."

"All right." Daniel suddenly sounded extremely alert and extremely businesslike. "I can be there in under ten minutes. I want you two to stay away from the house. Do not, under any circumstances, attempt to confront the Bellamys yourselves. I don't think they have a history of violence, but you need to leave this to law enforcement professionals. Am I making myself clear?"

"As crystal," Jan said. "We just turned around and are going to drive back past the house to the intersection where Granite meets East Cottage. We'll wait there."

It took several minutes for the house to come into sight again, this time on their left. Elaine was about to drive on by when out of the corner of her eye she saw the side door of the house closest to the driveway open.

Mickey and Marvin Bellamy appeared, with Gleason Wattings walking slowly between them.

"Pull over!" Jan exclaimed.

Instinctively, Elaine swerved so that her car was pulled sideways across the entrance to the Bellamys' driveway. "Pretend we have car trouble," she said breathlessly.

Jan was already bouncing out of the car. "Open the hood," she said in a low tone. "Quick."

Elaine fumbled for the hood release, hearing the muffled "pop" a moment later. As she opened her door, she unobtrusively dropped her keys directly into the snow drift by her right rear tire. Should something go wrong, she didn't want the brothers to be able to take her car and make a getaway.

"Hi, Mickey. Hi, Marvin." Jan waved at the three men as she and Elaine scurried to the front of the car and peered inside it.

Mickey Bellamy stumped down the driveway toward them. "What's the trouble here?"

"The engine was knocking," Elaine said, "and it quit on me just as we hit your driveway. Lucky for me I was able to pull off the road."

"Want me to take a look at it?"

"That would be great," Elaine said. She politely stepped aside, and Mickey bent over beneath the hood, muttering to himself. After all, she thought, it wasn't as if he was going to be able to do anything terrible to it—she'd just had it serviced in January, and it was in tiptop condition.

Jan looked up the driveway and appeared to do a double take. "Hello, Gleason." She waved again at the two men he'd left standing near the cars. "Hey, you really ought to give your mother a call. She's been looking all over the place for you."

Mickey, beneath the hood of the car, reared up so quickly he smashed his head on the underside of the hood. There was an audible "clunk" that made both Elaine and Jan wince.

With an exclamation of pain, Mickey folded to his knees in the driveway, hands held protectively over his head. After another second, he slumped sideways.

Elaine bent over him, truly alarmed. "He knocked himself out!"

Marvin came down the driveway, leaving Gleason standing beside the car. As he bent over his brother, Elaine rushed up the driveway to Gleason. "Do they have weapons?" she asked in an urgent whisper.

Gleason shook his head. "Just a kitchen knife, but Marvin dropped it." He indicated a sizable butcher knife lying in the snow.

Elaine immediately kicked it beneath a bush at the side of the house.

"I'm tied though," Gleason said.

Elaine stopped and looked at him. His hands were bound behind his back with what looked like torn rags from T-shirts, and his ankles were hobbled as well. He was only wearing one shoe. "The police are on their way," she assured him.

"Thank you," he said in fervent gratitude, turning to rest against the fender of the car. "I'm starving," he said. "They haven't fed me much all week."

"You almost managed a phone call," Elaine said.

Gleason grimaced. "I almost got away altogether on Monday. Almost. That was when they stopped feeding me. Mickey was mighty annoyed about that."

"Where's your shoe?" Elaine asked him.

"Out here somewhere. I lost it when Mickey tackled me and dragged me back into the house on Monday." He shook his head. "Man, he hit me pretty hard out there on the ice. My head's still not right."

"I'm sure you'll get medical attention," Elaine assured him. "Just hang in there a little longer."

Sirens screamed in the distance, and Marvin's head jerked up as Elaine walked back down the driveway to stand shoulder to shoulder with Jan.

"It's time to let Gleason go," Jan said to the young man, not urgently. "The police will be here very soon."

Marvin sighed. "It was getting too hard to keep him anyway." He looked anxiously at his brother, prostrate in the snow. "Is he gonna be okay?"

"He might need to see a doctor, but I imagine he'll be fine," Jan said. "Were you two behind the break-ins of Mr. Wattings's ice shanties before you decided to kidnap Gleason?"

Marvin's face turned a dull red. "Yes, ma'am. Mr. Vennard, he said he'd pay us fifty bucks for each one we done. He even said we could keep and sell whatever fishin' rods we found. But we ain't sold any yet," he said sadly.

"How did you come to kidnap Gleason?"

"That was sort of an accident, see." Marvin's face was earnest. "Mickey said as how we should bust up another ice shanty last Sunday night, so we started to, but Gleason came along and found us. So Mickey conked him on the head and took him back to his car. I went and got in Gleason's Jeep after a bit and drove it back here."

"That's why we only saw one of them coming off the ice with Gleason," Jan said quietly to Elaine.

The sirens were growing louder, and a moment later, the flash of emergency lights could be seen coming toward the house. Trooper Benson was out of his cruiser the moment he pulled to a stop, and two more state cops were right behind him. As Daniel stopped to speak with Jan and Elaine, the others went up the driveway to Gleason.

"There's a knife under the bushes," Elaine called after them.

Daniel sighed. "I told you to stay away from them," he said to the two women. "You listen like my kids do."

"We had to do something." Elaine defended Jan and herself. "They were leaving."

"Why were you leaving?" Daniel asked Marvin.

"Mickey said we might have to hide him better." Marvin shrugged.

"What'd you do to this one?" Daniel asked the cousins, indicating the unconscious Mickey lying beside the front tire of Elaine's car.

"He knocked himself out," Jan said.

Daniel looked at Mickey more closely. "That takes talent."

"Also, Gleason may have a head injury," Elaine said, "so they'd better both get medical attention."

"I have the EMTs on the way," Daniel said, "because I wasn't sure what we might find. I'm going to send you home now. I'll be by to take statements in the morning."

# CHAPTER TWENTY-FIVE

Tuesday morning at Tea for Two was much like any other. Elaine, after a morning devotional in which she gave thanks for Gleason's safe return to his family and offered prayers for the Bellamy brothers, unlocked the door and stepped back to admit Macy and Rue, the first two customers of the day.

"So we want all the details," Macy said immediately. "Heard you were in on the bust."

"The bust?" Elaine had to laugh. "You mean the arrest of the Bellamy brothers?"

"And Joe Vennard," Rue added. "I can't believe he took advantage of those two poor souls. I bet they'd never have thought of kidnapping Gleason if he hadn't hired them to break into Bud's huts in the first place."

Elaine had to concede that might be an accurate assessment.

"But they came up with the plan to kidnap Gleason all on their own," Macy said. "Worst decision they ever made."

"I have a feeling Mickey did most of the thinking," Elaine said. "Marvin doesn't really seem capable of planning something like that. I felt sorry for him, if you want to know the truth."

The door opened again.

"Elaine!" A massive flower arrangement, with denim-clad legs sticking out beneath it, walked through the door. "How can I ever thank you and Jan enough? Where is she?"

"I'm here." Jan had come through the kitchen door into the hallway.

The flowers lowered enough that Elaine could see Shelba Wattings's eyes peeking over the top. They were sparkling with tears, but she was smiling as she handed off the flowers to Archie so that she could hug each cousin.

"How's Gleason?" Jan asked her. "Was he admitted to the hospital?"

Shelba shook her head. "He was checked out and released. He has a concussion, but they expect a full recovery, and soon."

"I heard he wanted to call his girlfriend first thing," Macy said. Elaine rather wished Macy hadn't heard quite so much. Had the woman slept at all last night or had she been on the phone spreading gossip until dawn?

Shelba refused to rise to the bait. She merely nodded. "He did, and we invited her to come and stay with us while Gleason recovers. She's helping me make all his favorite foods. Those two crooks barely fed him."

"We're so thankful to hear that he's going to be fine," Jan said, an arm around Shelba's shoulders. "And I think it's lovely that you've asked Marlene to be a part of his recovery."

The door opened yet again, decanting Freddie Donnett into the hallway. "Hello. I heard Gleason was found."

"He was, and he's going to be fine."

Freddie spotted Shelba, and her face reddened, probably from the memory of the way she'd failed to recall Gleason being in her class the week before. She said diffidently, "I thought when Gleason's up to visitors, maybe I'd go see him and offer to catch him up on what he missed in class last week."

Shelba's face lit up. "That would be nice. He's a little upset about missing his classes." She smiled at Freddie. "He's feeling pretty good. If you'd like to have tea with me, I'll take you over to the house and you can talk to him today."

"That would be nice," Freddie said. "Thank you."

"Come on in and take a table," Jan said. "We have an interesting special tea from China today. It's called pu-erh tea, and it's aged to undergo a secondary fermentation process after production. Today we're featuring an organic caramel toffee pu-erh tea, and I've made some good old-fashioned monkey bread with caramel sauce to complement it. Would you like to try that?"

"Sounds fabulous." Freddie started toward the west parlor with Shelba.

As they drifted into the east parlor, Elaine and Jan stood for a moment in the foyer, admiring the lovely flower arrangement that Archie had placed on a side table.

"That was sweet of Freddie to offer to tutor him," Elaine said.

"And gracious of Shelba," Jan agreed. "I'm so happy that Gleason's home and going to be okay."

"I know." Elaine looked up at the house around them. "And I'm glad for another reason as well."

"What's that?" Jan looked curiously at her cousin.

Elaine sighed. "I can't stop thinking about the fact that Elmer Wood was a boarder right here in this home. We need to keep digging. The crazy thing is, Des Murphy's grandfather, Arthur, lived here then too." She shook her head. "Could that mean there's a connection?"

"I see where you're going with this." Jan asked. "I feel as if we're on the verge of figuring this whole thing out."

"We must be," Elaine said. "We just need to connect a few more dots."

Jan smiled. "Then we'd better get back to it."

The front door opened, and a young couple Elaine had never seen before entered.

"Good morning," she said. "Welcome to Tea for Two."

# ABOUT THE AUTHOR

Anne Marie Rodgers is the author of nearly sixty novels, including more than a dozen for Guideposts. A best-selling, award-winning writer, she is also deeply committed to animal rescue and rehabilitation, specializing in neonatal animal care for many species as well as giant-breed dog rescue. A recent transplant to Savannah, Georgia, "Grandmarie" enjoys lots of time spent with her two young granddaughters.

# ROSE'S GERMAN BLUE CHEESE & WALNUT BAKED APPLES WITH PEPPERED HONEY

1 tablespoon rum flavoring (to taste) plus apple juice or cider to make ¼ cup

¼ cup raisins

1 cup honey

1 teaspoon thyme

1 teaspoon ground black pepper

1 teaspoon lemon zest or zest from half a lemon

½ cup chopped walnuts

¼ cup unsalted butter

½ cup blue cheese

1 teaspoon chives sliced

1 teaspoon parsley sliced

4 large baking apples

Preheat the oven to 325 degrees.

Heat the apple juice or cider with the rum flavoring until warm. Remove from heat and add the raisins, and soak until soft and plump.

In a small pot over medium-high heat, combine the honey, thyme, pepper, and lemon zest. Simmer for three minutes. Set aside.

In a small pan over medium heat, toast the walnut pieces until heated through. Stir in the butter, rum-flavored liquid, and raisins. Remove from heat, then add the blue cheese and herbs.

Slice off the very bottom of each apple to make a flat surface. Remove the top third of each apple and hollow out the core with a spoon. Stuff the apples with the walnut mixture, place on a baking tray lined with parchment paper or foil, and bake for at least twenty minutes or until the apple flesh is tender when poked with a clean knife.

Place on a warmed plate and drizzle with the peppered honey mixture. Near the end of your baking time, you can add the apple tops with stems to make decorative lids for the apples.

READ ON FOR AN EXCITING SNEAK PEEK
INTO THE NEXT VOLUME OF TEAROOM MYSTERIES!

# *Tea Is for Treasure*

Jan had a secret.

She didn't like keeping secrets, especially from her cousin Elaine, who was now busy preparing the tearoom for opening. It was a cozy Tuesday morning and the kitchen smelled of cinnamon and cloves. She'd gotten up early to start the baking, and the cooling racks on the kitchen island were full of mini maple croissants, a favorite among their guests at Tea for Two.

Rose, one of the tearoom's two employees, had arrived a short time ago and tied on her apron before getting started on the tearoom's cookie of the day. The young server and baker stood at the kitchen counter, carefully measuring sugar for the lemon meringue cookies. She wore a butter-yellow apron over her tan slacks and white polo shirt, her wheat-blonde hair pulled back into a neat ponytail.

Rose had never made meringue cookies before, but she'd wanted to give them a try. And Jan had encouraged her, pleased at how Rose's confidence in the kitchen was growing each day.

Then she turned her gaze back to the window over the sink, reaching out to part the lace curtain. Gray clouds hung heavy in the March sky, but a hint of sunlight shimmered behind them.

It had rained in Lancaster for the last three days, a soft spring rain that had slowly soaked into the ground, leaving it wet and spongy. She and Elaine had laid out extra throw rugs in the entrance hall between the double parlors that comprised the tearoom so their guests could wipe off any moisture or mud they might carry in on their shoes.

Raindrops still dripped from the porch roof beyond the kitchen window, but Jan sensed the sunlight struggling to break through the clouds foretold a clear day ahead. The daily high temperatures in March could range from the low thirties to the mid sixties, and today was a chilly one. So she'd dressed in a heavy-knit blue turtleneck sweater and gray slacks, along with a long silver pendant necklace.

Jan leaned closer to the window but didn't see any sign of the mail truck on the road. She'd hoped the postman would arrive before the tearoom opened at ten o'clock so she could intercept him. She didn't want Elaine or Rose to see the letter she was expecting.

"Oh no!" Rose exclaimed.

Jan turned around to see the younger woman standing in front of the oven and pulling out a cookie sheet. "What's wrong?"

"My meringues look more like little pancakes," Rose said with a groan. She set the cookie sheet on top of the stove, then removed her oven mitts. Frustration flared in her blue eyes. "I don't understand—I followed the recipe to the letter!"

Jan gave her an empathetic smile as she walked over beside Rose and took a look at the flattened cookies. "Meringues can be a little temperamental. Even the weather can affect them."

Rose glanced at the window. "But it stopped raining last night. Is there still too much moisture in the air?"

"No, I don't think that's the problem," Jan told her, placing her hands on her hips. "Did you let the eggs come to room temperature before you beat the egg whites?"

"Yes," Rose said with a nod.

"And you made sure the mixing bowl was spotless?"

"I wiped it clean." Rose turned and leaned against the counter. "And I used a glass bowl, because you taught me that fat particles can get into the microscopic cracks in plastic bowls and diminish the volume of the egg whites."

"You've got a great memory." Jan chuckled. "That was my next question."

Rose was an avid learner with natural talent. She'd recently started attending culinary school at night to hone that talent, giving her a busy schedule.

"The most common reason for egg whites to deflate," Jan explained, "is overbeating them or beating them too quickly."

"Oh," Rose said slowly. "That might be what happened. I set the mixer at the highest speed because I wanted to get these into the oven quickly so I could get started on the next batch."

Jan picked up the turner spatula and slid it between a meringue cookie and the parchment paper, lifting it off the pan. Then she took a bite, savoring the sweet, lemon flavor of the delicate cookie. "It's delicious," she proclaimed. "So just take it a little slower beating the egg whites on the next batch, and I'm sure they'll turn out just fine."

"Will do," Rose said, looking ready to take on the challenge. "Should I throw these out?" she asked, pointing to the flattened cookies.

"Absolutely not," Jan said a smile. "They might not look good enough to serve to our customers, but there's no reason we can't enjoy them in the kitchen. Half the fun of baking is eating the flops."

Rose laughed as she headed off to make the next batch while Jan scooped the deflated meringue cookies onto a plate.

A few moments later, Elaine walked into the kitchen. "We're all set in the tearoom. How's it going in here?"

"Great," Jan told her, putting a kettle on to boil. "Rose is working on the lemon meringue cookies and I just finished mixing up another batch of tea leaves for our Hello Spring tea."

She and Elaine loved to mix their own special tea blends, as well as serve the classics. Now that March had arrived, they'd decided to celebrate spring with a lighter tea combining the flavors of orange peels, lavender, and rose hips.

"At least the rain's finally stopped, so I'm expecting a bigger crowd than we've had the last few days." Elaine smiled. "As soon as Archie arrives, we'll have all hands on deck."

Jan nodded, taking another peek out the kitchen window. Archie Bentham worked part time at the tearoom. An older British man with the air of a distinguished professor, Archie had earned multiple degrees and traveled the world before retiring and settling down in Lancaster with his wife.

Jan was about to drop the curtain when she saw a flash of light from a windshield on the road. A few seconds later, the mail truck came into view.

"Mail's here!" Jan called out, her voice sounding shrill to her ears. "I'll get it." She hurried to the back door even though Elaine was closer. But when she glanced back at her cousin and Rose, she was relieved to see both women placing pastries on the silver serving trays and paying no attention to her as they chatted happily together.

"Calm down," Jan whispered to herself, slipping a windbreaker off the hook by the door before stepping onto the screened porch. She closed the door behind her, then saw Earl Grey snuggled cozily on a plump yellow cat cushion.

Now that the weather was warming up, he spent less time in the little home they'd made for him out of a Styrofoam cooler covered with Mylar and filled with straw to keep him warm during the winter.

He opened one sleepy green eye as she walked past him, then closed it again, undisturbed by the imminent arrival of the postman.

Jan stepped outside and started walking toward the front of the house as the mail truck pulled up in the driveway. Then she waved to the postman, Orin Bond. "Hello there! You're here early today."

Orin smiled as he grabbed his mailbag and stepped out of the truck. "I got an early start." A stocky man in his fifties, Orin had been born and raised in Lancaster. After enlisting in the army right out of high school, he'd served twenty years before returning to Lancaster and taking a job at the post office. During the tourist season, he shared mail duties with Russell Edmonds, who delivered mail by boat to the cottages along Chickadee Lake.

"At least the sun's peeking out today," Jan said, happy to see the clouds dispersing as the sunbeams skated across the icy lake. "Maybe it will dry up some of this mud."

Orin chuckled as he walked toward her. "I sure hope so. I got stuck yesterday. Gavin Richardson had to pull my mail truck out with his tractor."

"Oh dear, that's not fun."

His blue eyes twinkled. "Well, it wasn't all bad. He towed me to his dairy farm so I could hose the mud off the tires, then Annie sent me on my way with a piece of peach pie right out of the oven."

Jan laughed. "Sounds like you should get stuck more often." Then she leaned closer as he dug into his mailbag. "I'm expecting a letter."

"Well, let's see what we have here." Orin gazed down at the stack in his hand, separating out a few pieces of mail and dropping them back into his bag. Then he handed the stack to Jan.

He stood there while she thumbed through it, his gaze curious.

"Looks like mostly bills," she said, trying not to sound disappointed. It wasn't there. Her secret would have to wait another day.

She took a deep breath and smiled. "Thanks, Orin. I don't have any pie for you, but we do have some lemon meringue cookies that flopped." Her smiled widened. "But they taste delicious."

"I better pass." Orin stepped toward his truck. "I'm not really supposed to eat on my route, with the exception of peach pie," he said with a grin. "But I might get in trouble if they find cookie crumbs in my mailbag." Then he slapped one hand to his forehead. "I almost forgot. I have a package for you."

"You do?" she said, wondering if it was the tea leaves they'd ordered yesterday.

Orin walked to his truck and pulled out a cardboard box about the size of a bread box. "Sorry to say, it must have fallen in a mud puddle sometime during transport. The label got a bit dirty." He handed the box to her. "I made an incident report, so you can file a report if there are any damages."

She stared down at the label, noticing the return address was unreadable.

Then her gaze moved to the postmark. "Looks like it came from New York City."

"Sorry again about the water damage," Orin said.

"No problem. It doesn't look as though the package itself got wet, just the label." She tucked the package under her arm.

Orin gave her a wave then climbed into his truck. "Have a nice day, Jan."

"You too!" she called back, watching as he pulled out of the driveway. Then she saw three cars heading toward the tearoom, recognizing one of them as belonging to Macy Atherton, a regular customer at the tearoom. She hurried back to the house, giving Earl Grey a quick pat as she walked through the screened-in porch and into the kitchen.

"There you are," Rose exclaimed, standing by the stove with an oven mitt on her hand. "The cookies are almost ready and Elaine wants us to make an extra pot of the Hello Spring tea. Macy called ahead and said she's got quite a crowd coming today."

Jan nodded, turning into Elaine's office and depositing the mail and the package on the desk before slipping off her windbreaker and heading back into the kitchen. As she tied on her apron, she made a mental note to tell Elaine they'd received a package addressed to the tearoom. Then she pushed up her sleeves, washed her hands, and got to work.

Two hours later, Jan carried a silver tray into the tearoom. She'd been on the run since the tearoom opened and more people kept walking through the door. Archie and Elaine were serving customers in the west parlor while she and Rose tended to customers in the east parlor.

Macy Atherton frowned as Jan approached her table. "I was beginning to think you'd forgotten about me."

Jan smiled as she set the tray on the table. "I could never forget you, Macy."

One of their most frequent and loyal customers, Macy's communication style was more vinegar than honey. And today, for some reason unbeknownst to Jan, Macy was in a sour mood.

"And I think you're going to enjoy these lemon meringue cookies," Jan told her.

Macy looked doubtful as she picked up one of the meringue cookies and took a bite. She chewed thoughtfully for a moment, her dour expression slowly clearing. "Why, yes, they do have a nice, sharp flavor." Then she looked at the remaining cookie in her hand. "Perhaps next time you could work a little more on presentation. They should all have a nice dome shape. As you can see, this one has a tiny dimple in the top."

"I'll pass that along," Jan said, keeping a cheery note in her voice. The sound of the front door opening behind her made Jan glance over her shoulder. Two women she didn't recognize walked inside. She turned back to Macy. "My, we're certainly busy today. Not that I'm complaining."

"You have me to thank for that," Macy said, sitting proudly up in her chair. "I have several new guests staying at the cottages and recommended Tea for Two to them. So you and Elaine need to be at the top of your game."

Macy ran the Green Glade cottages on the shores of Chickadee Lake, along with her son, Shane, and daughter-in-law, Zale.

"It's not even tourist season yet," Jan said, glancing around the room. She'd noticed several new customers sitting among the regulars and had just assumed there was a gathering of some kind happening in town. "Are they here for some kind of reunion?"

"No," Macy said, leaning closer and lowering her voice. "They're actually part of a club and call themselves Finders

Keepers. Apparently they like to travel together around the country looking for treasures—rare antiques and collectibles, I suppose."

Jan smiled. "That sounds like fun. And there are plenty of places around here to find nice antiques and vintage pieces. They'll love Oldies But Goodies, Gift Me, A Little Something, and the Sugar Plum . . ."

"There is also another couple staying at Green Glade to celebrate their anniversary." Then Macy frowned. "And I can't forget the ornithologist."

"Oh, you have a bird-watcher?"

"Yes, and he's quite a persnickety fellow," Macy said with a sniff. "Always complaining that his cottage is too hot or too cold. Or that someone parked in his spot." She shook her head. "I just don't understand people who find fault with everything."

Jan stared at her, trying not to smile at the irony. "Yes, it is a mystery." She picked up Macy's teapot. "I'll make some more tea for you and be right back."

"Make sure it's hot enough this time," Macy called after her.

Jan carried the empty teapot to the kitchen, enjoying the hum of conversation emanating from the tearoom. Moments like this reminded her why she and Elaine had decided to open a tearoom together almost a year ago: to bring people together in conversation and fellowship—while enjoying delicious teas and treats.

"Ho, there," Archie said, almost running into Jan as they met at the swinging door leading into the kitchen. The tray in his hands was piled high with maple croissants, lemon meringue cookies, and raspberry biscotti. "We almost had a bit of a spill."

"Almost," Jan agreed, laughing. "Macy misses you, by the way. She's more cantankerous than usual today."

He chuckled. "Well, I have my hands full," he said, nodding toward the tray as he walked away, "with some hungry customers."

Elaine appeared behind her, carrying an empty tray. "Looks like we have a traffic jam."

"We sure do," Jan said, laughing. Then she remembered the mail. "Oh, Elaine, I wanted to tell you we got a package in the mail addressed to the tearoom."

"Is it the tea leaves we ordered?" Elaine asked, following Jan into the kitchen.

"No, it's from New York City, but there was some water damage on the label, so I couldn't tell who it's from."

"That's interesting," Elaine said cheerfully, setting the tea tray on the counter. Then she turned back toward the tearoom. "Let's take a look when we have a spare moment, shall we?"

"Sounds good." Jan set down the empty teapot, then looked over at Rose. "Your lemon meringue cookies are a hit. Even Macy likes them."

Rose beamed. "That's high praise indeed." She placed her hands on her hips. "I just put the last batch in the oven. As soon as those are done I can help you out in the west parlor."

"Perfect," Jan said, putting on some water to boil and wondering how long it would take before they could open that mysterious package from New York.

As it turned out, Elaine and Jan's spare moment didn't arrive until they'd closed the tearoom at four o'clock.

"The last customer just left," Elaine said, walking into the kitchen. "We were hopping today!" She smiled as she untied her apron. "I'm surprised we didn't run out of tea."

Jan laughed as she washed the last teapot while Archie and Rose finished wiping down the counters. "It was almost as busy as tourist season. I guess folks wanted to be out and about after all the rain we've had for the past few days."

"The more the merrier as far as I'm concerned," Elaine said, placing a lid on the bowl of raspberry biscotti. "Although I feel as if I haven't had time to sit down all day."

Archie pulled out a chair, then gave a formal wave of his hand toward Elaine. "Your throne, milady."

They all laughed as Elaine took a seat. "Now that's more like it. Why don't we all sit down and enjoy a break? We've earned it after a day like today."

They all followed Elaine's lead, taking a seat at the table and sharing a pot of tea and the lemon meringue flop cookies that Rose had baked early in the day. Jan enjoyed the light crunch of the meringues and the tart bite of the lemon flavor.

After a few minutes, Elaine turned to her. "What about that package you mentioned earlier?"

"Oh my, I almost forgot," Jan said, rising from her chair. She walked into the office and retrieved the package, then carried it back to the kitchen table. She set it down, then reached for the kitchen scissors and cut the parcel string holding it together.

Elaine pulled it toward her and studied the label. "It's just addressed to Tea for Two. I guess that means it's for both of us."

"Then you should open it together," Rose suggested.

Jan nodded, intrigued by the mystery of it all. She and Elaine both began to pull apart the brown paper covering the box. Then Jan used one blade of the scissors to slice through the packaging tape holding the cardboard lid flaps together.

Elaine pulled the lid open, revealing layers of bubble wrap and loose newspaper scraps. "Something fragile must be inside."

Jan reached into the box and carefully pulled out the large ball of packaging material, bound together with plastic tape. "The sender sure isn't making this easy for us."

Elaine leaned closer, her blue eyes wide with anticipation. "I wonder what it is?"

"So do I," Rose chimed in, her hands wrapped around her teacup.

Jan and Elaine began peeling away the packaging. "I think it might be a teapot!" Jan exclaimed as she finally glimpsed white bone china through the bubble wrap and plastic tape.

"I believe it is." Elaine removed the last of the packaging to reveal a lovely white china teapot adorned with an exotic floral design in vibrant shades of coral and sage green.

Jan looked up at her cousin. "Are you sure you didn't order this?"

"I'm positive," Elaine replied, looking equally perplexed.

Jan looked over at Archie, who had friends and connections all over the world. "Perhaps one of your friends sent it to you, now that you work here. But how would they have our address?"

Archie's mouth curved into a sheepish smile. "I've told quite of few of my mates about this place. In fact, an old school chum, Nigel Fox, is on his way here from England right now. We've kept in touch all these years and now he's renting a cottage at the lake and planning a nice visit."

"If he's coming by way of New York, maybe he sent it," Rose said.

"I doubt it. Nigel is a collector, but has never been interested in pottery or dishware of any kind." Archie chuckled. "In fact, all of my mates have ribbed me a bit about working in a tearoom. But I quite enjoy my time here."

"And we're lucky to have you," Jan told him as Elaine nodded in agreement.

"Well, whoever sent this teapot has wonderful taste." Rose stood up and lifted the dainty lid off the teapot. "It's so pretty." Then her eyebrows arched in surprise as she stared into the teapot. "There's something strange inside."

# FROM THE
# GUIDEPOSTS ARCHIVE

This story, by Sabra Ciancanelli of Tivoli, New York,
originally appeared in *Guideposts*.

T eam Ria will find the loot!" my niece Regina declared.
She brandished a compass and a journal, items from the
treasure-hunting kit her mother, my sister Maria—Ria for
short—had assembled as a Christmas gift. Now we were putting
them to good use. Somewhere amid the browning oak trees
and rocky shores of Catskill Point Park was a golden doubloon
that had lain hidden for seventeen years—and we wanted to
find it. We needed to. *God, we need something to keep our minds off
missing Ria,* I prayed, holding back tears as I watched Regina
look under benches and picnic tables with my sons and my
brother's children. Had it really been six months since Ria
died, so suddenly, so utterly unexpectedly, in her sleep? I took
a deep breath of the chill autumn air and touched the photograph of her that I kept in my coat pocket. How I wished she
were still here with us. Ria was all about treasure hunts and
family time.

A few days earlier, my sister Laura had sent me an e-mail with the subject "Want to look for treasure?" I followed the link in the e-mail to a newspaper article "Treasure Hunt Unsolved for Nearly Two Decades." Officials in nearby Greene County had created the treasure hunt back in 1991 to promote tourism to Catskill, New York. Although there had been plenty of interest at first, over the years the treasure had been forgotten by all but a few dedicated hunters. The prize that Greene County had put up for finding the golden doubloon—a specially made jeweled crown valued at over ten thousand dollars—seemed like it might never be claimed.

Ria would have loved this! I thought. She loved everything about the ocean, waves, seashells...but especially pirates. Every summer our families rented a cluster of cottages on the beach in Wellfleet, Cape Cod, and on our last vacation, Ria planned an elaborate treasure hunt for the kids, burying clues and making a large X in the sand with rocks and flotsam above a big treasure trunk filled with goodies. She even threw Mom a pirate-themed birthday party complete with skull-and-crossbone hats, swashbuckling outfits and plastic swords. It was nutty...but that was Ria. Life was one big adventure, full of hidden clues and joyful surprises.

The picture in my pocket was from Mom's party—Ria dressed like a regular Captain Hook. It seemed like her goofy ideas and energy were what brought our family together, our center of gravity. Who else but Ria could get us all digging through sand for clues to buried treasure or wearing eye patches, laughing as we did our best pirate shouts: "Avast, matey!" Now that she was gone, every family gathering was tinged with sadness. Her oldest daughter's graduation, Regina's birthday. I even dreaded Christmas, because we always spent it at Ria's. The treasure hunt was the first thing we'd gotten excited about in a while. We were all in: my husband, Tony, my two sons, Solomon and Henry, my brother, Paul, my sister Laura and their families. Even Mom, who had been hit the hardest by our loss.

As the kids searched, decked out in pirate swag, I thumbed through the treasure story concocted by the tourism office, which held the clues to finding the now-legendary doubloon. Mom, Laura and I had read it earlier. "Captain Kidd and The Missing Crown" was filled with details of the infamous pirate's travels, and about the cargo, crew and supposed longitude and latitude of his stops. I reread the ending, which said the treasure was buried "somewhere on the banks of the Hudson River." The hand-drawn map depicted Catskill Point but lacked the usual X for buried treasure.

All day we scratched around in the dirt. Lifted up rocks. Searched behind buildings and through bushes. But every shiny glint turned out to be a crushed soda can, a penny, a gum wrapper. "That doubloon could be anywhere," Mom said. I nodded. In seventeen years, no one had found it. Had it been washed away somehow, irretrievably lost like Ria?

We resumed our search the next weekend. Team Ria gathered at a restaurant called, of all things, Captain Kidd's. We'd learned from the locals that the restaurant had once been owned by an organizer of the treasure hunt. Aha! Was the doubloon hidden on Captain Kidd's property? Regina tore ahead to a larger-than-life statue of the captain himself. Pushing aside leaves, we looked to see if there was a hidden compartment. "Is that a doubloon on his boots?" Solomon asked excitedly. No, just gold-colored buckles. We joked at how silly we must look. How would we explain ourselves if the owner came out?

Laura was sure she had it figured out when she spotted a big pig statue across the bridge from Catskill Point. The clues were filled with references to St. Anthony, who, according to our research, was often accompanied by a fat pig. But we checked it out and discovered that the statue had been a promotion for the movie Babe...and had been placed there seven years after the hunt began. "*Arrgh*," we said.

Later that week we got together at Laura's and went over the story, map and our notes. "Maybe there's a hidden code," someone suggested. Taking out Scrabble tiles, we rearranged the letters of the names of the story's characters. Among the many combinations possible, one stood out: "low tide marker." We decided to zero in on the Hudson's shoreline at low tide.

The next few weekends were filled with trudging the shoreline of the park and even taking kayaks out on the river, searching land only accessible at low tide. The kids splashed each other and had a great time, but we still came up empty. It's just a silly treasure hunt, I tried to convince myself. Inside though, I ached for Ria's presence in my life. Lord, will it always feel like this? I asked.

I came home from hunting one day to find my refrigerator on the fritz. Great, just what I need. Tony pulled the refrigerator away from the wall and fiddled with the back.

"Look what I found!" he said, holding up a postcard. On the front was a treasure map, on the back, "We already miss you guys! Can't wait for next year. Love, Ria." She had sent it from Cape Cod last summer.

I shook my head and smiled. "Who else would send a postcard to the people she had just vacationed with as a surprise for them to come home to?"

All of a sudden the fridge hummed back to life. Tony scratched his head and looked puzzled. "I didn't really do anything yet," he said. I stuck the postcard to the front of the fridge with a magnet. We had to keep looking. Ria would have wanted it.

By our next outing, only a few stray leaves still clung to the trees as our crew of fifteen, ages two to sixty-two, hiked through a nature preserve just north of Catskill Point. The sun retreated behind a steel gray cloud, as if to hide from the rain that soon began. We trudged along, tugging our hoods over our heads, and I couldn't help but laugh. What other family does this? The laughing spread to my brother and sister. Ahead on the trail, Regina giggled with her cousins. Hiking in the rain in search of buried treasure? We had to be nuts, as nuts as Ria.

*Oh, Ria!*

It didn't feel as if we were missing something. We were celebrating all the joy and optimism that was my sister. It didn't matter if we found the doubloon. This was the way to get past the sadness: living our lives a little bit like Ria had.

Back at the car, sopping wet, I whispered a prayer of thanks.

A few days later Laura called. "Are you sitting down?" she asked.

Her husband, Michael, was walking their puppy that morning. "He felt guided to look under a big rock buried in the riverbed," Laura said. There wasn't any one clue, any logical explanation as to why he picked up that particular rock of the hundreds of large rocks on the edge of low tide. But when he did, the doubloon—worn and blackened by years underwater—was underneath.

Our family was awarded the jeweled crown right before Christmas. It had been kept for seventeen years in an old cake box under the bed of one of the organizers of the hunt. It's in a safe-deposit box now, though Mom keeps the box it was stored in at the top of her stairs. "It makes me smile every time I see it," she says. Me too.

Hunters who had searched for years sent us e-mails and phoned us, from as far away as California. "How did you find the treasure?" they asked.

"We had lots of help," I tell them. A sister nuts for pirates and treasure hunts. An encouraging postcard at the right time. A nudge toward a certain rock. And the crown wasn't the most precious treasure we found. We discovered Ria's joyous spirit, alive in all of us.

# A NOTE FROM THE EDITORS

We hope you enjoyed Tearoom Mysteries, published by the Books and Inspirational Media Division of Guideposts, a nonprofit organization that touches millions of lives every day through products and services that inspire, encourage, help you grow in your faith, and celebrate God's love.

Thank you for making a difference with your purchase of this book, which helps fund our many outreach programs to military personnel, prisons, hospitals, nursing homes, and educational institutions.

We also create many useful and uplifting online resources. Visit Guideposts.org to read true stories of hope and inspiration, access OurPrayer network, sign up for free newsletters, download free e-books, join our Facebook community, and follow our stimulating blogs.

To learn about other Guideposts publications, including the best-selling devotional *Daily Guideposts*, go to Guideposts.org/Shop, call (800) 932-2145, or write to Guideposts, PO Box 5815, Harlan, Iowa 51593.

# Sign up for the
# Guideposts Fiction Newsletter

## *and stay up-to-date on the fiction you love!*

You'll get sneak peeks of new releases, recommendations from other Guideposts readers, and special offers just for you . . .

### *And it's FREE!*

**Just go to Guideposts.org/Newsletters today to sign up.**

**Guideposts**     **Visit Guideposts.org/Shop or call (800) 932-2145**

# Find more inspiring fiction in these best-loved Guideposts series!

### Sugarcreek Amish Mysteries
Be intrigued by the suspense and joyful "aha" moments in these delightful stories. Each book in the series brings together two women of vastly different backgrounds and traditions, who realize there's much more to the "simple life" than meets the eye.

### Miracles of Marble Cove
Follow four women who are drawn together to face life's challenges, support one another in faith, and experience God's amazing grace as they encounter mysterious events in the small town of Marble Cove.

### Secrets of Mary's Bookshop
Delve into a cozy mystery where Mary, the owner of Mary's Mystery Bookshop, finds herself using sleuthing skills that she didn't realize she had. There are quirky characters and lots of unexpected twists and turns.

### Patchwork Mysteries
Discover that life's little mysteries often have a common thread in a series where every novel contains an intriguing mystery centered around a quilt located in a beautiful New England town.

### Mysteries of Silver Peak
Escape to the historic mining town of Silver Peak, Colorado, and discover how one woman's love of antiques helps her solve mysteries buried deep in the town's checkered past.

**To learn more about these books, visit Guideposts.org/Shop**